D1577758

COUNT ON ME

BAYTOWN BOYS

MARYANN JORDAN

Cover Design by: Graphics by Stacy

Cover and model photography: Eric McKinney

ISBN ebook: 978-1-947214-54-5

ISBN print: 978-1-947214-55-2

❀ Created with Vellum

Author's Note

Please remember that this is a work of fiction. I have lived in numerous states as well as overseas, but for the last twenty years have called Virginia my home. I often choose to use fictional city names with some geographical accuracies.

These fictionally named cities allow me to use my creativity and not feel constricted by attempting to accurately portray the areas.

It is my hope that my readers will allow me this creative license and understand my fictional world.

I also do quite a bit of research on my books and try to write on subjects with accuracy. There will always be points where creative license will be used in order to create scenes or plots.

Jerking awake, Scott Redding bolted up in bed, kicking at the covers with his right leg, unable to move his left. A weight sat on his chest as he clawed toward consciousness. Managing to toss the covers to the floor, he reached down to rub his aching leg and dug his fingers into his left thigh. Massaging downward, his fingers passed his knee and then came to nothing.

Eyes open wide now, he flopped back onto the mattress, a curse leaving his lips. Wiping his hand over his sweaty face, he rolled over and moved to the side of the bed. Grabbing his crutch, he stood and limped into the bathroom. Wetting a small towel, he washed his face and neck, the cool water helping to cleanse the night-mare from his mind.

As always when dreams woke him, he forced his thoughts to travel down a different path. Makowitz, Torgenson, Bullock, Kandle, Roberts... all good men. Most still alive. Some still active. Blowing out his breath, he remembered the early morning runs, most during pre-dawn over the rough Afghanistan terrain. There was a hill where they would stop and watch the sunrise. It always struck him as strange to watch the sun lift in the sky and know that it was the same sun that rose over his home near the Chesapeake Bay back in the States. The same sunrise that his grandfather always watched.

He knew the dangers, but surrounded by fellow soldiers, he always felt safe. But then, traveling from one post to another, the truck in front of him ran over an IED. The larger vehicle lifted into the air, landing partially on the front of his. Seeing the hulking metal coming toward him was the last he remembered.

He awoke in the camp hospital, but his world was fuzzy. All he could remember was walking on the beach on the Eastern Shore of Maryland with his high school girlfriend and hoping she would let him get to second base. Or further.

The next time he regained consciousness, he was in a hospital in Germany. His parents were standing near his bed, but confusion marred his reality. He could not understand why his mother was crying. The covers were pushed back, and when he looked down, his naked right foot lay on top.

And below his left knee was nothing.

No pain. Just nothing.

Days turned into weeks. Weeks turned into months. Surgery. Rehabilitation. Anger mixed with acceptance. *At least I came back.* One of his buddies had been killed in the blast along with two more in other vehicles. And that did not include those injured along with him.

His living nightmare had been almost two years ago. Most of his team had moved into his memory, part of his past that remained firmly there. Now, he had created a new life for himself, firmly ensconced in Baytown. New home. New friends. New job.

The nightmares came rarely now, but knowing that sleep would be elusive, Scott used his crutch for balance and went back into the bedroom. Soulful brown eyes stared up at him from a large pillow on the floor. "Hey, Rufus. Gonna get up now. You want to come?"

His dog stood and stretched. Then, giving a full body shake that made his ears slap against the side of his head, he followed Scott into the kitchen. Rufus was a rescue. He had been a young hunting dog at one time, but an accident had taken one of his legs. His owner gave him to the shelter, but they had a hard time finding someone to take him on. As soon as Scott and Rufus lay eyes on each other, it was as though they knew they were a match. Rufus' tail began to thump on the floor, and Scott grinned widely, taking him home that day.

"You hungry, boy?"

The question was purely rhetorical. Rufus was always hungry. As soon as the kibble went into his bowl, the dog immediately began to crunch. Flipping on the coffee pot, Scott scrambled eggs, microwaved a few slices of bacon, and popped bread into the toaster.

Sitting at his table, he watched the morning sun rise on the Eastern Shore again, but now he was in Virginia. And he thought of those in uniform who were still overseas, watching the sun rise from where they were.

3

Ruffling his hand over Rufus' head, he said, "Come on, boy. Let's go for a little run."

Scott sat in the office that his grandfather used to occupy for so many years, recently updated. His grandfather had adorned the wall behind his desk with his degrees and associations in heavy frames that now were replaced by local artisans' paintings of shore scenes. And on the credenza behind the desk now sat framed pictures of both his family and his military family, the team he served with in Afghanistan.

In some ways, it still seemed surreal to be back in Baytown, occupying the office that he had visited so often when a child. Scott loved his grandfather but never anticipated following in his footsteps. Instead, he had craved adventure, and the desire to travel far outside the bounds of the tiny town had called him to join the military after high school. His gaze landed on the photograph of his former team, and his lips curved slightly at the youthful faces, cocky smiles, and the surety that they would all come home safely having fought for God and country. *Oh, the folly of youth.*

"Good morning, Scott."

The greeting startled him out of his musings, and he looked up as Lia McFarlane stood in the doorway, smiling at him. Her long, dark hair was pulled back in a low ponytail, and her warm eyes twinkled. She had always been attractive, but since falling in love with

Aiden McFarlane, her face now held a glow from deep within.

"Good morning," he replied, smiling in return.

She walked in and sat down in one of the leather chairs in his office, and her gaze drifted around the room as his had earlier. Lia had come to Baytown, buying out his grandfather's accounting business when he retired. Scott knew his grandfather would have preferred to sell it to him, but Scott was finishing his master's degree and not ready to take on the business' responsibilities. As soon as he finished, he'd contacted Lia and she hired him as an employee, then, several months later, offered him a partnership, which he'd accepted gratefully.

"I'm glad we were able to expand and update the office." She quickly looked back over and smiled. "Your grandfather's office was perfect for him, but for us, it was a little…"

"Stuffy? I think that's the word you're looking for," he said, and they both laughed.

When the building next door became available, they bought it and renovated the entire space. They each had a large office, Scott taking over the one that had been used by his grandfather. Besides Lia's office, there was now another for a future accountant, if needed. They also had two conference rooms plus an employee work-room. The ever-efficient secretary, Mrs. Markham, had an updated reception area as well.

Just then, Mrs. Markham walked in with a small tray in her hand. Setting it on his desk, she handed a cup of coffee to both he and Lia before taking the third cup for herself. Settling in the other chair, the three sipped in companionable silence for a moment. This was something new that Lia had begun several months ago... a chance for each working day to start with the three of them sharing coffee together.

Scott enjoyed his morning cup of coffee as much as anyone, but over time, he'd begun to appreciate the pleasant way to start each morning.

"Any luck with house hunting?" Lia asked, turning to Scott.

He shook his head. "No, not yet. I'm driving the real estate agent crazy, but I think my biggest problem is I just can't define what I'm really looking for. The historical houses in town are nice, but the ones already restored are fairly expensive. I'm not into doing the restoration work for the ones that are more moderately priced. Plus, I don't really want to be right on top of my neighbors."

"So, you'd like a little space?" Mrs. Markham asked, peering at him over her cup.

"Yes, I see myself in a place that has a little bit of land around it. Breathing room, I guess you'd call it."

"I'm sure there's lots of places in the country outside of Baytown that are for sale," Lia added.

He sighed heavily. "So far, nothing has resonated with me."

Mrs. Markham looked at her watch and startled. "Oh, my goodness. I didn't realize the time." Looking up at Scott, she said, "Your client will be here in a few minutes." She stood and gathered the empty coffee cups before carrying the tray out of the office.

He looked at his online calendar and his brow scrunched. "Beau Weston? Is he a new client?"

Shaking her head, Lia replied, "I'm sorry. I meant to tell you that I'm handing him over to you. He's been around forever, and your grandfather used to be his accountant. He's a wonderful man, and we got along fine. But I have to say that when he heard that Thomas Redding's grandson was here, he seemed happy. Plus," she shrugged with a smile, "he runs a farm, and with you being tax accountant, I think you're a better fit for him."

Scott thought that he and Lia made a good team. His specialty was tax accounting, focusing on businesses, and her specialty was fraud. They both handled the customers' tax questions in preparation but utilized their specialties as much as possible.

Lia continued, "In fact, I think he mentioned the American Legion when I met with him last year. You might have already made his acquaintance."

She had barely left his office when Mrs. Markham showed at his doorway and said, "Mr. Redding, your appointment is here." Standing to the side, she ushered in an older gentleman, introducing, "This is Beau Weston."

In stepped a large man, dressed in clean overalls and a white, short-sleeved, buttoned shirt. His cheeks were ruddy and he had a shock of white hair on top of his head, wide smile peering out from a trimmed, white beard, and blue eyes that fairly twinkled. Scott had an image of Beau easily playing Santa Claus. And he could not help but grin.

2

"By God, you look just like your granddaddy did when he was younger. Nice to meet you," Beau exuded, grabbing Scott's extended hand.

Still grinning in return at the firm and friendly handshake, Scott indicated for Beau to have a seat.

"Can I get you anything? Coffee or water, perhaps?" Mrs. Markham asked.

Beau shook his head and replied, "Thank you muchly, but I've already had my allotted caffeine for the morning. My Reba, God rest her soul, has been gone several years, but my granddaughter has taken her place, making sure I eat right. She lets me have two cups of coffee in the morning and that's it."

Laughing, Mrs. Markham closed Scott's door as she left the room.

Beau turned around in his seat, settling his gaze on Scott. "I've missed the last couple of meetings, but I do recognize you from the American Legion. I know your granddaddy was mighty proud when you joined the military."

Chuckling, he shook his head slightly. "I believe my family eventually came around, but I can assure you when I first joined right out of high school, neither my grandfather nor my parents were very happy."

"Oh, that was just the fear talking," Beau said, settling deeper into his seat. "I don't believe your daddy served, but your granddaddy did, so he knew what it could be like. But make no mistake, he was proud."

"Thank you for that." Scott relaxed, feeling an immediate camaraderie with the older man. Beau's affable personality set him at ease, and while most people wanted to immediately get down to business, it was fine with Scott if Beau wanted to chat a little bit.

"Heard you talk at one of the meetings about your injury. You've got my admiration, Scott. Anyone who can go through what you went through and come out of it doing as well as you did... well, like I said, you've got my admiration."

Shrugging, Scott patted his thigh and said, "Mr. Weston, I figure I'm lucky. I had some friends who didn't make it back."

Beau nodded slowly, the light in his eyes dimming slightly. "Yeah, me too. Did a tour in 'Nam." He patted his leg as well and chuckled. "My knee gave out over there. To this day, I can tell the weather depending on how my knee feels."

The two men offered knowing smiles, the connection tangible. One of the things Scott had learned from participating in the multi-generational American

Legion was that their service branches may be different as well as the battles they fought, but there was always a camaraderie amongst servicemen and women.

Moving the conversation back to the reason Beau was visiting, he said, "I understand you have a farm? I apologize for not being prepared ahead of time, but I just found out that you would be my client."

"Oh, that's fine," Beau said, waving his beefy hand to the side, dismissing Scott's concerns. "I like Mrs. McFarlane just fine and got no problem working with a woman, but she told me that you were real good with taxes. Plus, I was excited to meet Thomas's grandson."

"Well, why don't you tell me a little about your business?"

Scott was not sure Beau's smile could have spread wider, but as he began talking about his farm, it was obvious how much he cared about his land.

"The farm's been in my family for over a hundred and twenty-five years," Beau began. "Farming is the only life I've known... the only life I've ever wanted. I met my wife when we were in high school. She was a pretty girl from the town, and I was just a country boy. Couldn't believe she said 'yes' the first time I asked her out. Reba and me got married right after high school. Her daddy wasn't happy, but Reba knew her mind. We moved into the farmhouse with my parents and eventually built a small house of our own on another part of the land. Once my parents passed, we moved back into the bigger farmhouse."

"What do you raise?" Scott hated that he had not read up on the Weston farm.

"When our farm was at its biggest, we had over four hundred acres, raising corn, cotton, and potatoes. I also kept a few cows, had a prize bull, plus pigs and chickens." His smile slid from his face, and he rubbed his fingers over the whiskers on his chin. "Years ago, during one of the recessions, I sold off a hundred acres to Luca Giordano, the Tomato King."

Eyebrows lifted, Scott did not have a chance to ask about that title before Beau began chuckling.

"I see you haven't heard that before," Beau said, his smile back on his face. "The Giordano farm began snapping up farmland about thirty years ago. The Eastern Shore is known for its tomatoes, and he had direct contracts with companies like Campbell's for their tomato soup." Nodding his head, he added, "Big business being in tomatoes."

"I knew that tomatoes were one of the crops that grew prevalently around here, but I never thought about it being so important," Scott replied. "I confess that I was gone for many years and have only recently come back to the Eastern Shore. It seems like there's much I need to learn."

Waving his hand again, Beau said, "I get along fine with Luca. We chew the fat when we see each other. But about five years ago when Reba died, I sold off another 50 acres. It was getting harder to have workers, and I sure as hell ain't getting any younger. My son... well, my son doesn't work the farm." Beau's eyes brightened. "But I've got my Lizzie. And I'd do anything for her."

"Lizzie?"

The crinkles next to Beau's eyes deepened as he said

with obvious affection, "My granddaughter. Elizabeth. Named after my mother. Works the farm with me, and I want to make sure I can secure her future."

"I'm assuming you want me to start working on the taxes for this year for the farm."

Nodding, Beau leaned forward and placed his forearms on Scott's desk, holding his gaze. "Yes, but I'm hoping there's more you can help me with. I don't want to have to keep selling off land. Lizzie's not just working the land because she's got nothing else to do. She's got farming in her blood. She's got some newfangled ideas, and we've got a few more goats and damned if she isn't talking about getting a couple of alpacas." Leaning back, he sighed heavily, and it appeared his large body seemed to deflate. "I'm hoping you can help me find ways to save a little money and keep the farm going. She deserves that legacy and security."

"Is there any other family that's involved in the farm that I should know about?"

Beau's expression resembled a hound dog, and it dawned on Scott that Beau was not a man to hide his emotions. Curiosity abounded, and he anxiously awaited Beau's response. As seemed usual for Beau, he did not make him wait.

Shaking his head slowly, Beau said, "Me and Reba hoped to have a bunch of children, but she had several miscarriages early on, and we just figured it was God's way of telling us that was not His plan. So, we stopped trying, not wanting to have any harm come to her. By the time we were about forty, married for twenty years..." Chuckling, he said, "You can probably guess where this story is going."

Scott's lips curved in response, and he breathed easier seeing Beau's smile back on his face.

"Reba didn't even tell me for months that she was pregnant, assuming she would miscarry. When it finally looked like she was going to start showing, she told me. Won't lie... we were both scared, but she delivered a sweet baby boy. Named him Robinson after her father and called him Robbie. We were older parents and probably doted on him too much, but he had chores and worked the farm before and after school." His brow scrunched as he added, "You know how I said my granddaughter has farming in her blood? I can't explain what that really means, except to say that some people take to farming and other people just don't. My son? Robbie just never took to farming."

Scott watched as genuine confusion seemed to settle on Beau, as though the older man could not imagine someone not loving a life of working outdoors with animals and the soil.

Beau continued, "Don't get me wrong, I don't think farming is for everyone. I wouldn't have minded what Robbie wanted to do. He could farm, do mechanics, build houses, go to college. Anything he wanted to do would've been fine with me and Reba." Sighing heavily, he said, "But that boy was just lazy. Bone lazy. By the time he was a teenager, he got caught stealing when he was trying to sell the items to a pawnshop. Did a few days in juvenile detention, then he was handed back over to us. We tried everything we knew... love and

14

tough love. If he didn't want to farm, I got him a job in town working with one of the mechanics. Half the time he wouldn't even show up. Reba spent more time on her knees in prayer for Robbie than she did pulling up weeds in the garden. Thought he'd grow out of it, but at eighteen years old, he left, and we didn't hear from him for several years. One day, he shows up on our doorstep with a pregnant wife. We thought he'd turned a corner, and for a few years, it seemed like he had. Reba was ecstatic, and we welcomed his wife, Jane, into our home, pleased as punch that she was a hard worker and dedicated mom." Beau's face brightened once again as he said, "Lizzie became the joy of our lives."

"I hate to ask, but is Robbie still around?"

Beau's smile dropped from his face. "By then, it was clear that Robbie was an alcoholic. Most of the time he wasn't working, and we supported Jane and Lizzie. That wasn't hard because Jane worked the farm right along with us. By the time Lizzie was about ten years old, Robbie up and left. I'm afraid we had a big fight. Robbie said he was tired of living on our charity and I told him he could start working anytime he wanted. He wanted to take Jane and Lizzie, but Jane put her foot down. Said she was tired of having a bum for a husband, and she wasn't going to go off with him. He left, and we've never heard from him since. He signed the divorce papers that Jane had served to him, and even though he was my son, I was so proud of Jane for standing up for herself."

"I'm real sorry to hear that, Mr. Weston." Scott often heard people's histories and stories when they came in to talk about taxes. How much money people make and spend is so personal, and when he worked on their taxes or financial plans, clients would often fill him in on everything going on in their lives. He was not surprised by Beau's confessions but was intrigued. "Is Jane still part of the farm?"

"No, and I can't say that I'm sorry. By the time Lizzie graduated from high school, Jane had met a real nice man who was a minister in Richmond. They got married and she moved there with him, but Lizzie wanted to stay with us, which thrilled us. A couple of years later, Reba took ill and died soon after. Devastated me. Devastated Lizzie."

The two men sat in introspective silence for a few minutes before Beau seemed to snap out of his thoughts and suck in a deep breath, holding Scott's gaze once again.

"I'm an old man, and Reba's death was a stark reminder that none of us know how long we have on this earth. So yes, I need help with the taxes, and I'll take any assistance you can offer for making sure Lizzie can hang on to her legacy."

Scott's interest was piqued. Tax preparation was necessary, and he knew he was good at his job, but the idea of helping Beau and his granddaughter gave him a renewed sense of purpose. "Well, sir, I'll start reviewing all the financials for the farm and see what we can come up with."

With his smile firmly back on his face, Beau placed his hands on the arm of the chair and hefted himself upward. "That's all I can ask. And while I appreciate the respect, please, just call me Beau."

Shaking hands, he watched the older man leave his office, his mind already running through ideas of how to help the Weston Farm.

3

SIX MONTHS LATER

The hot sun was beaming down, causing heat waves to rise from the asphalt road as Scott drove home from work. He had moved from the rental condo in The Dunes into a small rental house north of town. He had finally told his real estate agent that he was going to rent until he could find the perfect house. His rental house was much better than the condo but still did not feel like home.

As he came to an intersection, his way was blocked as the electric company was cutting overhanging limbs from a tree. Tossing a wave toward the workers, he turned down another lane to travel a different way home. With the air conditioner blasting, keeping the interior of his SUV cool, he felt sorry for the men and women who were working outside. He had planned on taking an afternoon run but decided he could wait until tomorrow morning.

Turning a corner, he saw a wooden sign proclaiming Weston Farms. He and Beau had stayed in contact as he found numerous tax benefits that would help the overall financial status of the farm. Beau did not make each monthly meeting of the American Legion, but Scott had seen him several times, the older man always greeting him warmly.

As he continued the drive, he saw Beau standing near the fence by the edge of the road. He pulled to the gravel shoulder, waving as Beau squinted in the sunlight to see who had arrived. Recognizing him, Beau waved as well, pulling off his hat to wipe his brow with a hand-kerchief.

Climbing from the driver's seat, Scott walked over to the edge of the fence, shaking Beau's hand, observing him sweating profusely. "Beau, I know you're used to working outside, but it's ungodly hot right now. Are you sure you're okay?"

"You sound like my Lizzie," Beau chuckled. He took a big breath and said, "You're right, though. It's mighty hot for this time of year. I surely can't work the way I did when I was a younger man."

His gaze drifted behind Beau to where a large animal was ambling toward them. Eyes wide, he asked, "Is that a llama?"

"Alpaca," Beau answered. "We've got three of them now."

Uncertain what to say, he was also uncertain how Beau felt about the odd-looking animal. The alpaca wandered over and nudged Beau's hat off his head. Beau huffed, re-settled his hat, and said, "Stop that, Caesar!"

Blinking, Scott was unable to hold back his laughter. "Caesar? His name is Caesar?"

Shaking his head, Beau chuckled as well. "This here is Caesar." Pointing toward the distance where two other alpacas were standing under the shade of a tree, he added, "The one on the right is Cleopatra, and the other one is Mark Antony." He lost the battle of holding in his own laughter, and said, "My Lizzie… she's got an imagination."

Looking to the left, Scott saw a separate grazing area where goats roamed freely, younger goats frolicking around the pasture. Off to the right, nestled in between several large trees, sat a white, two-story farmhouse, complete with a wide front porch and two brick chimneys on either side. Several trimmed box hedges were in front of the porch, flowers blooming between each one. The house gave off a vibe of comfort and days gone by. His breath caught in his throat as he stared at the simple structure, resplendent in its simplicity.

"Would you like to come in for some lemonade?" Beau asked. "Lizzie has gone into town to the grocery, but I'm sure she's got either lemonade or sweet tea in the refrigerator."

It was on the tip of his tongue to take Beau up on his offer but realized that by doing so he would pull Beau away from the work on the fence that he had been involved in before Scott drove along. To a farmer, time was money, and he certainly did not want to interfere with Beau's business.

"That's a nice offer, Beau, but I really need to get home. I'll let you finish your work."

Shaking his hand goodbye, Beau added, "I wanted to thank you for all your help with our taxes this past year.

With the changes coming along that Lizzie and I would like to make, we're still solvent, and I can keep from having to sell Luca more of my land."

"Don't mention it. I'll see you soon." Observing Beau wiping the sweat from his red face again, he added, "Don't work too hard and take care of yourself." With a wave goodbye and a final longing look at the farm, Scott climbed back into his car, blasted the air conditioner once more, and drove home. Pulling into the gravel drive of his small rental, he thought back to the Weston farmhouse, wondering if his real estate agent could find a house like that for him.

Six Months Later

Scott welcomed Beau into his office, shaking the older man's hand, concerned to find his grip not as sure as it had been. At quick glance, Beau's appearance was very much the same as the first time he met him. Clean overalls. Worn but clean white buttoned shirt. The corner of a handkerchief was sticking out from his back pocket. But upon closer observation, he could discern that the older man's face was more gaunt than full. His overalls hung on a frame that was less robust than before. But when he stared into Beau's face, the blue eyes twinkled as bright as ever.

Ushering him to a seat, he waited until Beau was

settled, making sure he had the water Mrs. Markham offered. "I was fascinated to get the papers you sent over a few weeks ago. I see that Weston Farm is now selling goat milk products. It's still operating at a loss, but I have every confidence that could eventually turn a profit."

Beau nodded his head slowly as a smile spread over his face. "My Lizzie is a thinker. It's funny because she has very little confidence, and yet, her ideas are sound. There was no way we were going to be able to continue farming the way my father and grandfather and those before them had done. Raising crops, I was not going to be able to market them at a profit with the competition from the huge farms all around. So, when she decided to get goats and those crazy alpacas, she started making goat milk products, and after shearing the Alpacas sell their fleece. I know she's disappointed that it's not bringing in a lot of money so far, but if anyone can do it, it's my Lizzie. Never seen a harder working young woman, with the exception of my Reba."

"She sounds like an amazing person," Scott replied, seeing the obvious pride in Beau's exuberant praise of his granddaughter. "Perhaps sometime we can look at her business plan and see how we can make it more profitable."

Beau's eyes opened wide, and he bobbed his head up and down in affirmation. "I'd welcome that, and I know my Lizzie would, too." After he spoke, his brow slowly furrowed as he rubbed his chin. "Well, maybe she wouldn't at first. She tends to get prickly with a lot of suggestions, taking it to heart that maybe she's not doing very well. But I know if you met her, she'd cotton on that you know what you're talking about. Like I said, she can be a bit stubborn, but she's a smart woman."

"Then I look forward to meeting her sometime, hopefully soon," Scott said, finding he sincerely meant his words.

"That'd be real nice," Beau agreed, sighing heavily. "Lizzie's kind of a loner. She works hard and hasn't got a lot of time for making friends. With her mom gone now, she's even more alone."

"Her mother's gone?"

"Oh, I probably said that wrong. I don't mean she died. She and her husband took a missionary position and moved overseas for a few years."

Scott breathed easier, not sure why he felt so relieved that Lizzie had not suffered more loss.

The two men reviewed the financial reports that Beau had sent over, giving Scott a chance to clarify any points of question. After an hour, as he was ushering Beau from his office, he said, "Make sure you take care of yourself."

Clapping him on the back, Beau replied, "Working hard is the only life I know, and when the good Lord decides to take me, I hope He takes me quick and easy, doing what I love best."

Goodbyes said, Scott stood at the outer door of their business, watching Beau walk down the sidewalk toward his old pickup truck. A strange melancholy moved over him, and he shook his head, anxious to dislodge the uncomfortable thoughts that had settled in his mind.

Mrs. Markham interrupted his musings, saying, "If you have a few minutes Scott, Lia said she needed to meet with you about the Parson estate."

With a polite nod toward their efficient receptionist, he walked down the hall, forcing thoughts of Weston Farm to the side, ready to tackle another client's needs.

Four Months Later

Ginny McFarlane, the newly elected Commander of the local American Legion, called the meeting to order. Scott had only been a member since moving to Baytown but was heartened to observe the meeting room was almost filled to capacity. The members' ages ranged from twenty to some in their nineties. There were men and women who had served in World War II, both in Europe and the Pacific, Korea, Vietnam, Desert Storm, the Gulf wars, and the many deployments in between all of those.

When deciding to move to Baytown to work with Lia's accounting business, he was thrilled to discover the very active American Legion. There had been a group of boys raised in Baytown, all leaving high school for the military. Most found their way back, discovering that the small, coastal town had everything that they wanted as adults. With the American Legion active, they also invited former military friends who did not have a place to call home to come live in Baytown. He quickly developed close friendships with many of the members and participated in most of their activities.

The AL sports teams for youth had been one of their most beloved endeavors. Offering all youth the opportunity to play in the AL baseball league had given many of the disadvantaged youth in the area a chance to participate regardless of their family's financial ability to assist. And for many of the members, they coached, enjoying the camaraderie the teams offered. An added bonus was the way the community came together to support the young people, filling the bleachers and providing snacks for the kids.

Scott had been athletic when he was younger... baseball, football, running, and swimming. The PT in the Army kept him fit, but it was the idea of playing on a team that brought about excitement. The highs of winning together combined with the shared encouragement when they lost. Now, with his special prosthetic, he had the ability to run again and often found that running alone allowed his mind to wander over the many changes in his life.

Startling when he heard his name called, he realized that he had been daydreaming during much of the meeting. He was the Post Service Officer, and it was time for him to report on the newest activity plans. Standing, he made his way to the podium.

"We are very close to our first annual American Legion 5K, 10K, and fun run. Our goal is to encourage anyone who wants to participate by having the three different distances. The kids and those who would like to walk or run for a very short distance can participate in the fun run. Those who are more used to a longer distance can participate in either the 5K or 10K. I've got all three mapped out and have already spoken to Mitch and Colt to get their approval and assistance."

Both Mitch and Colt nodded at his acknowledgment and Scott grinned, knowing that his job was much easier with both the Baytown Police Chief and the North Heron Sheriff part of the American Legion.

"The courses will start and end at the North Heron Fairgrounds. We originally thought of including an area of Baytown, particularly the ballfield, but the runs would be limited due to keeping everyone off of Highway 13 which is heavily traveled. If we start and end at the fairgrounds, we're able to utilize back roads that are easier to police with less traffic and provide a scenic background for the runners."

Opening for questions, he was thrilled with the overall enthusiasm.

"Will there be a registration?"

Nodding, he said, "Runners can register early, or they can register that morning. Anyone under the age of eighteen must have parent permission."

"How safe will the fun run be for the kids?"

"To make sure we don't have any children running on the roads, the fun run will take place inside the fairgrounds. Only the 5K and 10K will travel along the country roads."

"I sure as hell can't run... damn, I can hardly walk," one of the older members chuckled. "How can we help?"

Grinning widely, Scott replied, "Glad you asked!" The meeting participants broke out in laughter, and once it subsided, he answered, "The American Legion Auxiliary will be providing water bottles and energy bars for the participants. They will also be conducting a bake sale to raise money. Anyone willing to volunteer to monitor the racecourse, I'll have a sign-up sheet for the end of this meeting. I know some of you will be running, but we can use people all along the way to help direct the runners along the roads, having golf carts around in case someone becomes fatigued or injured. I know Zac is coordinating the EMTs and paramedics in the area to provide assistance. Mitch, Colt, and Hannah will provide security."

Hannah was Easton's Police Chief, a nearby small town, and Zac was Baytown's Rescue Captain, once again proving that members of the AL were pillars in the community and perfect for arranging wide-scale activities.

When there were no more questions, he nodded toward Ginny and moved back to his seat. Sucking in a deep breath, he let it out slowly, filled with enthusiasm and energy for the upcoming event.

His mind was on what still needed to be done, and he almost missed Ginny's final comments.

"As we come to the end of the meeting," Ginny said, "I want to let you know that we just received notice that we have lost one of our members. Beau Weston has been a member of our AL Chapter since it started. He's been a resident of North Heron his whole life, living and working on Weston Farm. His granddaughter,

Lizzie, found him on the farm earlier today, unresponsive. He was pronounced dead at North Heron Hospital soon after. I spoke with Lizzie briefly, but she was distraught and obviously had not had a chance to consider his services yet. As soon as those are firm, we'll get an email out to everyone."

Ginny concluded the meeting, but Scott heard nothing as he fought to suck air into his lungs at the news. As soon as he could, he escaped the gathering, skipping the usual trip to Finn's Pub with his friends, wanting to be alone.

A few hours later, lying in bed as sleep eluded him, the news of Beau's death still whirled in his mind. While he had only known Beau for a couple of years, he enjoyed their conversations and had looked forward to a time when he could meet with Beau and Lizzie about the plans for their farm.

Rolling to the side, he stared out the window of his small house, the cloudless night allowing the stars to shine. Heart heavy, he remembered Beau's words. *When the good Lord decides to take me, I hope He takes me quick and easy, doing what I love best.* He supposed Beau had gotten his wish and smiled at the thought of the old farmer dying the way he wanted. But then his mind turned to Lizzie and how alone she must feel. *Damn, Beau's last wish is his granddaughter's nightmare.*

4

The day was cloudy, but thankfully not rainy. The sun would occasionally peek through the thick white clouds, sending an immediate ray of sunshine toward the mourners below, then just as quickly pull the warmth away as it hid once more.

Scott stood to the side, surrounded by other members of the American Legion. He had not been surprised to see the small church where Beau's funeral service was held to be standing room only. The minister spoke of Beau's undying love for his country, his farm, and his family. He spoke of the long line of Westons that had settled on the Eastern Shore in the 1800s. He spoke of Beau's loving wife, Reba, and how the two were now joined once again.

Several older members of the American Legion also gave eulogies, speaking of the man who would drop everything to come to the aid of a friend. Scott listened carefully to the words others said of Beau, not surprised to find that the man he'd enjoyed talking to was someone that others found easily relatable as well.

Now the crowd had moved to the cemetery for the final ceremony. Scott leaned toward the side, hoping to catch a glimpse of Lizzie. Her blonde hair was so pale it appeared almost white against her dark, navy dress. Sunglasses covered a third of her face and a tissue was constantly lifted to wipe her tears and nose, keeping him from being able to discern her features. He wondered if she would have Beau's piercing, intelligent blue eyes. He also wondered if, in better times, she shared Beau's bright smile.

She was standing next to a woman with short hair that was the same color as Lizzie's and a tall man. He assumed they were her mother and stepfather, but it struck him how she still appeared very alone. A single, solitary figure amongst many. It also caught his attention that there were no women her age standing nearby, and he remembered Beau's comment that she had little time for friends, spending most of her time on the farm.

On the other side of the gravesite, he noted many of his friends from Baytown, some having been raised in the area as Lizzie had been. He did not know how old she was but wondered if she had attended high school with some of the Baytown men and women.

Just as he had bonded with many of the men in the American Legion, he knew that many of their wives had formed a tight-knit group and would quickly swoop in if they saw a need. Staring at Lizzie, it was obvious to him there was a need. And while the women would befriend her, he hoped there was a place for him as well.

He needed to talk to her about the farm, taxes, the estate, and especially her plans for the future. Seeing her lift the crumpled tissue to wipe a stray tear once more, he knew that discussion would have to wait. At least for a few days until she would be less exhausted.

When the service was finally over, he watched an honor guard from the American Legion step forward to take the American flag that draped Beau's casket, fold it, and present the neat triangle to Lizzie. Clutching the flag, she stepped forward and placed a single rose on Beau's casket before moving to stand next to the minister.

The gathering disbanded, everyone heading to their cars, and the men from the funeral home directed everyone as they exited the cemetery. Assuming she was well-tended, he looked over his shoulder, seeing her standing with just the minister and the couple. He waited by his truck, allowing the rest of the mourners to pass by, offering chin lifts to those he knew.

Looking back to the gravesite, he watched as the couple led her away. Instead of settling into the back of the funeral home's black Cadillac, she climbed alone into the old truck that he had last seen Beau driving. He hated to be caught staring but could not drag his eyes away as she drove by, her fingers tightly clutching the steering wheel and her sunglasses-covered eyes facing straight ahead.

The urge to follow her and comfort her was strong. *But what would I say? She doesn't even know me. Surely, when she gets home, there will be others to see to her needs.*

Convincing himself that he was right, he climbed

into his truck and headed into Baytown, knowing most of his friends would be gathered at Finn's Pub.

Twenty minutes later, he was sitting at a table next to Lia, her husband Aiden working behind the bar. Ginny, married to Brogan, the other McFarlane brother also behind the bar, sat next to Lia. Nearby were their other friends from Baytown: Mitch Evans, Grant Wilder, and Lance Greene, all members of the Baytown Police Department, and their wives Tori, Jillian, and Jade. Zac was with his wife, Maddie. He remembered that she was a counselor with the mental health group in town and stored that tidbit of information away in case Lizzie needed it.

Gareth Harrison was married to Katelyn, the third McFarlane sibling who owned Finn's Pub. Callan Ward, a Baytown native, now worked for the Virginia Marine Police. Hunter Simmons was a detective for North Heron County, working under Sheriff Colt Hudson. Hunter's wife Belle and Colt's wife Carrie were sitting with Rose, owner of Sweet Rose Ice Cream Parlor. Her husband, Jason, was off to the side, sitting with one of the newer members of the American Legion, Joseph. Jason owned an auto mechanic shop along with a tattoo shop next door. He worked there rarely, but Joseph was now the main artist.

Excusing himself, he walked up to the bar, ordering another beer. Eschewing small talk with Aiden and Brogan who were both busy behind the bar, he made his way over to Jason and Joseph. Shaking their hands in greeting, he said, "I wondered if you had a chance to fit me in for a consult sometime."

Both men nodded, and Jason asked, "I remember you talking to us about more ink. Are you ready?"

Nodding, he said, "Yeah, but I'll have to get the race over with first. I can't have irritated skin while running. I've seen your work and know you'll do a great job."

Joseph replied with a chin lift, and Scott knew there was very little he would get from the large, taciturn veteran. "I appreciate it. I'll give you guys a call."

Veering toward the tables where most of the women gathered, he asked, "I want to ask you about Lizzie Weston. Did she go to school with any of you?"

Jillian nodded and replied, "She was a couple of years younger than us, but I can honestly say I barely remember her." Sighing heavily, she added, "I really hope that's because she was quiet and not because I was so much in my clique that I ignored her."

Belle placed her hand on Jillian's arm and said, "Jillian, you can't take that on. Everyone in high school is cliquish. It's just the way teenagers are."

Katelyn piped up, "It might be, but that doesn't make me feel any better."

Belle added quietly, "I do remember her, but barely. I was very shy in high school, and Lizzie lived in the county, not in town."

Tori, her gaze holding steady on Scott, asked, "What are you thinking?"

"I spent time with Beau, both at the American Legion and professionally as his accountant. He had a lot of friends, and there were a lot of us there today. But I couldn't help but notice that Lizzie didn't seem to have a group of friends with her. Of course, it seemed like that was her mother standing next to her, so she'll have company."

"I don't think so," Jillian said. "I overheard some people talking when they were in my coffee shop saying that her mother and stepfather won't be able to stay because of a mission trip overseas."

Silence met her news and then, almost in unison, the women immediately began to toss out ideas.

"We can take some food."

"We can visit her."

"We need to invite her to the American Legion Auxiliary."

Chuckling, Scott said, "I'm not sure she's up to being overwhelmed at the moment. But I wanted to mention it. Beau indicated that she spent most of her time working the farm, and that may not have left a lot of time for socializing. I just hate to think about her being alone."

"Scott, I usually try to visit the family when there's been a death of a client," Lia said. "Since you were so close to Beau, I think that would be appropriate for you."

Nodding his agreement, he said, "I had already planned on doing that." Looking at the women, he said, "Why don't I visit her tomorrow, and then I'll let Lia know how she's doing and what she needs. Lia can then pass that on to the rest of you."

The friends all agreed, and he decided to forgo the beer he had just bought and said his goodbyes. Stepping out of the pub, the cloudy day finally gave way to a misty rain. He turned up the collar on his jacket and headed to his SUV. Once inside, he drove home, his mind on the visit he planned to make with Lizzie the next day.

Lizzie sat alone at the kitchen table, a dull ache in her heart as well as her head. Several women from the church had brought casseroles that would still be sitting on the counter if her mother had not wrapped them and placed a few into the refrigerator and the rest into the freezer.

She had offered thanks for the food, her grandfather's words ringing in her mind. *"Lizzie, always accept the gifts of others with gratitude, even if you don't want it. If someone wants to give, allow them that charity."*

Her mother had wrapped her arms around Lizzie once more, and the two women grieved as they clung to each other. "I loved him so much," her mother said. "He was more father than father-in-law to me. I'm only glad that he and dear Reba are finally together."

Her stepfather had offered to take care of the animals that evening, but it was all Lizzie could do to keep from rolling her eyes at the thought of kind but *citified* Richard trying to take care of the goats and alpacas. She loved her stepfather and appreciated his offer, but he was unused to farm work and would never be able to properly handle the animals.

"Mom, Richard, you don't need to stay. I know you

need to fly back soon. Why don't you come back in a few months when you can stay longer, and we can all remember Papa Beau and not cry so much." Her parents had just made it in for the funeral but did not have many days for bereavement leave.

"Oh, baby, I don't want to leave you here alone—"

"Mom, I don't mind. Really. You two are needed there. I'll be fine, and I have the farm to keep me busy."

They chatted for several more minutes, her mother extracting a promise that Lizzie would call every day. That seemed to placate them, and when she finally closed the door, she stood for a long moment with her hand still on the doorknob and her forehead pressed against the solid wood. She had been uncertain if it was possible for her to cry any more, but as she slid to the floor, it was evident that acute grief produced an unlimited number of tears.

Once spent, she stood and climbed the stairs. Stripping out of one of her few good dresses, she pulled on her jeans and a flannel shirt. Jerking on a thick pair of socks, she went back downstairs, through the kitchen, and into the mud room where she slid her feet into her work boots.

Stepping outside, she ignored the mist falling, knowing there were animals to feed, eggs to collect, and goats to milk. Unlike other jobs where bereavement leave was expected and taken, farm work did not stop even when your heart was breaking.

Now, several hours later, the animals were in the barn, fed and milked. The hens were roosting, their eggs collected. She had walked around the fence line, checking to make sure the pastures were secure, and she was now sitting at the kitchen table.

She had no desire to eat, feeling nauseous at the idea of food. She simply sat with her forearms resting on the table, her hands clasped together. The house was eerily quiet. She waited, almost expecting to hear her grandfather walking through the back door, the heavy clump of his boots hitting the floor. She wanted to glance to the side and see him walk into the kitchen, his wide smile greeting her. He would have talked about the animals, what needed to be repaired on the farm, how the garden was doing, and even news and gossip from the neighbors.

But he was not there, and the bone-chilling acknowledgment that he would never greet her that way again moved over her. She let out a long, shaky breath. Standing, she moved to the back door to check the lock, then repeated the action with the front door, something that he had done each night.

Walking up the stairs, she stopped outside the room that was his, the one he had shared with Grandma. The night he died, she had come in from the hospital and closed his door, unwilling to peer inside. Now, she hesitated with her hand on the doorknob, then slowly backed away. *Not now. Not tonight.*

Her room was across the hall, and she went inside, stripping out of her work clothes. After a quick shower, not willing to wait for the water to warm, she pulled an old, soft T-shirt over her head. She barely glanced at the unrecognizable woman in the mirror. Climbing underneath the covers, she lay for hours, but sleep did not come. Her chest heaved and another cursed tear slid down her cheek, wetting her pillow.

She wondered if she would rest any that night, knowing that early the next morning she would need to rise as she did every day. The farm and the animals would not wait for grief.

5

The next morning, Lizzie pried her swollen eyes open, wanting to do nothing more than pull the covers over her head and not move. In the distance, she could hear the bleating of goats and sighed heavily as she sat up in bed. Looking around her room, she could almost pretend that it was just another day. A day where she and Papa Beau would rise early, greet each other before both going out for the pre-breakfast chores. Once done, they would meet back at the house where they worked side-by-side fixing a hearty breakfast, downing it with strong coffee. They would sit at the table and discuss the day, then, once the breakfast dishes were cleaned, they would head back out, each taking care of what needed to be done on the farm.

But now, sitting in bed, there was nothing but silence in the house, and a weight settled on her chest so heavy she wondered how her body did not cave in. The bleating continued and, not giving in to the overwhelming grief, she flung the bed covers back. Dressing quickly, she ran a brush through her hair before tying it back then pulling her ponytail through the back of a baseball cap.

Repeating the actions that were rote, she headed outside. The back door led to a brick patio, and from there, a worn path led to the gravel drive. The animals heard the sound of her boots approaching as she walked toward the barn, their bleats increasing in volume.

The two-story structure held enclosures for the alpacas and the goats. Sunlight sent rays through the dust as it beamed through a few loose boards. A large metal bin contained some of the food. Tools were now on the second story along with some hay. Throwing open the door, she observed the goats all vying for attention, pushing against each other in an effort to be fed first.

After she carried the feed out into the fenced grassy area near the barn, she opened their gate. Rushing her, they pushed their way over the dirt path to get to the food. "Get back, you sillies," she grumbled. Watching for a moment to make sure they behaved, she then turned to the alpacas. They were humming and bending forward, eager for her to pet them.

Feeding them next, she let them out into their field. In the pen near the barn, she fed and watered the pigs. Next were the chickens, who were already scratching for their feed before she had put it down. Stepping into the coop, she gathered the eggs using the same basket her grandmother had used years before. The handle was worn, but she could not bring herself to replace it. "I suppose one day when it falls apart and I drop all the eggs, I'll know it's time to get a new one," she mused aloud to one of the hens still sitting in her laying box.

Walking back up the drive, she carried the eggs to the house. It had not eluded her notice that she had talked to the pigs, goats, alpacas, and chickens. But there was no human to greet.

Fatigue pulled at her, making her feet feel like lead, and she leaned her hip against the counter after setting the eggs down onto the worn counter. The house was as silent as a tomb. And while she usually craved the calm, she could not stand the natural desire to listen for her grandfather's footsteps, knowing they were not coming. She had no inclination or money for a fancy gadget for music but flipped on the old radio that Papa Beau kept on the kitchen counter. He had it set for a country station, which was fine by her. Turning the volume up, she drowned out the silence as she fixed a cup of coffee and a slice of toast.

Sitting down to her meager breakfast, she knew she would become hungry soon but had no desire to cook for just herself. She was not even sure she could choke down the toast past the lump that had settled in her throat since the moment she had found Papa Beau lying near the fence.

Lost in her thoughts, she jumped at the sound of a knock on the kitchen door. The way the house was situated, the front door was rarely used and the welcoming kitchen door was next to the drive. Gritting her teeth, she considered not answering it, having no desire to play hostess to more of the well-meaning church ladies. But, with the radio blaring, it was obvious that she was home. Dropping her chin to her chest, she sucked in a deep breath before moving to the door and flinging it open.

Expecting to see several gray-haired women, she blinked in surprise at the man standing before her. For some reason, her gaze dropped to his feet, finding shiny black shoes, so different from what her grandfather's old, scuffed work boots looked like. Her gaze traveled up his legs, his muscular thighs encased in dark blue pants. His abs were trim leading up to wide shoulders, all covered in a tailored, light blue, neatly-pressed shirt, a navy print tie knotted perfectly around his neck.

But it was his face that caused her gaze to stutter to a halt. Strong jaw, neatly shaven. Full lips with a tiny scar running through his upper lip. And sky-blue eyes. She blinked again, her hands still on the open door, and tilted her head in silent question.

"Lizzie?"

Jerking slightly, she nodded. "And you are?"

His lips curved ever-so-slightly as he introduced himself. "I'm Scott. Scott Redding. I was your grandfather's accountant, and I just came by to offer my condolences."

It took several seconds for his name to register, then recognition hit her. "Oh, yes." She shook her head slightly, remembering her grandfather's opinion of the young accountant. *'Oh, Lizzie, Scott has some wonderful ideas for the farm.' 'I've just been into town, Lizzie, and met with Scott. He's a smart boy, that one.'*

"I began to wonder if Papa Beau was going to adopt you."

She watched as Scott blinked, and she rushed to explain. "Every time he came in from a meeting in town or the American Legion, he was full of effusive praise for you."

His shoulders visibly relaxed. "I was very fond of him as well. I can't imagine how hard this is for you. I lost my grandfather a few years ago, but he and I never had the chance to work together like you and Beau did."

His warm voice soothed over her, and she witnessed the crinkle between his brows and the way his gaze held hers. She lifted her hand and rubbed her forehead, willing the pain to subside. Suddenly aware that she looked bedraggled next to his dapper appearance, she added, "Thank you for your condolences. I realize at some time I'll need your services, but, for now, I fear I'm not up to discussing what needs to be done."

If he was surprised at her dismissal, he did not react. Instead, he inclined his head slightly and said, "I understand. We can set up a time to go over the estate taxes. If there's anything I can do to help, please let me know." He glanced over his shoulder, then turned back and added, "I can certainly help with some of the chores around the farm and—"

A snort slipped out at the thought of the professionally-dressed accountant attempting to corral the goats. "I... uh... that's not necessary. I have my routine with the animals, and they're used to me. But thank you... um... I'll call to set up an appointment." She stepped back and closed the door, hating to appear rude but afraid if she did not sit down, she might fall down with fatigue. She tip-toed toward the sink and peered out the window. She watched as he sighed heavily before turning and walking toward his vehicle parked to the side of the house.

Instead of climbing in immediately, he stood, hands on his hips, and stared out over the farm for several minutes. She had no idea what he was thinking, but curiosity held her attention as she continued to watch out the window.

He walked over to the first fenced pasture. Caesar ambled toward him, and her breath caught in her throat as she battled the need to rush out and keep the errant alpaca from trying to take a bite out of her visitor. She watched in surprise as Scott lifted his hand toward Caesar, and instead of nipping at his fingers, Caesar leaned forward and sniffed. Scott then smoothed his hand over Caesar's head and down his long neck.

The bizarre sight of the dapper accountant standing on the dusty path next to a barbed-wire fence lined with weeds and petting the large alpaca sent a strange emotion moving through Lizzie's chest. The heavy weight that had pressed down upon her since finding Papa Beau lying on the ground was still present, but ever-so-slightly lighter.

With a final pat, Scott walked to the other side of his SUV and climbed inside. Unable to tear her eyes away, she watched as he turned around on the gravel drive and pulled out onto the road. She stood motionless at the kitchen sink for several more minutes, her mind swirling and her heart aching. Her stomach growled its protest from only having coffee and toast.

Pulling open the refrigerator door, she reached

inside and grabbed one of the casseroles, unheeding its contents. Nuking it in the microwave, she sat down at the table with a glass of water and ate on automatic pilot, not tasting the food.

Alone. All alone.

Glancing into the rearview mirror as the large, white farmhouse slowly disappeared from view, Scott shook his head. *Well, that was a disaster.* Mentally kicking himself over his choice of clothing, he had assumed that showing up in his business clothes would be a sign of respect. But it had made him appear pompous, and even though his offer to help was sincere, she viewed him as unable to help on the farm.

The sight of her had given him pause, although he had to admit he had no idea what he'd expected. Her eyes were red-rimmed, but that was normal with someone who had most assuredly cried a great deal recently. Her complexion was clear although pale, even though she worked in the sun. A ball cap covered her hair, and even though he could not see the back of her, he assumed the blonde tresses were pulled into a pony-tail. Her clothes had a bit of dirt on them, and considering that she was standing in her socked feet, he assumed she had left her boots at the door when she came in from her morning work.

Standing so closely, he could see that her height brought her to his shoulders. Her jeans fit snugly over her hips and long legs, but the unshapely shirt hid her curves. Growling aloud, he chastised himself for thinking about her curves when she was clearly upset.

Sighing again, he could not keep the vulnerable expression on her face out of his mind. He admired the steel in her spine and the proud lift of her chin as she declared her independence, but her blue eyes held a sea of pain.

He wondered about the women's offer to help and hoped it would be well-received. Ten minutes later, he parked along the street in front of the McFarlane–Redding Accounting offices. Stalking in, he nodded toward Mrs. Markham and headed directly to Lia's office.

Glad that she did not have a client, he knocked on the doorframe before walking straight into the room and plopping onto one of the chairs in front of her desk. Scrubbing his hand over his face, he sighed.

"I get the feeling that your visit with Lizzie did not go so well," Lia said, closing the file on her desk and giving him her full attention. "What happened?"

"I'm an idiot."

A chuckle sounded from Lia as she lifted her hand to attempt to stifle the noise. "I hardly think you're an idiot."

"Oh, yeah? I show up in these clothes, the ones that are perfectly acceptable for our office, then proceed to offer to help her with chores on the farm. Let's just say she was not impressed with my offer."

"I'm sure she was just overwhelmed."

Slumping in the chair, he shook his head in dejection. "So, any advice on how to help?"

Now it was Lia's turn to observe him carefully, tilting her head slightly to the side as she held his gaze. "Well, you could just leave her alone."

"That's part of her problem," he protested. "She is alone!"

"Hmmm," Lia murmured. "Just how interested are you in helping Lizzie?"

Sitting up straighter, he defended his interest. "I liked her grandfather, and I liked how he talked about her. He had so much admiration for her, and yet wanted to make sure that things were set up so that she would be taken care of. I want to make sure that his wishes are carried out."

"Well, you can keep it just professional. Wait several weeks and then make an appointment to stop by or have her come here. Go over the taxes, the estate, and see what you can do to help her financially."

"It doesn't seem right to just let her flounder on the farm alone. Beau once said that she doesn't get out much and had little time to make friends."

Tapping her fingernail on her desk as she appeared deep in thought, Lia said, "I know that Jillian, Tori, and Belle were planning on making a trip out to see her soon. Maybe that will give her some female companionship."

He scrubbed his hand over his face and nodded. "You're probably right." Pushing himself to a stand, he walked back into his office. He was soon buried underneath a pile of papers, entering the sums and figures into his computer, but his mind continually drifted to the Weston Farm... and Lizzie.

6

Lizzie struggled to get out of bed the next morning. The weight on her chest had not dissipated, and while her mind accepted that it would be a long time before she could think of Papa Beau without feeling crushed, she wondered how she was expected to keep going. She had worked the previous day, pushing herself beyond her limits, hoping that fatigue would take the place of her sadness. All it had done was make her tired in addition to being sad.

She spent the morning tending the animals before driving the golf cart around the property to check the pasture's gates and fences. Several of Papa Beau's farming friends had called during the week, offering to help her with anything she needed. She appreciated their gestures but politely turned them down, knowing they had their hands full with their own farms.

Getting out periodically along the fence row, Lizzie checked to make sure the pasture was secure for animals. Papa Beau had been so careful, and she did not want to ignore a potentially loose area in the fence so that the goats or alpacas could get out. There might not be a lot of traffic on the road that went by their farm, but she would hate for any of them to have an accident.

The goats were frolicking in their field, and as she drove through the next pasture, all three alpacas followed her. She could not help but smile as she watched their antics, their long necks bending as they placed their heads closer to hers so that she could run her fingers over their fleece.

"Caesar, it's going to be shearing time soon. It's getting hot and I don't want you, Mark Antony or Cleopatra to be miserable." Moving on to the next gate, they followed her as she continued her conversation with the alpacas. "I was going to get Papa Beau to help me with the shearing, but I'll have to see if I can get someone else to help. I just don't think I'm ready to try to do it by myself."

Glancing into the pasture where the goats were, she grinned as several of the kids hopped around, climbing on the wood stumps that she and her grandfather had placed out for them. Sucking in a deep breath, she let it out slowly, then tilted her head back so the sun beamed down on her face. The ever-present ache was still there, but she realized how much freer she felt outside.

The sound of crunching gravel had her turn to see a shiny black pickup truck coming to a stop nearby. Even from a distance, it was not hard to see the words Giordano Farms emblazoned on the side of the truck. Licking her suddenly-dry lips, she watched as Luca

Giordano climbed from the driver's side and walked toward her.

His hair was silver, combed back neatly. Clean-shaven, his face gave no indication of his age other than the deep lines emitting from his eyes. Years of working in the sun had etched themselves where he had squinted. He was wearing khakis, neatly-pressed, along with a navy shirt, his farm's logo embroidered on the pocket. Boots were on his feet, worn, but not scuffed. He looked the part of the farmer who no longer had to work the land but had an empire under him to do so.

She watched as he approached and lifted her chin slightly, waiting to see what he had to say.

"Ms. Weston," he began, "I wanted to come by and express my condolences. I enjoyed talking with and doing business with your grandfather. I considered Beau a friend, and his presence will be greatly missed."

Breathing in and out through her nose as she pinched her lips together for a moment, she nodded. Clearing her throat, she replied, "Thank you. Yes, he will be missed."

His gaze left hers and drifted over her shoulder toward the pastures where the alpacas were staring at them and the goats were munching on the grass.

Turning back toward her, he said, "This place will be too much for you to handle." She bristled, but he threw his hand up in a placating manner. "I'm not trying to be insulting, Ms. Weston. With the animals you're raising, you'll never be able to bring in enough money to keep this farm going. Beau would not have wanted that for you."

Tilting her head to the side slightly, she tried to lock down the trembling that was moving through her body. Whether it was from adrenaline, fatigue, or rage she had no idea but was determined to remain calm on the outside. "I know that my grandfather wanted me to continue our farm and do it in any way that I saw fit."

"That may have been what he said to you, but I know he had concerns."

At that, she jerked as though slapped. *Had Papa Beau talked to Mr. Giordano? Had he thought that I couldn't do this?* Tamping down her panic, she shook her head. *He would have never done that.*

"I'm sure he had concerns because he loved me. But I'll be fine. Just fine."

Luca held her gaze for a long minute, his neutral expression giving away nothing. Finally, he inclined his head slightly and said, "Well, Ms. Weston, I wish you all the best. But please, remember me. Your grandfather sold me a number of acres over the last few years. He was paid a fair market price, and I'm more than willing to do the same for your farm."

She had been determined to not show weakness but wrapped her arms tightly around her waist as though to ward off his words, his offer, and his insinuations—and to quell the quaking of her body. With a short, jerky nod, she replied, "Thank you for your condolences. Now if you'll excuse me, I need to get back to work."

His lips curved into a smile, and he nodded his goodbye. She watched as he climbed back in his truck, executed a perfect three-point turn, and drove out of her lane and down the road. When he was finally out of sight, she fought the desire to collapse onto the ground and scream out her frustration. Just then, the humming from her alpacas caused her to turn and watch as they trotted over to the side where she had feed set out for them.

Refusing to give in to the conflicting emotions of fear and anger that Luca had brought forth, she went back to work. An hour later, the goats had been milked, all animals fed, and the barn mucked out.

She walked back to the three alpacas, once again running her fingers through their fleece, knowing that it would be time to shear them soon. She had seen goats and sheep being shorn and learned that the process would be very similar to the alpacas, except their size made the chore much more difficult to manage.

Cleopatra came to her readily, and she chatted for a few minutes with the beautiful animal, her mind still in turmoil.

Glad for an early morning run before the day became muggy, Scott jogged around the track at the nearby middle school. He was not alone, seeing quite a few of his friends running as well. Several were local law enforcement and keeping in shape was a requirement for their job. Others just liked the exercise.

"I figured I'd better get out here and start running if I was going to keep up with you at the AL race," Jason called out.

"Well, hell, if it isn't the bionic man," Aiden shouted, coming up beside him.

Laughing, he said, "You'd better believe this contraption gives me ability, but I'm not sure I've got the speed of the bionic man."

Looking to the side, he saw Joseph's eyes drop to Scott's blade prosthesis. "I'll come in to see you once I get this race over with. I want something new around my leg near the amputation, and would like to get some ideas from you." Joseph silently nodded, then continued to run.

As they ran around the track, he was soon surrounded by his group of friends, laughing and joking as they paced themselves. Many were married or engaged, and from their conversations, he discerned that impending fatherhood was first and foremost on their minds.

As the group slowly disbanded, he continued to run several more laps, now alone. Not one to wallow in self-pity, he had already faced the realization that it would take a very special woman to see past his amputation. In the last several years, he had found that some women's interest in him waned almost immediately when they discovered that he was missing part of his leg. A few had even sworn that it would not make a difference until they were in the middle of getting hot and heavy but then could not get past the stump. Recently, he had not even attempted dating, deciding that his hand on his cock was going to have to make do until he could find the right woman.

As he slowed down and made his way to his SUV,

the vision of Lizzie came to mind. She was beautiful, but it was obvious she had no idea of her appeal. She was strong, and yet, her vulnerability was not hidden.

Sighing as he sat down on the back of his opened SUV, he pulled off the carbon-fiber c-blade with a suction suspension socket. It had taken a lot of trial and error to find the proper fit, but now that he was used to running with the prosthetic, he appreciated the engineering. Twisting around, he grabbed his walking prosthesis, sliding on the variety of socks and sleeves. As he drove home to shower, Lizzie stayed on his mind, and he wished that he had made a more favorable impression on her.

Walking into his rental, he grinned at the enthusiastic greeting he gained from his dog. Bending, he gave Rufus a good rub down. Opening the back door, he threw a ball into the small yard, laughing as his three-legged dog bounded out of the house and across the grass, snagging the bright yellow ball in his mouth. Trotting back, he dropped it at Scott's feet, who continued to throw it several more times before they finally went back into the kitchen.

After pouring kibble into Rufus' dish, Scott headed to his shower. With the use of a shower chair so that he did not have to maintain his balance on the slippery tile, he quickly scrubbed off the sweat. With the aid of his crutch, he made his way back into the bedroom. Sitting on the edge of his bed, he pulled on his boxers before he rubbed unscented powder over his residual limb. Gliding the liner on next, he then added several socks to make this fit comfortable. Standing, he stepped into his below the knee prosthesis and pressed down until he heard it locked into place. Sitting again, he slid his socked feet into his dress shoes before moving to his closet and choosing a shirt and tie to go with his dark pants.

Letting Rufus out once again to do his business, he finally headed to his office. It was time to determine how he could help Lizzie—and, hopefully, get to know her better.

7

A week had passed since Papa Beau's funeral, and Lizzie wondered when she would be able to wake up and face the day with something besides a grimace at what needed to be done without her beloved grandfather around.

Forcing her body to go through the motions, she made it through her early morning chores, then pushed herself to take a shower and find something appropriate to wear. Her grandfather's lawyer had asked her to come by, and he would go over Beau's will with her. Standing in front of the mirror in her bedroom, she stared at her reflection. Her hair was brushed and pulled back with a headband. She was wearing a pair of dark slacks with a blue blouse. Boring, but acceptable. She lifted her gaze but hated seeing the haunted look in her eyes, so she quickly turned away.

Grabbing her purse, she headed out to Beau's old truck. It wheezed to life as she crossed her fingers over the steering wheel. She hoped she would not see anyone in town she knew, not wanting to make conversation. She had nothing new to say. *Yes, I'm fine. Yes, I miss him, too. Yes, I'll call if I need anything.* Glad to find a parking place outside the lawyer's office, she executed a horrible parallel parking job. Climbing from the truck, she glanced down to brush a few stray strands of straw from her pants. *That's what happens when you drive in a farm truck.*

Looking at the old brick-front office, she pulled on the door and stepped in, nodding politely toward the receptionist. Mrs. Grassley had been working with the lawyer for as long as she could remember.

"My dear, Lizzie, I'm so sorry about your grandfather," the receptionist said, standing from her desk and offering her hand. Clutching it for a moment, she said, "Follow me. Mr. Barker is ready for you."

Lizzie was grateful that Mrs. Grassley had not gone on and on about her grandfather but assumed that the elderly receptionist had watched many grieving relatives move through the lobby toward the lawyer's office. Obediently following, she was ushered into the office and smiled slightly toward Preston Barker, Beau's long-time friend and lawyer.

He stood and hurried around his desk toward her, his hand extended in greeting. "Lizzie, I know how difficult this is for you. I'm so glad you could come in today." He led her toward a comfortably-worn leather chair and continued, "I loved Beau dearly. I miss him so very much."

With her hand warmly clasped in his, she allowed his words to move through her, fully understanding that she was not the only one grieving. Her slight smile was sincere as she said, "I know what good friends the two of you were. I'm glad you were in his life."

He sat down at his desk again, glancing at the folder of papers in front of him. He was dressed as she had always seen him, a dark suit with a white shirt and dark tie. His white hair was thin on top, and the lines on his face were deeper than she had remembered. She looked down at her hands in her lap, remembering Papa Beau claiming, *"Never trusted lawyers too much, except my old friend Preston. He's about the best friend I ever had."*

The only sound was the tick of the old clock on the wall, and she waited for him to speak. He looked up and glanced at the clock, saying, "We only have one other person that we're waiting for, and he—"

Mrs. Grassley appeared in the door and said, "Right this way, Mr. Redding."

Lizzie's head swung around toward the door where she watched in shock as Scott walked into the office. He smiled at Mr. Barker before turning his attention to her.

"Lizzie," Preston said, standing from behind his desk, "I've asked Mr. Redding to be here. It was your grandfather's wish that he be present at the reading of the will."

Saying nothing, her heart began to pound with nerves. *Did Papa Beau not trust me with the farm?* Trying to force her expression to calm, she offered what she was sure was more of a grimace than a smile.

Preston nodded toward the other chair and said, "Scott, please take a seat." Turning his attention back to

Lizzie, he said, "My dear, let me do the reading, and then I think everything will be clear."

Nervous, she sat, her back ramrod-straight, her hands now clasped even tighter in her lap. Not trusting her voice to speak, she remained silent, staring toward Preston, refusing to look to the side.

The lawyer shuffled a few papers around and then said, "I'm sure it's no surprise that everything now belongs to you, Lizzie. He knew that your mother was taken care of since she married and so there was no money left for her. What makes it all better for you... on advice from Scott, Beau had already placed your name on his accounts and the farm deed so that you won't have to pay inheritance taxes. This means the land, the house, the animals, and all the possessions contained on the land or in the house are yours. He had a checking account and savings account at the Baytown Bank, and a small trust fund for you as well."

She was not surprised that her grandfather had left everything to her, but the news that Scott had saved her a great deal of money in taxes—along with his presence in the room—made her feel unbalanced. Uncertain why Papa Beau wanted him there, she remained perched on the edge of her seat, heart racing, palms sweating.

Preston slid his glasses off of his face and, pulling out a handkerchief, began to clean the lens. Once again, the only sound in the room was the ticking of the clock. Uncertainty filled her, and she glanced to the side, observing Scott staring at her, a concerned look on his face. Just when she could take the suspense no longer, she opened her mouth to speak when Preston replaced his glasses back on his face and cleared his throat.

"Of course," he began, "your grandfather knew that there would be things that we hate to deal with but need to when someone passes. That's why he asked for Mr. Redding to be here. He seemed to think that you would try to do things on your own, and he wanted to take that burden from you."

At those last words, Lizzie sucked in her lips tightly to quell the quivering while blinking back the tears. She swallowed deeply, afraid to speak for fear that her words were turned to sobs. She was glad to hear that the reason her grandfather wanted Scott present was because he could handle all the accounting for the farm. Blowing out a shaky breath, she nodded.

Preston continued, "And your grandfather knew that times were changing, and you had some good ideas about what to do with the farm. He knew it wouldn't survive trying the same old farm methods from his time or his father's time."

She remembered her grandfather's incredulity when she first wanted to buy goats and alpacas, but she'd showed him the research she had completed on how they would be able to use some of their pastureland for those animals and then use the fleece and milk to make products to sell. She had held her breath, wondering what his response was going to be, but Papa Beau had simply smiled and said, "I think you've got something there, girl." Chuckling, he had added, "I sure would like to have seen my daddy's face at the idea of one of them alpacas in his fields." As the memory moved through her mind, she focused her attention back on Preston as he began to shuffle papers on his desk again.

Clearing his throat, Preston lifted his gaze toward her. "Beau also wanted to make sure you had someone who could help you with a good business plan. That was the other reason he wanted Scott here... not just for taxes but to work with you to make sure the farm was solvent."

At that, she blinked, her body jerking as though slapped. "He's supposed to help *me* formulate *my* business plan?" She swung her head around to stare at Scott. "But you don't know anything about farming! Or what I want to do!" Not giving either man a chance to speak, she jumped to her feet, looking down at Scott. "For all I know, you're going to tell me to bow to the pressure of Luca Giordano and sell the farm just to make money off the land and then I'll end up with nothing!"

Scott stood quickly, his hands out, saying, "Lizzie, I would never tell you to sell. That's your land and your heritage."

Preston hurried around his desk once again, his hands out toward her. "Lizzie, please, be calm. Beau was just looking out for your interests. He would never want you to sell the farm. That was why he knew that if he was not around to assist, he felt Scott was the perfect person to give you sound business advice."

Dropping her chin to her chest, she shook her head slowly back and forth, staring at her feet as the heavy weight on her chest pressed in deeper. Her voice barely a whisper, she said, "He thought so little of me? That I couldn't do things on my own?"

Preston placed his hands on her shoulders and gave a little squeeze as he leaned in close. His words, spoken steady and strong, said, "My dear, Beau would have done anything for you. You were the light of his life. He loved your ideas and was excited about what you wanted to do. He didn't make this request because he didn't think you couldn't handle things. The only reason he wanted you to have Scott's assistance is so you wouldn't feel so alone. That terrified him, Lizzie… to think that you'd be alone."

He gave her shoulders a little shake, and she lifted her chin to stare into the watery eyes of her grandfather's friend. "But I am alone," she whispered. Holding his eyes, she nodded slightly, her voice barely audible now. "Thank you for your time, Mr. Barker." Taking a step back, she turned and picked up her purse and walked out of the room, avoiding Scott's gaze. She passed by Mrs. Grassley but said nothing as she walked out to the truck.

She drove in silence, her mind in turmoil. Looking ahead, she saw The Diner, a popular restaurant in the county near the little town of Easton. The old-fashioned restaurant held many fond memories. As a girl, her grandfather would stop there on his way back from the feed store, and he would buy her a milkshake, complete with whipped cream and a cherry on top. She would happily slurp the sweet concoction while Papa Beau chatted with the owners, Joe and Mavis. Years later, she befriended one of the waitresses, Carrie, a single mom who worked long hours but always managed to have a smile and a friendly word.

Without thinking, she jerked on the steering wheel and pulled into The Diner's parking lot, suddenly filled with the desire for something familiar... something she had shared with Papa Beau. Glad that the breakfast crowd was over and the lunch crowd had not descended upon the popular restaurant, she pushed open the door, hearing the familiar bell announce a new customer.

Carrie was behind the counter, her eyes hitting Lizzie at the same time that Joe and Mavis looked up from the back. Her breath caught in her throat as doubt slid through her, the acute loss of Papa Beau taking over. Carrie moved to her, her eyes warm as she pulled Lizzie into a hug.

"Let's get to the counter, sweetie."

With a jerky nod, she allowed Carrie to guide her over to the counter where she settled onto one of the old stools. She looked through the kitchen's pass-through window and caught Joe's eyes. He held her gaze for a long moment then lifted his chin in greeting. It was a simple movement, but she understood the unspoken words of condolence and found his silent gesture to be comforting. Offering him a slight smile, she nodded in return.

"You look like you could use some coffee, darling," Mavis said, coming up behind her, resting her hand on Lizzie's back. "You also look like you could use some food."

"Do you feel like you can eat anything?" Carrie asked.

She was about to deny their offer when the scent of bacon, fried potatoes, and scrambled eggs hit her, and she sighed. "Yeah, it smells really good. But… um… not too much."

While Mavis went to the kitchen, Carrie poured a cup of coffee and then settled on the stool next to her. "I didn't want to hover at your grandfather's funeral, but I'm glad you came in today. I was actually going to call you later. I wanted to see how you were doing and see if there was anything I could help you with. Of course, Jack has school during the day, but he would love to come help you on the farm in the afternoons." Chuckling, she added, "He may only be eleven, but I know he'd be a good worker and would love being around animals."

Often preferring solitude, Lizzie found that she liked the idea of the irrepressible Jack helping on the farm occasionally. Nodding, she replied, "Let me get my head together about everything I need to do, and I'll give you a call. Actually, I would love to have him help. The animals love company, and I'm not sure that I can give them my full attention right now."

Carrie slid her arm around Lizzie's shoulders and gave her a hug. "I want to ask how you're doing, but that would be such a foolish question. But can I confess that I'm worried about you?"

Tilting her head to the side, she repeated, "Worried?"

"I know that you've always worked hard, throwing yourself into anything that Beau or the farm needed. But I'd really like you to come to one of the American Legion Auxiliary meetings with me sometime. I think it would be good for you to get out, even one night a month, and make some new friends."

She opened her mouth to refute Carrie's suggestion, but Carrie wasn't finished.

"I know about hard work, Lizzie. I know about working every moment that I could to make enough money so that Jack and I had a roof over our heads and food on the table. But, unlike your job, my job allowed me to be around good people here. I want that for you, too."

The sting of tears hit her eyes, and she wondered if that was going to continue to happen every time someone mentioned her grandfather or how they wanted to help her. Grabbing her napkin, she wiped her nose quickly but was saved from replying when the bell over the door sounded once again. Glancing over her shoulder, she watched as Colt Hudson, the tall, power-fully-built sheriff strode in and without missing a beat gave Carrie a kiss, then turned to Lizzie and said, "Good to see you out and about. If you need anything, don't hesitate to let us know."

Her smile was sincere as she nodded her acknowl-edgment, then looked down at the plate that Mavis had set in front of her. It was not overflowing with food, for which she was grateful, hating to be wasteful. She nibbled the toast, forked in a few spoonfuls of the eggs and hashbrowns, and munched on a piece of crispy bacon. As she listened to Colt and Carrie's joking conversation, she was so pleased that her friend was now married to a man like Colt. And, if she was honest with herself, she had to admit that she was a bit envious.

Shaking away that last thought, she finished her breakfast and accepted another round of hugs before leaving. Pulling into the drive by the Weston Farm sign, she breathed a little easier. Papa Beau's will, along with the knowledge that he liked her ideas for change, eased the weight off her chest slightly again.

As she climbed from the car, she looked toward the pastures with the goats and alpacas and smiled. Then her gaze drifted to the fence row that always needed checking and repairing and the outbuildings and barn that needed to be kept up as well. Nibbling on her bottom lip, she sighed. Hurrying inside, she changed into her work clothes and headed back out. If Scott Redding was going to look over her ideas for the farm, he would find it in perfect order.

Scott left the lawyer's office, his shoulders rounded in a slump and his head aching. Deciding to stop into Jillian's Coffee Shop and Galleria to get a cup of coffee, he stepped into the now-familiar old shop. Jillian's parents had restored the rundown storefront to its original glory. The black-and-white-tiled floor and highly-polished cherry paneling with brass sconces on the wall gave off a warm and welcoming vibe. The morning crowd had left, and he made his way toward the barista. Shelves on the back wall caught his attention, and he bypassed the coffee, walking over to see what Jillian had for sale. Sea glass jewelry, handmade coasters, and bottles labeled 'essential oil' filled some of the shelves.

An idea hit him, remembering Beau once telling him that Lizzie made goat milk lotion and soaps. At the time, he'd had no idea what those were... truth be told, he still had no clue. But they seemed like something that Jillian would be able to sell.

"Hey, Scott," a female voice sounded from behind, and he turned around to observe Jillian approaching. A beauty with long, dark blonde hair, she was dressed in her typical bright colors. Glancing down, he spied her baby bump and grinned, knowing her husband was crowing proudly to anyone who would listen about their baby-to-be. "I saw you come in and thought you might want some coffee, but it looks like you've got gift shopping on your mind."

Rubbing his chin, he smiled in greeting and asked, "Do you think you could sell goat milk lotion and soap?"

Jillian stopped and blinked in surprise, her gaze darting from his face over to the shelves he had been perusing. "Uh... are you looking for some?"

His face reddened with blush, and he chuckled. "Sorry, it's not for me. Actually, I'm not even sure what it is."

Jillian's brow furrowed even more. "But you think I should sell it?"

Shaking his head, he said, "I'm sorry, Jillian. I'm afraid my mind is muddled, and I'm not making any sense."

Her face relaxed into a smile and she said, "Come on over, have a cup of coffee, and maybe I can help un-muddle your mind."

He followed her to one of the small tables and soon had a cup of freshly-brewed coffee in his hands. Sipping appreciatively, he carefully considered how much he wanted to tell her. It was important to maintain confidentiality and professionalism with Lizzie's information but he needed to gain more information before talking to her again.

"I know someone who makes homemade goat milk lotion and soap. I know they sell them at the farmers' market, and I know that they want to expand their sales base. I'm not at liberty to say more right now, but I'm just trying to get an idea if there is a market for local businesses to sell the products."

Jillian was already nodding enthusiastically before he finished and said, "Absolutely. My customers love buying local products, and with as many visitors and tourists as we get in this town, they would snap those items up!"

With that validation, he smiled, relaxing deeper in his chair as he sipped his coffee. Lost in thought, he looked up when Jillian cleared her throat and saw her staring at him, her head tilted to the side.

"Do you want to tell me who makes the goat milk products? Will they bring some samples in for me?" She reached into her back pocket and pulled out a business card. "Or you can just have them email me or give me a call."

Pondering what to say, he finally admitted, "Here's the problem, Jillian. I need the suggestion to come from someone other than me." Seeing her startle, he threw up his hand and continued, "Don't ask, because there's certain things I can't tell you in order not to violate confidentiality. But let's just say that I know that Lizzie

71

Weston sells these products at farmers' markets, and I think it would be good for her to have some other avenues."

Eyes wide, Jillian nodded. "I was going to see her soon anyway. A couple of us thought that we would visit, see how she's doing, and invite her to the AL Auxiliary. It would be very easy to find out what she produces and let her know that she can put them here to sell."

Relaxing once more, he nodded. "If you could do that, it would be wonderful. I'd really appreciate it."

Shrugging, she met his smile with one of her own. Tossing her long braid over her shoulder, she stood and smoothed her hands over her growing baby bump. "Hey, don't thank me. I love getting my hands on local products that I can sell here. It's a win-win for every-body." With a pat on his shoulder as she moved away, she headed behind the counter.

Breathing easier, he finished his coffee and headed to his office. Once settled at his desk, he thought over the comments Lizzie made in the lawyer's office. *"For all I know, you're going to tell me to bow to the pressure of the Giordanos and sell the farm, just to make money off the land and then I'll end up with nothing."* Her distraught face filled his mind.

Determined, he fired up his computer, deciding to find out everything he could about Luca. If she was getting pressure to sell, he owed it to her and Beau to do everything he could to look out for her interests.

Thirty minutes later, he picked up his phone and

called Harrison Private Investigations. "Gareth? It's Scott."

Gareth, like himself, was not an original Baytown Boy but had moved to Baytown to live after leaving the military service. Now married to Katelyn McFarlane, he ran a private investigation company with his wife.

"I need you to do some digging for me. I've tried, and I'm coming up blank." Giving Gareth a quick rundown on what he needed, he disconnected the call and leaned back in his chair, scrubbing his hand over his face. The image of Lizzie's face as she left Preston's office haunted him. He had fought the urge to pull her into his arms, offering his comfort and strength. *I might not know farming, and while this started because of my promise to Beau... now it's Lizzie that's captured my attention.*

8

Walking out of the barn, Lizzie wondered how long she would be able to accomplish everything on the farm without hiring help. She remembered Carrie's offer of her preteen son but feared she would spend more time supervising him than him helping her. *Maybe I could invite Carrie and Jack over for a friendly visit, and that would give me an idea of how he is around animals.* Standing on the dirt path, she sighed heavily. *I'm going to need more than just a part-time young boy for help.* With no new ideas forthcoming, she walked back to the house for lunch.

After a ham and cheese sandwich eaten at the kitchen counter, eschewing dining alone at the table, she decided to spend the afternoon making goat milk lotion. Whenever she took her products to the local farmers' market, she always sold out. She loved experimenting with new fragrant oils, something she used to do in the evenings while Beau watched the news or read the newspaper before going out and checking the farm one last time before bed.

Hearing the crunch of gravel outside, she winced at the idea of more visitors. She knew she had been rude to Scott, but it was easier to take her frustrations out on him than the church women bringing food. Stalking to the door, she was surprised to see three women walking toward her.

She recognized two of them, having attended Baytown High School about the same time that they had. Jillian Evans had been the blonde homecoming queen, beautiful and reported to be very sweet. Lizzie had never been in Jillian's high school orbit though, and with little time and little extra money as an adult, she had also never been in Jillian's Coffee Shop. She was married to Grant Wilder, the former homecoming king who was now a Baytown police officer. And she was very pregnant.

Looking from Jillian to the woman standing next to her, she recognized Belle Gunn. That member of the trio surprised her, remembering that Belle had grown up in the poor section of the town's trailer park. She had a hard time imagining they were now friends, but it had been many years since high school. Belle was also married now, but Lizzie did not know her husband.

The third woman had vibrant red hair, and Lizzie had seen her in town. Stunned to see them walking toward her, she blinked as though the apparition would disappear.

As soon they reached her, their faces filled with generous smiles, Jillian said, "Lizzie, I'm Jillian. This is

Belle and Tori. Our husbands knew your grandfather from the American Legion, and we just wanted to stop by to offer our condolences."

Swallowing deeply, she dipped her chin in acknowledgment. "Thank you. I appreciate it."

"We also wanted to see if there was anything we could help with. I know that many people say those words when someone has passed away, but we truly would like to offer or arrange any assistance," Tori said.

Uncertain what they could possibly do to help, she shook her head. "It's very kind of you to offer, but... um... this is a... a working farm. I'm afraid that right now, the animals are used to me, and I have my routine. I think it's best if I stick to that."

Assuming the women would turn and leave, Belle surprised her when she said, "One of the nurses at the nursing home where I work brought in some Weston Farm goat milk lotion. I didn't make the connection until right now. It was wonderful! I had her go back to the farmers' market to buy some more because it was so soothing for some of our patients."

The praise lessened the weight on her chest just a little, and while her smile was tight, she acknowledged the comments. "Thank you. Yes, I make it here in my kitchen." Shrugging, she surprised herself when she blurted, "I was getting ready to make some right now."

"Oh, can we watch?" Jillian asked, her eyes bright with interest.

"Or better yet, can we help? I'd love to buy some to take back to the Sea Glass Inn. My guests would love this!" Tori exuded.

Company was not what Lizzie expected, but she could not think of an excuse against the exuberance from the three women. "I... uh... I guess so." Turning to walk back through her kitchen door, she rounded the counter where she had her supplies already laid out and said, "There's really nothing for you to do."

"Watching would be wonderful," Belle said, her soft voice filled with enthusiasm. "I'm always so impressed with people who have creative abilities."

She opened and closed her mouth several times, but no words came out. Flummoxed, she began mixing the ingredients, finding herself explaining what she was doing as she began the task.

"Um, here I have pasteurized goat milk in this bowl, and I add an equal amount of distilled water, stirring until it's mixed well. Over here, I take the stearic acid and add it to the avocado oil and sweet almond oil that I mixed together just before you came. Next, we add the emulsifying wax."

"This is absolutely fascinating," Tori said, leaning over the counter and sniffing appreciatively. Her eyes met Lizzie's and she smiled. "Thank you so much for letting us watch."

Nodding ever-so-slightly, Lizzie took the large bowl and placed it in her microwave. "I have to heat this for about two minutes so the wax and acid melt in the oils." She pressed the buttons on her microwave, continuing to stare dumbly at the bowl turning around and around, not wanting to look at the women waiting patiently for the next step.

When the microwave dinged, she took the bowl out

and set it back on the counter. She lifted up another bowl and began dumping the thick contents into the bowl of warmed oil. "This is Shea butter. I just stir it in, and it will slowly melt." After a couple of minutes, it had melted, and all of the ingredients were well-mixed. She began to relax, her visitors appearing to enjoy her impromptu lessons. Moving back to the bowl of goat milk and distilled water, she said, "We'll microwave this for about a minute to get it warm."

Once that was accomplished, she poured the oil mixture into the milk mixture, stirring as she went. "You can see that it's beginning to thicken, but we'll help that along and make it smooth by putting it in the blender."

Pouring half of the bowl's contents into the appliance, she pulsed the blender several times and then checked the ingredients. Pulsing a few more times, she then poured it into another large bowl. She finished with her complete, thickened mixture.

"It seems kind of runny," Jillian said, scrunching her nose as she leaned over the bowl and peering down.

"You don't want it to be too thick at this stage or you won't be able to pour it into the bottles."

"Is it ready?" Belle asked, eyes bright.

"Not yet. We have to add in the preservative." Once she stirred it thoroughly, she began to add in the fragrant oils.

"Ooohh, that smells wonderful," Tori gushed, leaning over and inhaling deeply. "How did you ever learn to do this?"

"YouTube," Lizzie replied. When the others looked at

her in surprise, she could not help but smile. "Honestly... you can learn to do anything from YouTube."

Bringing over her clean, clear bottles, she stuck a funnel into the top of one and began pouring the lotion, filling the bottle to almost the top. Placing in the pump lid, she screwed it on tightly. She continued until she had ten bottles filled. Opening a folder she had on the side of the counter, she pulled out labels that she had made. They were simple round labels with the words *Weston Farm Goat Milk*. She carefully centered them on the bottles and pressed them to stick. Pulling out another sheet of labels that listed the ingredients, she pressed it to the back.

Looking up at the women that were staring at her, she suddenly felt foolish. Shrugging, she mumbled in defense, "It's not much, but I like making it."

"I think it's brilliant!" Belle enthused. "My only hobby is knitting, but I love this! If you ever want some help, please let me know. I'd love to come over and assist."

Jillian tilted her head to the side, tapping her forefinger on her chin as though in thought. "Lizzie, would you consider letting me sell some of your goat milk products from my coffee shop?"

"From your coffee shop?" It was hard to keep the incredulity from her voice, not understanding what a coffee shop would do with lotion.

Laughing, Jillian said, "Oh, I should explain. It's really a coffee shop and galleria. I have all kinds of things that I sell there that are locally made. Everything from sea glass jewelry and paintings to woodcarvings. I get a lot of vacationers and out-of-town visitors and they love everything that's local. I have no doubt this would sell like crazy!"

Before she had a chance to reply, Tori added, "I'd like to buy some from you now so that I can offer it to the guests that stay at my inn."

Shrugging, Belle said, "Around the holidays, we like to bring in local artisans to let our nursing home patients purchase items that they can give to their family for Christmas gifts. Most cannot get out to stores and it makes them feel less helpless."

The women all stared at her, but Lizzie's mind locked up. Papa Beau had often told her that she should produce more of her products, but she had always replied that there was never enough time. Just the memory made the tears sprang to her eyes and she blinked furiously trying to keep them at bay.

Embarrassed, she did not have a chance to speak before Belle wrapped her arm around her and led her over to the kitchen table, ushering her to a seat. Stunned, she watched as Tori put on a kettle of water and Jillian searched until she found the teabags. While they made cups of tea, Belle sat on the other side of her, setting a box of tissues nearby.

She dried her eyes and breathed deeply, willing the agonizing pain to lessen. Gaining control of herself, she looked up as Tori and Jillian set mugs of tea on the table. Sucking in a deep breath, she let it out slowly before asking, "I don't understand why you're here. We weren't friends before. You never even knew me way back in high school, and I've never been to your shop in town."

She knew the words sounded rude as soon as they left her mouth, but confusion had mixed with grief and she was too tired to try to guess anyone's motives. Waiting for them to stand up and flounce out of her kitchen in disgust, they remained still. Slowly lifting her gaze, she noted each of them staring at her with expressions of what could only be described as kindness.

Speaking first, Jillian said, "It's been many years since high school, Lizzie. I would hope that you would never hold anything against me from that long ago."

Now embarrassed, she shook her head and said, "No. I'm sorry to have even implied that. I was several years behind you in high school." Shrugging, she said, "I always had to work on the farm, so I did very little in high school other than attend. I didn't really have time for friends or activities. And since then, there was always so much to do here."

They were quiet, and she swallowed deeply before adding, "Farming is what I love, but it's... hard. The farm used to be much larger, but my grandfather was forced to sell off many acres because he wasn't able to produce and sell crops at prices competitive with some of the major farms in the area. We worked from sunup to sundown every day. No days off. No vacations. And it's as though it's all slipping away."

Taking a sip of tea, the ease of unburdening herself, even just a little, made her feel calmer instead of more embarrassed. "But enough about that. I don't know how much I can produce, but I would be very interested in selling more of my products. Besides the lotion, I make goat milk soap." Looking at Jillian and Tori, she said, "I should be able to make enough that I can provide it to you. That would keep me from having to spend time working a booth at the farmers' market."

The women seemed genuinely excited, and they all stood, taking their empty mugs to the sink. Getting ready to leave, they offered her hugs, which she accepted awkwardly. Trying to think of something socially acceptable to say, she glanced down at the baby bump pressing between her and Jillian and asked, "When are you due?"

Jillian's face brightened as she smiled widely and said, "This fall." Laughing, she added, "There's a bunch of us that are expecting right now."

Not understanding who she was referring to, she remained quiet. Belle must have noticed her confusion.

"There's a group of women our age who belong to the American Legion Auxiliary, and quite a few are pregnant now," Belle explained. "The Auxiliary is for family members of current or former military. There are people of all ages that attend the meetings and support the activities. My grandfather was in the military, like yours, and so you would be eligible to join. There's no membership fees or dues or even obligations." Reaching out and placing her hand on Lizzie's arm, she gave a light squeeze. "I know you don't have a lot of free time, but I hope you'll consider coming to the next meeting. I'd be glad to come pick you up so you wouldn't feel like you're walking into the room all by yourself."

Touched by her invitation and the understanding that she would have never walked into a meeting of strangers by herself, she simply nodded, not knowing what else to say. "Carrie Beaumont also asked me to come."

Belle added, "I know right now all you feel is pain. My grandmother raised me, and when I lost her, I felt like I had lost the biggest part of me."

Swallowing deeply, Lizzie breathed through her nose in an effort to still the tears that once again threatened to fall.

"Think about joining us, and I'll check with you before the next meeting," Belle said.

She had to admit that she was curious as she listened to the conversation about the American Legion and the Auxiliary, especially when they talked about the activities they participated in. It seemed the fundraising race that Scott was organizing was first and foremost on everyone's mind.

"The race will be coming right past your farm," Jillian said. "It starts and ends at the North Heron Fairgrounds."

"The auxiliary is going to be selling baked goods and other things at the end of the race," Tori said, looking over at Lizzie. "You should bring some of your goat milk products to sell."

Before she had a chance to reply, the others joined in with their encouragement as well. "Think of it this way," Belle said. "There will be a lot more people at the park than ever come to the farmers' market."

As the idea took hold, she smiled, saying, "Looks like

I need to get busy making some more before next weekend."

With a sincere thanks for their visit, she walked them outside and watched as they climbed into their car.

Just before closing her door, Jillian turned and said, "If I were you, I'd talk to Scott Redding. He's a wonderful accountant and is also great with financial planning. He would have some wonderful marketing ideas for your products."

Lifting her hand in a slight wave, she watched as they drove out of her driveway and down the road. Thinking over Jillian's advice, she snorted. *I wasn't very appreciative of him. I don't know if he'd be willing to help me with anything.*

She needed to clean the kitchen from the lotion-making mess, but the goats were bleating, and the alpacas were no longer wandering around their pasture but were standing at the fence staring at her. Sighing heavily, she thought, *There's no rest for the weary.*

9

"Shit!"

It was earlier than Lizzie normally started her chores, but, not sleeping well since her grandfather had died, she climbed from bed as the predawn sky was just beginning to lighten. Dressed and fixing a cup of coffee, she had glanced out the window and spied some of her goats wandering in the yard.

Shoving her feet into her work boots as she ran outside, she observed the barn door open. Cursing her stupidity for not checking the door the night before, she prayed none of her goats had left the yard and gotten into the road.

Trying to calm her panic, she rushed around, pulling some of them away from her grandmother's shrubs and cursed as she noted that several were stomping through the small flower bed.

"Get out of there!" she grumbled, clapping her hands and attempting to herd them back toward the barn. Belatedly, she realized they would come for food.

Jogging toward the barn, she looked over her shoulder and saw most of them following her.

Once in the barn, she quickly ascertained that the baby goats were still in their pen. The adult goats were following her, and she moved them into their pasture, filling their feed dishes. With a quick count, she heaved a great sigh of relief at having all of her goats.

She flipped an empty bucket over and plopped down unceremoniously on her makeshift seat, resting her elbows on her knees and her forehead in her hands. The sun was just beginning to paint the sky pale blue, rose, and peach, but she did not see any of the beauty.

Giving in to the emotions churning through her, she felt tears running down her cheeks and swiped angrily at them. Standing quickly, she snatched the bucket from the ground and stomped back to the barn, cursing her stupidity for not securing the animals the previous evening.

Standing in the barn, she looked around at the securely-pinned goat kids and the alpacas. Casting her mind back to the night before, she could have sworn that she locked their pen as usual. It was her practice to always give the stable gate a hard jiggle to make sure it could not be pushed open.

Could someone else have done this? Looking around, she saw no signs that anyone had been in the barn and knew she was simply looking for an excuse for her own shortcomings. Dropping her chin to her chest, she stared at her worn, dusty boots and remembered Papa Beau's words. *"Don't beat yourself up for a mistake. Just learn from it and move forward."* Swallowing deeply, she lifted a hand and pressed it against her heart, willing the ache to lessen.

The goat kids began to bleat louder, and once more a sigh left her chest. Picking up another bucket, she pushed all thoughts to the side as she began her chores.

The early morning was not humid, for which Scott was grateful. He ran along the path that he had charted for the fundraising runs. Starting at the Fairgrounds, he planned a 5K along this stretch of road, and a separate 10K race would start in the same place but would meander along several other country roads. The fun run for the kids would be held in the Fairgrounds so that it would be easier for adults to make sure the children stayed safe.

He had decided on this path after he had visited Beau, realizing the beautiful lane with farmland on either side would make the perfect backdrop for the runners. Now, he wondered if Lizzie would be outside working, possibly catching a glimpse of him.

Self-doubt crept along his spine as he thought of what her opinion of him would be if she saw him running in his blade. Aiden had not been far from wrong when he jokingly called him the bionic man. The first time he had ever seen someone running with a blade had been when he was in rehab after his amputation. At that time, he was not sure he would ever walk again, much less run. Watching the man practicing in his blade, Scott had been first appalled at the balance necessary and then intrigued with the idea of success.

Dogged determination kicked in, and he anxiously awaited the first time he was fitted with a blade and tried it out.

As he continued to run down the road, he passed the Weston Farm but did not see Lizzie in the yard or near the fence. A strange mixture of disappointment and relief moved through him. He would have loved to have seen her again, and yet, hated to see the look on her face when she realized he was an amputee. Lifting a hand to wipe the sweat from his forehead, he continued down the road until the farm was out of sight.

Lizzie finished her morning chores with the goats and now stood in the pasture with the alpacas. Finally, calmer from the early morning goat escape, she leaned against the fence and breathed the fresh air deeply into her lungs. The humming sound they made filled her with joy, and she laughed at their antics. Making sure they had feed, she lazily ran her fingers over their fleece. Her mind began to wander, and as so often recently, it wandered to Scott. She could not figure out why he continued to invade her thoughts.

He was certainly handsome, and he had always been exceedingly kind to her. Sighing, she realized that thoughts of him were pointless. He had offered to help, and she'd shoved him away.

The alpacas crowded around her, each trying to see

if she had more treats for them. Suddenly, all three twisted their long necks, swinging their heads to the side. She turned to see what had captured their attention. In the distance, she could see a lone man running, his lower left leg replaced by a blade prosthetic. He was not close to her, but even at her distance she could see that his body was muscular. With a ball cap covering his head, the brim creating a shadow over his face, she had no idea who he was and had not seen him running along the lane before. Not wanting to be caught gawking, she turned and moved with the alpacas back to the barn.

"I'm not going to feed you now," she insisted as she began mucking out their stalls. A few minutes later, she peeked out of the barn and could see that the man had passed her farm, continuing to run down the road. His T-shirt was wet with sweat and clinging to the muscles in his back and upper arms. His running shorts were molded to his taut ass and thick thighs.

His gait was steady, and her gaze dropped to his legs. It was fascinating to watch him run on the prosthetic blade. She had certainly seen runners with a blade on television but never in real life. There was a strange, other-worldly appearance to the appendage, and she wondered how difficult it would be to get used to it. She continued to stare, thoughts of the man running through her mind.

I wonder when he lost his leg. Her grandfather had talked about a farming accident with a young man a few years back, and as she searched her memory banks, she remembered that the accident happened with his arm.

There are a lot of veterans in the area. When coming home from an American Legion meeting, Papa Beau would mention the young men coming back from their service or moving to the Baytown area.

I wonder if he was a runner before. If he was a veteran, she felt sure that running has been part of his life. *It must have been agonizing to learn how to walk again, much less run.* She thought of the news reports that would show the physical therapy and training required just to learn to stand, balance, and walk with the prosthetic leg.

As he disappeared into the distance, she turned, leaning heavily against the barn door, the air in her lungs leaving her body in a rush. She closed her eyes tightly, the image of the man still burning inside. *What fortitude he has to come back from a devastating injury to not only live but take life at a run.* Embarrassment slid through her as she thought about the self-pity she had felt since Papa Beau died.

Certainly, she grieved and knew that was normal and healthy. *But to wallow in self-pity... Papa Beau would never have wanted that.*

Opening her eyes, she looked around the barn, mentally categorizing what needed to be done on a daily basis as well as the general upkeep of jobs that would need to be completed. She walked back outside and turned slowly in a circle. Working long hours, she was able to continue all of her tasks on the farm plus some of what her grandfather used to do.

She dropped her chin to her chest as the reality sunk in. A weight pressed on her chest again as she accepted that she was going to need help, especially if she was going to be increasing her sales for the goat milk products that she so wanted to do. And then there was the shearing of the alpacas.

But where do I come up with the money to pay someone to help? An image of Scott landed right in the middle of her thoughts. With hands on her hips, she continued to stare at her old, scuffed boots. She had been so angry to find out that her grandfather specifically wanted Scott to help her figure out the finances for the farm. But the reality was she needed him. Wincing, she thought of how she had not been very welcoming or accommodating. Pinching the bridge of her nose with her forefinger and thumb, she squeezed her eyes even tighter before sucking in a deep breath and lifting her head.

Squaring her shoulders, she knew what she needed to do. She was Beau Weston's granddaughter and would not allow Weston Farms to go under.

Before she had a chance to reconsider, she finished her morning chores. Once complete, she double-checked to make sure the animals were secure in their pastures and hurried into the house to shower. Taking care to dry her hair smooth, she braided it so that it hung down her back, out of her way. Looking into her closet, she had few clothes that might be deemed appropriate for visiting someone in their office other than what she wore to the lawyer's the other day. Deciding it did not matter, she pulled on a pair of clean jeans, a simple, unadorned T-shirt, and a pair of sneakers that had seen better days but had not become dirty with farm work. Grabbing her purse, she headed to the truck.

Within fifteen minutes, she was driving down Main Street of Baytown, passing Jillian's Coffee House and Galleria. The dark green awning over the few tables that sat on the sidewalk looked inviting, and she wondered if her goat milk products would really sell there. Turning onto a side street, she was able to find parking near McFarlane–Redding Accounting.

Walking with a purposeful stride, she pulled open the front door and stepped inside, her gaze landing on a perfectly-coiffed older woman sitting behind a wooden desk. The woman looked up, smiled pleasantly, and asked, "May I help you?"

Uncertainty filled her and her stomach knotted. She clutched the strap of her purse tightly, and blurted, "Uh… I was going to see… but I don't have an appointment. Uh… I'll just…"

"You're Elizabeth Weston, aren't you?"

Jerking her head up and down in reply, she said, "Yes, ma'am."

The woman stood and extended her hand. "I'm Mrs. Markham. I knew your grandparents from years back. I'm very sorry for your loss, my dear."

Expecting the usual sting of tears that tended to hit when anyone referred to her grandparents, she found Mrs. Markham's warm tone and sincere expression to soothe over her. Letting out a breath she did not know she was holding, she smiled slightly. "Thank you. I appreciate that."

"I assume you're here to speak to Mr. Redding?"

"Yes ma'am, I was. But it can wait. I came on impulse and didn't even consider that I needed an appointment."

She looked down at the neat desk and wondered how to go about making an appointment. "He can call me, or I can just do it now, or—"

"Actually, he doesn't have any appointments this morning, so this is wonderful timing. Give me just a moment, and I'll announce you."

Her mouth formed an 'O,' but no words came out as Mrs. Markham disappeared down the hall before Lizzie could change her mind. She looked around the elegant reception room, several comfortable leather chairs arranged in one corner with large potted plants decorating the space. The walls were adorned with paintings of seascapes in heavy wooden frames. As though drawn to the image of the shore, she moved closer to the wall, studying the exquisite painting of sand dunes, tufts of seagrass, gentle waves rolling in, and gulls flying overhead.

A longing deep inside squeezed around her heart. She had been born and raised a few miles from the Chesapeake Bay but had rarely visited the shore in recent years. She lifted her hand, fingers extended toward the painting, but stopped before they touched the canvas, curling inward as she placed her hand over her chest.

"Lizzie?"

Jumping, she whirled around and saw Scott standing with Mrs. Markham. Her gaze made an immediate assessment, something she seemed to always do when in his presence. And, as usual, he did not disappoint. His tall, muscular frame was covered in a tailored light-blue shirt, rose-colored tie, and dark slacks. His blue eyes held hers and she swallowed, uncertain why her mouth was suddenly dry.

An embarrassed blush flooded her face, and she babbled, "I was just admiring the painting. It's… uh… quite lovely." Relieved when they merely smiled, she continued, "I apologize for just dropping in. I can make an appointment—"

"Not at all." Scott's smile was wide. "I'm glad to see you. Please, let's go to my office."

With a small nod directed toward Mrs. Markham, she followed as Scott led them down the short hall. Her gaze dropped to his ass and she wondered what was wrong with her. When he reached his office, he turned and waved his hand to usher her in ahead of him. As she slid by him, she looked up, realizing this was the closest she had ever been to him. He was tall, easily a head taller than her. His jaw was square and firm, his eyes clear and warm as they held her gaze. His shoulders and chest were broad, something she was now noticing with intimate detail.

He was handsome, no doubt about it, and yet, that thought only served to make her more self-conscious. Taking a seat, she clutched her purse in her lap, glad to have something to do with her hands.

She was surprised when he did not walk around and sit behind his desk but instead settled into the chair that was angled toward her. If he did this to put her more at ease, he failed miserably. She almost snorted aloud at the thought that his close proximity seemed to be muddling her brain once again.

"Are you okay? Is everything okay with the farm?" he said, leaning forward slightly, his gaze intense.

His words moved slowly through her, the tension that had coiled inside loosening. Hurrying to assure, she said, "Yes, I'm fine. The farm is fine. Well, at least I want it to be fine. That's why I'm here, so it can be fine." Realizing she was babbling again, she smiled nervously. "I guess I should stop using the word *fine*, shouldn't I?"

He chuckled, and it struck her that it served to ratchet up his handsomeness level. Forcing her thoughts back to why she came, she said, "I realize that I haven't been very nice to you. I want to apologize for that." She watched as he lifted his hand to wave away her concerns, but she rushed, "No, please, I need to say this."

He nodded his acquiescence and leaned back in his chair, never losing hold of her gaze, giving his full attention to her.

"I… uh… I… oh, my goodness, I'm not sure what on earth I'm trying to say."

He reached out and touched her arm gently. "Just start talking, Lizzie. Say whatever's on your mind."

With that encouragement, she began again. "For a while now, it was just my grandfather and me. The farm changed over the years as it was harder to get anyone who wanted to work on a farm full-time. Papa Beau turned to migrant workers, but they were not always able to be here when we needed them. I don't blame him for selling off some of the land, especially when it became obvious that our small farm could not compete with the larger farms in raising crops."

She dropped her chin and stared at her hands clasped together for a moment, then sighed. "I had read about other animals that we could raise and ways that we could make money with them. Papa Beau was always good to encourage my ideas, but he also used to talk in such glowing terms about you whenever he came back from meeting with you. I suppose, in truth, I was a little jealous of you for holding a place of high regard in my grandfather's eyes when you had never worked on the farm."

"I understand that," Scott replied, and her gaze jumped up to his. "No, I really mean that. I think most of us are always trying to make our families proud, and yet sometimes our families tell everyone else of their pride but not us." His hand squeezed her arm gently as he added, "Lizzie, I can assure you that your grandfather was incredibly proud of you. Whenever he was here, he spoke of you."

The tension loosened a little more, and a slight smile curved her lips. "Thank you for that." She stared into his eyes and once more was struck with how handsome he was. Dark brown hair brushed to the side. A slight scar on his upper lip that only served to give his face character. And warm eyes that held hers. It had been a long time since she had given in to any desire other than just get through the day, but at that moment, she wanted to lean forward, close the distance, and touch her lips to his.

"So, what brings you here today? Please, let me know how I can help."

Blinking, she jolted slightly, embarrassment rushing

through her body realizing that while her mind was playing out the fantasy of kissing him, she was nothing more to him than a client her grandfather had willed to lend assistance.

Forcing her mind to the matter at hand and not her blossoming libido, she blurted, "A business plan." Seeing his unasked question in the tilt of his head, she explained, "I have an idea of how I would like to make the farm more profitable, but I don't know about making a business plan or marketing." She lifted her hand to rub her brow, hating to feel stupid, but she was desperate.

His hand was still on her arm, his thumb gently rubbing over her wrist. "Lizzie, I'm so glad you came to see me today. I cannot wait to hear about your ideas. I know that your grandfather was excited for you to take the farm in the direction that you saw."

"So... um... what do we do now?" she asked hesitantly.

"We go to lunch."

She opened her mouth then snapped it closed. Uncertain she heard him correctly, she repeated, "Lunch?"

"We can call it a working lunch. You can tell me all about your plans and we can feed ourselves at the same time."

Her gaze drifted over his crisp dress shirt and tie, pressed slacks, shined shoes, and then down to her simple T-shirt, jeans, and sneakers. "I don't think lunch is a good idea," she said, hating how her voice quivered.

Standing, he gently pulled her to her feet and with a wide smile said, "I think lunch is the perfect idea."

Before she could protest further, she was being escorted out of the office and down the street with Mrs. Markham's, "Have a nice lunch," ringing in her ears.

10

Under normal circumstances, Scott did not believe in high-handing anyone, particularly a woman. But it was obvious Lizzie had a hang-up about the difference in their lifestyles, and he was determined to break through that emotional barrier. She had sparked his interest just from hearing Beau talk about her in such glowing terms, but now that he had met her, he could not deny how much he wanted to get to know her better.

They walked down the sidewalk, and he glanced down to see her lips were tight—from irritation or nerves he was not sure. "I thought we'd cross over to the Seafood Shack. Their lunch crowd will be gone, so I think it will be quiet enough that we can eat and talk at the same time."

The only response he gained was a curt nod, so he continued his one-sided conversation. "I don't go there very often, but they have a great shrimp basket and clam basket. But if seafood is not what you like, they also have good burgers. Oh, and their fries are amazing.

They sprinkle them with sea salt and some kind of seasoning and give you a ton of them."

Looking over again, he could see her lips curving slightly. "Hey, are you laughing at me?"

A giggle slipped from her lips, and she looked up at him as they continued to walk down the street. "Papa Beau used to go on and on about food that he liked. You reminded me of him as you were talking about the restaurant."

Patting his stomach, he said, "It's true, I love to eat. Of course, I have to exercise to make sure I don't put on too much weight. But then, because I exercise, I have to make sure I eat. It's a win-win for me."

That gained him a small giggle, for which he was glad. By the time they reached the doors of the restaurant, she seemed much more relaxed. Entering, he watched her eyes scan the space quickly, and he knew it was the right place to bring her to put her at ease. The servers were in jeans and T-shirts with the Seafood Shack logo emblazoned on them. The few customers were also in jeans, several being local fishermen who had come in from their catch, wanting to have lunch before going back out. The atmosphere was casual, and he told the server that they needed to sit somewhere quiet so they could talk.

The tabletops were high, and he stood next to Lizzie as she hefted up into her seat. The server had picked the perfect spot, away from the bar and the TVs with constant sports playing. They were next to a window that overlooked the Baytown harbor and could observe fishing and pleasure boats coming in and out of the harbor.

Looking at the menu, Lizzie said, "I've never been here before, but I love shrimp."

"Then you can't beat their shrimp basket," he said. Gaining her nod, he ordered two shrimp baskets and iced tea.

As soon as the server left, he turned his attention back to Lizzie. A few wisps of pale blonde hair had escaped her braid and framed her face. Her blue-eyed gaze wandered over the eclectic interior of the restaurant before settling back on his face. Not wanting to give her a chance to throw the barriers up once more, he said, "Please, tell me what your thoughts are about the farm. You're right, I have no farm experience, so you're the one with the vision and information. But I can help with research and put an actual plan in place."

She reached into her purse and pulled out her phone, quickly tapping before turning it around to him. "Before I bought the goats and alpacas, I looked at what some other small farms were doing that was different." Nibbling on her bottom lip for a moment, she said, "As Papa Beau sold off many of the acres that he used to raise crops on, our overall acreage was cut almost by a third. But what we had left was wonderful pastureland and I thought about sheep but decided that goats would be better. I don't have the equipment for selling goat milk or making goat cheese, but I knew I could make other products with the goat milk. I also knew that alpaca fleece brings in good money. But there are other small farms that are doing all kinds of things... things that I know Weston Farms could do as well."

With that, she started a video on her phone, and he watched with great interest as a woman in another part of the state talked about her farm. As the woman walked around, he could see goats frolicking in the background with supervised children playing with the animals. She moved into the barn where the baby goats had recently been born and talked about cuddle time with the baby goats. In another clip, she showed the farm hosting a children's birthday party, a bridal shower party, and special days where the farm was open to the public for a small fee.

There were film clips of alpaca shearing, goat milk products being created and sold, and then something that took Scott by surprise... yoga classes with goats. As the film clip ended, he blinked, looked up, and asked, "Yoga with goats?"

Throwing her head back in laughter, Lizzie's eyes sparkled, and without the specter of grief overwhelming her, he was struck by her beauty.

"That's all you got out of that video? The goat yoga classes?" she asked.

Dumbstruck as he stared in awe at her, he jolted back to business. "No, no, it's just that was the last thing she mentioned and, well, I had no idea what she was talking about." Smiling, he softened his voice. "Is this something you'd like to do with Weston Farms?"

She nibbled on her bottom lip again, and he realized it was a nervous action that she probably was not even aware she did. Nodding, her hesitation moved in and he rushed to assure, "Lizzie, this is so incredible. I'm intrigued by this idea. Please, tell me more."

"There's nothing like it here on the Eastern Shore," she said. "I love the animals, and I think other people would love being around them as well." She shook her head ruefully and added, "I'm not sure what Papa Beau thought about my idea at first, but as time went on, he realized that times were changing for us. I really think this could be a sustainable small farm, Scott."

He watched the ever-changing emotions cross her face. Nervousness morphed into excitement, which then morphed into a pleading sense of acceptance.

"Lizzie, I love this." At those words, the tension lines around her mouth eased as her face softened.

Eyes wide, she asked, "Really?"

"Absolutely," he assured. "Look, you have what it takes to work with animals and run a farm. You have experience, tenacity, and brilliant ideas. In fact, I think that's why we make a good team. Each of us bring different skills to what you'd like to accomplish."

Visibly relaxing, they were interrupted when the server brought their shrimp baskets. They spoke little as they both dove in, and if her murmurs of appreciation were anything to go by, she was enjoying her meal.

As they finished, he began asking questions, not surprised when she offered well-thought-out answers.

"The farm obviously already has a business license," she said. "I would need to add an extra insurance policy and a waiver form for people to sign. I thought I would use our farm insurance agent and Mr. Parker for legal advice. I would not be providing food, so I don't need a license for that. Goat yoga is a different matter, but I would rather get some of the other activities started first before I take on that activity."

Chuckling, he shook his head. "Yeah, I'm afraid that's one area I know absolutely nothing about."

"It would be nice if I didn't have to travel to farmers' markets and stay all day long to sell my products." Her smile widened and her voice became animated. "Would you believe that Jillian Evans... I mean Wilder... came to visit me the other day and suggested that I put items in her shop! And Tori Evans came with her and wanted to purchase some for her Sea Glass Inn!" Shaking her head, she added, "I didn't even know they knew who I was."

Scott reached up and tugged at the collar of his shirt, heat infusing his face. Looking up, he found her eyes staring intently at him, and he could tell the instant the idea dawned on her.

Leaning back huffing, she asked, "Was that you?"

Lifting his hands in supplication, he said, "Please, Lizzie, don't be mad at me. I really wanted to help you but knew that you were not ready to let me do anything. I happened to go into Jillian's Coffee Shop and noticed her shelves in the back where she keeps local items to sell. I realized how nice your products would look on her shelves, so I mentioned it to her. That was all." Reaching across the table, he placed his hand on hers and gave a little squeeze. "I just wanted to take some of the burden from you."

She remained silent for a moment, thoughts working behind her eyes before she finally spoke. "It would be foolish of me to be angry with you over that, Scott. Having my products in some of the stores is exactly what I wanted, but I had no connections to move forward with that and very little time to work on them. So, thank you. I know you're just doing what Papa Beau asked of you."

A rush of air left his lungs, and he smiled, squeezing her hand again. "Lizzie, I liked and respected your grandfather and would do anything that he asked. But please, know what I'm doing, I'm doing for you."

Her brow scrunched as she held his gaze, but he was saved from further explanation when the server brought their check and a group of fishermen came in, loudly filling the stools around the bar. Quickly signing, he slid from his seat and held out his hand for her. Assisting her down, he gently placed his hand on the small of her back as he guided her out the door. He knew she was confused by his words but did not feel that she was ready to hear how she was filling his thoughts. Determined to keep it professional for now, he led her back to his office.

"I forgot to tell you that Jillian also had me sign up for a booth at the Fairgrounds for the race. She said there would be lots of people there... much more than at the farmers' market."

Unease snaked through him at the thought that she would see him before he had a chance to explain about his amputation... but then, maybe someone had already mentioned it. *But if not, then she might not—*

A touch on his arm startled him, and looking down,

he observed her hand on him and her brow wrinkled once more.

"Hey, are you alright?"

"Yeah, yeah," he rushed. "Just thinking about you selling your products at the race." She nodded, but her expression remained wary. He covered her hand with his as they stood outside his office saying goodbye.

She hesitated, nibbling on her bottom lip. "What should I do next?"

He had been staring at her lips, and it was on the tip of his tongue to say, "Kiss me," but quickly caught himself. "Um... call your insurance agent, and I'll talk to Preston. Once we know what licenses and insurance we need, we'll move forward on those. Go ahead and get some of your goat milk products to Jillian and Tori and we'll start getting word-of-mouth advertising from that."

Smiling, she nodded up at him, her hand resting warmly in his. "Thank you, Scott. For everything you're doing... it means a lot to me. Thank you."

Leaning close, he said, "Believe me when I say working with you is my pleasure."

He watched as pink tinted her cheeks, and she ducked her head as she turned and hustled to her truck. As she drove down the road, he could not keep the smile from his face. Rubbing the back of his neck, he wondered how to tell her about his amputation. *Before she sees my prosthetic or let it happen naturally?*

1 1

Lizzie heaved a sigh of relief on her drive back home, her heart lighter than it had been in weeks. Scott had accepted her apology and was willing to help her with her dream. In the distance, she could see her farmhouse, the sun illuminating the white front, and she was filled with the idea that her grandparents were smiling down on her.

Scott seemed to have led a charmed life, coming from a family with money and having a waiting job in his grandfather's accounting business, but his willingness to help her was no longer a bone of contention. She liked the way he focused on her and her ideas, not pushing them to the side. Spending time with the handsome man would certainly not be a hardship. That idea caused her thoughts to stumble. *No... I can't go there.* Losing her heart to someone out of her league would be ridiculous. *He's a businessman willing to help, that's all.* Sighing, she wished it could be more, but her grandmother's words came to mind… *"Lizzie, remember, if wishes were horses, beggars could ride!"*

A giggle slipped out and she shook her head. Her grandmother was right. It was better to stick to plans that could be worked on and not waste time on wishes that would not come true. Glancing at her watch, she knew the animals were anxious to be fed, and she could not wait to get her chores accomplished so that she could do more research on her business plan.

Pulling into her drive, she saw that there was a pickup truck parked at the end of the lane. Not recognizing it, she parked to the side of the house, glancing at the empty truck. The door was emblazoned with the logo of PD Development.

Curious, she walked around to the back, looking for the driver, startling when she saw a man walking toward her from the gate of one of her pastures. Dressed in jeans and a blue chambray shirt with his business logo embroidered on the pocket, his face was mostly hidden underneath a cowboy hat. Furious at his audacity, she stomped forward, eyes pinned on him.

His smile widened when he saw her, and he immediately called out, "Hello, ma'am. My name is—"

Throwing her hand up in front of her, she said, "I have no idea what your business is, but trespassing on private property is a surefire way to get ejected immediately."

"Ms. Weston, I apologize. I promise there was nothing I was doing other than just taking a look at your beautiful farm."

"Well, I'm a busy woman, so state your business so that I can get on with mine."

He pulled his hat off his head and held it in his hands as he continued, "My name is Paul Dugan, and I knew your granddad, Ms. Weston. Thought a lot of him and wanted to offer my condolences."

She offered him a nod but no words, waiting to see what else he had to say, and it appeared Mr. Dugan had no trouble filling the silence.

"I had presented Mr. Weston with a proposal several weeks before he passed, and he was in the process of considering my offer. You see, I own PD Development, and this land is just right for turning into a nice subdivision. Nestled between Baytown and Easton, lovely views, and driving distance to the Bay. We were setting up another meeting to discuss some of the particulars but were unable to do so. I know that he was very excited about what I was offering, and I wanted to wait a respectful amount of time before coming by and seeing you."

Narrowing her eyes slightly, she said, "Mr. Dugan, I have no idea what you're talking about. My grandfather did not mention you or any proposal that he was considering."

"Well, now, Ms. Weston, I don't think he wanted to worry you over any business details about our joint efforts—"

Heat began searing through Lizzie's blood as his words scored through her. Fists planted on her hips, she asked, "Are you seriously implying that my grandfather was considering a business proposal with *our* farm without talking it over with me? The last thing my grandfather would've wanted to do would be to sell this land!"

Shaking his head in a self-deprecating manner, Paul chuckled lightly. "Now, please don't get upset, Ms. Weston—"

Interrupting him once again, she ground out, "Now I know you're lying through your teeth." She noticed his face hardened at her words, but, too angry to hold back, she let loose. "You may have talked to my grandfather about some scheme of yours, but I assure you he was not considering it. This land has been in my grandfather's family for over a century and he would never have gotten rid of it—not to you, not to anyone. Now, Mr. Dugan, you can march yourself right back over to your truck and get off my land. As of right now, I consider you trespassing once again."

As angry as she was, she noted his hands gripping his hat tightly, and for the first time ever, she felt a snake of fear slither through her at the vulnerability of being in the country all by herself. Lifting her chin, she held his gaze, refusing to let him see her nervousness.

With a slight inclination of his head, he said, "I'll go, Ms. Weston. For now. But I think you'll find that you'll soon need help with this place. Good luck finding it. But my offer will still be around when you come to your senses, although the offer may not be as generous as it is now."

"Get off my land," she bit out between gritted teeth.

He walked back to his truck, and she watched every

step that he took, not taking her eyes off of him until he was no longer visible down the road.

Still shaking from the encounter, her good mood was smashed all to hell. With her fists still on her hips, she dropped her chin and stared at the ground for a long moment, wondering when she was going to catch a break. The image of Scott, a smile on his face, reaching across the table to place his hand gently on hers moved through her mind. *I need help, don't I, Papa Beau? Maybe, just maybe, you knew what I needed.*

The bleating of the goats brought her back to the present, and she called over her shoulder, "Hang on! I'll be right back!" Jogging into the house, she quickly changed into her old, worn work jeans and a T-shirt that had seen better days. With her feet now shoved into her work boots, she headed back out to the animals. Time to get them put into the barn and milked. Time to feed the goats, pigs, and alpacas. Time to feed the chickens and gather the eggs.

By evening, she was exhausted but anxious to make as many goat milk products as she could to take to the race next weekend.

Several hours later, Lizzie stood in her shower, the warm water sluicing over her body, washing away the dirt, sweat, and smell. Scrubbing her scalp, she luxuriated in the feel of the conditioner taming her long hair. Rinsing away all the suds, she turned off the water and stepped onto the bathmat, wrapping a towel around her body and another one around her hair. Using her goat milk lotion, she moisturized her entire body, including her face. As the steam dissipated and she was able to see into the mirror, she stared, wondering what Scott saw when he looked at her.

Her family had always said she was pretty, but she knew it was more the girl-next-door instead of the drop-dead-gorgeous variety. Still thinking about Scott, she wondered what his typical date was like. Beautiful women dressed in what her romance novels called an LBD for little black dress. Heels that would gain them inches and make their legs look longer. Makeup that included ruby lips and smokey eyes.

A snort slipped out when she remembered the last time she had *smokey eyes*, and it had nothing to do with makeup. It was the time that Papa Beau had started a fire in the fireplace, not realizing that an old bird's nest was blocking the chimney. As she rushed to throw open the windows in midwinter to air the smoke from the living room, she had to blink her watery eyes trying to clear the smoke from her vision.

Remembering how Papa Beau had sputtered his discontent at the birds in the chimney, she grinned, glad to finally have a memory that did not have her dissolving into tears. Her heart panged with sadness, but she cherished her memories.

As her thoughts slipped back to Scott, she sighed, deciding that it did not matter what Scott's typical date was like. His friendship with her grandfather was enough to cause her grandfather to ask for his help and Scott was nice enough to agree.

Pulling an old, soft T-shirt over her head, she combed her hair and crawled into bed. Bone-weary, she was not sleepy, so as her hair air-dried, she grabbed the romance novel that was on her nightstand and began to read.

Unfortunately, the words did little to help her sleep, but instead, she tossed and turned, her lust-fevered body dreaming of Scott.

The sun peeked over the horizon as Scott parked at the fairgrounds the morning of the American Legion charity race. The weather was calm, with gentle winds keeping the temperature perfect for a run. As volunteers were beginning to pull into the fairgrounds, he walked around, checking to make sure the event was on schedule.

Tents had been set up in rows on one side, ready for vendors to sell their wares. The AL had charged a nominal fee for a vendor to have a tent, and that money would offset the small fee that the North Heron Fairgrounds charged for the event.

Seeing some of his friends arrive, he walked over to greet them as well as make sure everything was on schedule.

"Good morning!" Katelyn called out. She was pushing a stroller, Finn gnawing on a plastic giraffe. Next to her was Tori, who tossed her hand up in a wave as she pushed another stroller, Eddie leaning against his restraints, waving his hands as well.

Heading toward them, he asked, "I was just going over to the children's area to make sure everyone is ready."

"Don't worry about it," Katelyn assured. "We've got it."

The fairgrounds included a large fenced area with a track around the edge. Scott deemed it perfect for the children's fun run. Volunteers would get the children lined up and observe them as they ran. Face painting and other games were available, all supervised by members of the American Legion and the Auxiliary.

As he continued his walk around the fairgrounds, he observed Zac and other members of the local rescue squads in place as well as the Baytown and Easton police officers and the North Heron Sheriff's deputies. Quite a few of them would be running as well, but others were on duty or race volunteers.

As he thought about the volunteers, he smiled. So many of his good friends were already at the fairgrounds or currently pulling into the parking lot. Brogan and Aiden were running in the 10K with him but had already been driving around the roads this morning to make sure everything was ready.

Ginny, Katelyn, Tori, and Maddie were assisting with the children's fun run along with others. Belle, Jillian, and Carrie were helping with the vendors and the Auxiliary tent bake sales. Rose was operating a tent, selling her ice cream, having already informed Scott that all of her proceeds were going to the fundraiser.

Jade, Lia, and Sophia were helping to coordinate the awards at the end of the race. Jason and Joseph were stationed at the intersection where the 5K runners would go in one direction and the 10K runners would continue on down the road.

"Good morning, Scott," a soft and now familiar voice sounded nearby.

Turning, he smiled as Lizzie walked closer. Clad in jeans that fit her hips and legs like a glove, the bottoms shoved down into cowboy boots made her legs appear even longer. She wore a jean jacket over a blue T-shirt, the color emphasizing her eyes. Her hair was loose, the sleek strands flowing down her back while the front was pulled into a clip away from her face.

His throat was suddenly dry, and he wanted to pull her into his arms and say... *what the hell do I say?* How do you tell someone that you're interested in that part of you is missing? How do you face the stare? How do you deal with the questioning—and maybe rejecting—specter that would move through their eyes? He had faced the results with a few other women, but no one he truly cared about. Jumping as he felt something on his arm, he glanced down and saw that her hand had reached out to him.

"Are you okay?" She leaned closer with her face turned up toward him. Concern knit her brow.

"Yeah, yeah," he rushed. "Just trying to keep track of everything in my head."

A slight smile crossed her lips as she nodded. "I think it's wonderful. I'm really glad that I can help and have a place to get more information out about Weston Farms products."

"Need help getting your tent set up?"

Shaking her head, she said, "No. I've got some rolling carts that I'll put everything in, so I'm fine. You have so much to do, you go ahead, and I'll see you later."

He wanted to stay and talk. He wanted to walk by her side, helping to carry the boxes or pulling the cart. Mostly, he wished he had already explained about his amputation. But he knew he was needed all over the place, so he simply nodded. "I'll see you later." He heard the regret in his voice, but as he walked away, she called out, and he turned to see her smiling.

"Good luck with the race. I'll be cheering for you."

Offering a chin lift, he turned and headed in another direction to check on the latest group of volunteers who had arrived. His heart was heavy, wondering if she would still be cheering when she finally saw him in shorts. Blowing out a breath, he pushed that thought down, heading back to work.

An hour later, he lined up with others at the starting line for the 10K, his prosthesis now changed to the blade. There were few stares because most of the legionnaires knew he was an amputee, and he wore shorts when coaching the AL ball teams so the kids were used to it as well.

He grinned at his friends as the starting gun fired and the race began, leading them out of the fairgrounds and onto the road where the deputy's cars blocked the traffic.

He pushed off, quickly gaining his balance and momentum as his blade hit the ground, the spring in the carbon fiber matching the calf and ankle of his right leg. As the pack of people dispersed, he easily settled into the speed he was comfortable with, finding several others running at about the same pace.

His lungs expanded with fresh air as the breeze

cooled his body. The occasional white cloud passed over the sun, giving the runners a respite from the sunlight although the temperature was not uncomfortable yet.

He and Aiden continued running side-by-side, few words passing between them as they each enjoyed the run. Scott was not attempting to win, just the thrill of competition and the beauty of the sport filling his mind.

Passing the halfway point, they waved to the volunteers who were nearby, offering water and words of encouragement.

"So, are you going to ask her out?"

Jerking his head to the side, he watched Aiden's shit-eating grin slide across his face. "What are you talking about?"

"Lia said you took Lizzie out to lunch the other day. I just wondered when you were going to properly ask her out."

"You're worse than the girls."

"Maybe, but when a friend of mine has a shot at a really good woman, I don't mind pushing."

Chuckling, the two men rounded the bend in the road and continued to run. "I'm working on it," Scott confessed. "Lizzie has had so much to deal with so I'm having to win her over a bit at a time."

"So, she's coming around?"

"Well, at least with me helping with the farm. Now I just have to see if I can get her to go out with me when it's not business."

"I remember when I was first interested in Lia," Aiden said. "We had a rocky start. I thought she was being uppity because she didn't want Emily to play ball with us. Instead, she was just nervous about Emily's hearing impairment and how that would work on the ballfield."

"What won her over?"

"Perseverance. And my charming, magnetic personality."

Barking out in laughter, Scott said, "I suppose for me, I'm going to have to rely on perseverance."

They caught up to a few of the other runners, and Scott estimated they were in the middle of the pack. Running on the blade gave him a sense of freedom, and with the sun beaming down, the wind at his back, good friends all around, and the idea that he could win over Lizzie, he smiled.

"I haven't had goat milk lotion in years."

Lizzie smiled as the older woman squirted some lotion from her tester bottle and rubbed it onto her hands.

"Oh, this is rose scented. I remember my mother using this."

"Do you make it yourself?" another woman asked.

She nodded. "Yes, I have goats at the Weston Farms, and I make all the lotion and soaps myself."

Business had been amazing that morning and she was selling almost everything she had brought, making four times what she had at the last farmers' market.

"Do you ever let anyone come by and visit the farm?" a woman buying some lotion asked as the little girl at her side stared at the picture of the goats Lizzie had placed on the table.

"Actually, I'm getting ready to open Weston Farms for events. I'd love to have children's days and parties where people could see the goats and alpacas."

"Alpacas?" the little girl repeated, her eyes wide.

Smiling at her, she said, "Yes, I have alpacas."

"Well as soon as you start doing that, please put something in the newspaper," the young mother said. "I'm always looking for something new and different for my kids to do. They would love to see that."

After taking the cash and wrapping up the lotion, she handed it to the young woman. "That's a good idea. I'll be sure to do that."

Another woman standing nearby said, "You could have people come in and participate in making the lotion. I'd love to do that."

Barely having time to listen while smiling and nodding and ringing up the sales, that comment struck Lizzie. *I could do that! I could have soap-making days!*

Jillian and Lia walked by, calling out their greetings. "How are sales?"

Looking down at her table, she laughed. "This is all I have left. I've sold everything else that I brought with me today!"

"Fabulous!" Lia cried, catching Lizzie's enthusiasm.

"The 10K race should end fairly soon," Jillian said. "As soon as you're ready, come on over to the finish line and we can cheer for everybody coming in."

It only took a few more minutes for the last of the lotion and soap products to be sold and bagged. With a wide smile and thanks given out, Lizzie's heart felt lighter than it had in weeks. In fact, maybe months. Even before Papa Beau died, she had been worried about finances. Slipping the money she had earned that day into her purse, she hung it crosswise over her body.

With nothing left on the table, she decided to follow the others to the finish line. She could come back and get her empty wagons later.

Walking past the other tents, she observed beautiful jewelry displays made with sea glass, booths with paintings, bird carvings, metal art, and every type of homemade item imaginable. Passing by the Auxiliary bake sale tent, she waved toward a few of the women she now recognized. Glancing at their tables, she was pleased to see that they had almost sold out as well.

At the end of the line of tents, she spied a crowd gathering and headed toward the large sign declaring the finish of the race. Upon arriving, it appeared that most of the people who ran the 5K race had already crossed the finish line, and now the first runners for the 10K race were coming into the home stretch. She did not recognize anyone, but, getting into the spirit of the day, she clapped her encouragement as they passed by.

Knowing that Scott was running in this longer race, she continued to look down the road, wondering when she would see him.

Another group of runners had just turned off the road and passed into the fairgrounds, and she began to search their faces. The group was running in a clump but began to stretch out as they came closer to the finish line. She recognized Brogan, and Aiden, and then Scott. His arms were pumping, his broad chest breathing deeply, and she began jumping up and down screaming his name. As Aiden moved slightly out of her view, she took in all that was Scott.

Halting in mid-jump, her body jarred as she realized

he was missing the lower part of his left leg and a running prosthesis was attached. Shocked, her voice halted in her throat as it slammed into her that he was the man she had seen running along her road. As though a vice was squeezing her heart painfully, she watched as he ran closer, now able to discern not only a look of determination on his face but his beautiful smile.

It was him. He was the one I saw. The one who made me realize that I have so much to be thankful for.

Her eyes began to sting, and she blinked back the tears, watching his powerful body move behind Brogan and Aiden approaching the finish line. Suddenly jolted into action, she again began screaming his name, jumping up and down.

It appeared he heard her because his head twisted, and for a few seconds their eyes locked. Continuing to scream his name, she waved her hands and watched as his smile widened, splitting his face. He crossed the finish line, and she began to push her way through the crowd, wanting to get closer. The runners were now walking through a line of poles with ribbons attached, staying in the chute as the volunteers were checking their times.

With a final push through the crowd, Lizzie managed to be at the end of the chute just as he walked through. "Scott!"

He looked over, and she saw uncertainty past through his eyes, so incongruent with the assuredness he normally exuded.

"That was amazing," she said, beaming up at him. "I

can't imagine running that far. I'm really proud of you." Seeing Aiden and Brogan standing nearby, their gazes pinned on her, she added, "Proud of all of you."

Scott moved closer, lifting his hand to tuck a wayward strand of hair behind her ears. "Lizzie, as hard as you work every day, you should be proud of yourself."

Her gaze dropped to his legs before she lifted her eyes back to his. "I can't imagine how hard that must be for you to run."

"I got used to it pretty quickly." He held her gaze, an awkward silence settling. He suddenly blurted, "How were your sales?"

Relief flooded her face. "Great! Would you believe that I sold everything I brought with me?"

They walked side-by-side away from the crowd, and he stopped. His smile beamed as he said, "That's great, Lizzie. How did this compare to the farmers' market?"

"Oh, my God, Scott. I sold three to four times more than I ever did at the market. It made me realize that I need to look for other avenues of selling besides just there."

He glanced over his shoulder before turning back and saying, "Listen, I need to go over to my vehicle. Can I meet you somewhere later?"

Her brow furrowed as she asked, "Do you need to get something?"

Hesitating for a few seconds, he swiped his hand over his face before pointing downward. "Honestly? I'm going to change my prosthetic. This is great for running but not good for walking."

"Oh." Her gaze dropped to his blade. "Um... can I walk with you?"

His smile widened and the tension in his shoulders seemed to relax. "I'd like that."

They walked side-by-side, and Scott was uncertain what had him more out of breath... running 10K or seeing Lizzie's easy acceptance of his amputation.

Her head inclined toward his prosthetic, and she said, "I'm sure you've heard this before, but when I look at the unusual design, I can't imagine how you run on it."

He never minded people asking questions as long as they seemed genuinely interested and not morbidly curious. "The way it's designed, it gives the body spring. It simulates a calf and an ankle. But, for it to work best, it needs the balance and speed of a run. That's why it's not very good for walking."

They reached his SUV and he unlocked the passenger door. Glancing to the side, he said, "If you give me a moment, I'll change prosthetics."

She nodded and moved around to the front of the SUV, giving him privacy. He had no problem changing the prosthetic in front of the guys. And while she had not seemed as though she would be embarrassed, he hated the idea of her seeing his stump now. Quickly removing the carbon fiber blade prosthetic, he slid on the pads and socks over his stump and attached his walking prosthetic. He had considered pulling on sweatpants, but the day was warm, and he preferred staying in his shorts. Glancing up, he caught her staring at him from a distance, smiling.

Making sure his SUV was locked after he slammed the door, he walked over.

With her head tilted, she asked, "Are you okay?"

"Well, the race was long, and I'm a little out of breath. But I'm in pretty good shape, so it wasn't too bad."

She shook her head. "That's not what I'm asking about, Scott. Are you okay with me seeing your prosthetic?"

Shrugging, he replied, "I know it's not visible when I wear my work clothes and long pants. But lots of people have seen it. I tend to wear shorts when I'm coaching the kids' ball games, so most of the people around here are used to seeing this one."

"Papa Beau never mentioned it, not that he would need to, so I didn't know."

She suddenly blushed and looked down, and the last thing he wanted was for her to feel embarrassed. With his knuckle, he gently lifted her chin, holding her gaze. "I lost my leg in Afghanistan, Lizzie. But I'm lucky. I came home. I also lost some of my friends, who never had a chance."

He wondered if he should have said that when her eyes filled with tears. "Lizzie, I'm so—"

Shaking her head, she spoke, her voice raspy. "Scott, I'm so sorry that you had to go through that. I can't even imagine."

"I shouldn't have mentioned it, though," he said,

stepping closer. "Your grief is still too fresh to take on anyone else's." The rest of the people at the fairgrounds faded into the distance as he continued to stare into her watery eyes.

She swallowed deeply, still shaking her head. "No, I'm glad you shared. I'm just embarrassed, that's all."

"Embarrassed?"

Her gaze left his, shifting to the side as she seemed to struggle with her emotions. His hands moved to her shoulders, gently squeezing, giving her time to pull her thoughts together.

She opened and closed her mouth several times before finally lifting her gaze back to him. "I'm not sure why, but I assumed you had had an easy life with things just given to you. That was foolish, and I'm sorry." Sighing heavily, she shook her head again. "I'm really not like that. Or, at least, I didn't used to be."

His fingers kneaded her shoulders, trying to relieve the tension he felt in her body. "Lizzie, there's nothing to forgive. But if it makes you feel better, then we can start over." Stepping back a foot, he lifted his hand and said, "You must be Lizzie, Beau's granddaughter. I'm Scott... a friend."

She quickly wiped away the moisture under her eyes and sucked in her lips. Finally, giving way to the laughter, she took his hand in her own. "It's nice to meet you, Scott. I've heard a lot of good things about you."

The feel of her fingers, warm in his hand, moved through him, and he wanted to pull her close, wrapping his arms around her body. Before he had a chance to act on his desires, they were surrounded by others. American Legion members were congratulating him on the organization of the fundraising race, Lizzie's new friends were checking on her sales, and invitations to join the picnic were abounding.

He managed to sit next to her while they ate, but soon his duties interrupted his time with her as he made sure the fairgrounds were left in the same state as he found them. By the time the legionnaires were finished with cleaning up, the parking lot was almost empty, and he noted her truck was gone.

Disappointment filled him, but he knew her animals had to be fed and cared for. Driving home, he hummed along with the radio, formulating his next plan. The plan that involved getting to know Lizzie even better.

13

A week later, Scott came in from his morning run, sweat dripping off of his body but anxious to get showered and on with his day. He and Lizzie had exchanged a few texts during the week, but since she had sold out of all of her lotion and soap, she was on a mission to replace her depleted stock, working late at night. Knowing her schedule left little time for the possibility of a date, he discerned a new way to spend time with her.

Met at the door by Rufus, he scratched his dog's ears, then said, "Boy, you're going to have some fun today." Glad to have a Saturday that did not involve an AL ballgame to coach, he could not wait to get out to the farm to surprise Lizzie.

Rufus had made his way into Scott's bedroom and now sniffed his boots. Laughing, he said, "If you weren't going with me today, you'd really be sniffing my boots when I got home." Grabbing his phone and wallet, he patted his thigh and said, "Come on, boy, let's go."

Rufus jumped into the cab of his SUV, and it did not take long before they were pulling into Lizzie's drive next to the large Weston Farms sign. As he drove toward the house, he suddenly wondered if showing up unexpectedly was a good plan. An inkling of concern that she might not be happy to see him oozed through his mind, but before he could turn around, he saw her at the back end of her pickup truck, hauling large bags, struggling under the load.

Rufus began barking, and Lizzie stumbled as she turned too quickly, dropping the bag back onto the tailgate as she stared at the source of the noise.

Dusty jeans, T-shirt covered by a short-sleeve plaid blouse, hair in a long braid down her back, and ball cap on her head. He grinned as he climbed from the truck, stalking toward her, thinking, *Absolutely fucking gorgeous*.

Rufus ran around, and Scott called him back, making the dog walk at his side. "Good morning!" he called out.

Lizzie stared, her gaze going from him down to the dog and back up again before her lips curved into a smile. "Uh… good morning. What are you doing here?"

"I had a free Saturday morning. I thought you could use some help, and I also thought that I need to have more of an idea of how the farm works to help you with your business plan." Her mouth opened and closed several times, but no words came forth. Jumping into the silent breach, he stepped closer. "And, Lizzie, I really just wanted to see you again."

She snapped her mouth closed at that, and he saw

her cheeks grow rosy, more from blush than the sun. Her gaze moved back down to the dog at his side. "This is Rufus. He's a shelter dog that I rescued, but sweet as can be. I promise he'll be good with the animals."

Rufus sniffed her hand and quivered with excitement. She looked concerned as she rubbed his head and scratched his ears. "I don't mean to be rude, but do you think he'll be okay out here?"

"Why?" Scott asked. "Is it because he only has three legs?" He watched as she nibbled on her bottom lip and added, "I promise I wouldn't have brought him if I didn't think he'd be great. And believe me, this dog can do anything that a four-legged dog can do."

Smiling, she nodded her agreement. She stuck her chin out slightly as she peered up at him. "So, you want to spend some time on the farm?"

"Absolutely. Just show me what needs to be done, and as we go about your chores, you can tell me about how things run."

She looked around in uncertainty, then said, "Well, I was hauling the bags of feed into the barn. I made a run to the feed store this morning."

Knowing her day began early, he wanted to help as much as he could. Moving to the back of her old farm truck, he hefted a bag of feed easily onto his shoulder and said, "Just point the way, ma'am."

Her bottom lip trapped between her teeth, she crinkled her nose as she dropped her gaze to his jean-covered legs. Not giving her a chance to become embarrassed, he said, "Lizzie, don't worry. I'm just like

Rufus... I can do anything that a two-legged man can do."

Holding his gaze for another moment as though pondering the veracity of his statement, she nodded and showed him where she kept the bags of feed. "I have to keep them in here and locked up," she said, indicating the metal bin inside the barn. "I can't afford to have the feed eaten by snakes or mice, and I certainly don't want the animals to get into it." Looking around, she added, "The barn is in good shape, but it could use a few repairs. And I know before I have people come to the farm, it really should be painted." Shrugging, she sighed. "I suppose I need to add that to my list of things to do."

He looked around and could see there were several boards that needed to be replaced, but the barn overall looked sturdy. Scott was sure that if Beau was still alive, he would have taken care of it. It did not take long for him to get all the bags put away, and he turned, seeing her beam.

"Wow, that was fast!"

"These bags weren't that heavy. My rucksack in the Army was much heavier, and we ran for miles with it."

"Until recently, I had no idea you were in the military. I mean, I guess I should since you belong to the American Legion, but it just never really hit me." Her face softened as she added, "No wonder Papa Beau bonded with you. He used to love talking about his days in the Army and always enjoyed swapping stories with others."

"I enjoyed his company as well." Wanting to keep the

mood lighter, he grinned while rubbing his hands together and said, "What's next on the farm?"

Grinning, she said, "How would you like to meet my goats?"

They started off in the small pasture where the baby goats were frolicking around, jumping and skipping over rocks and stumps. Rufus followed them in, and, obeying Scott, laid down on the grass and allowed the goat kids to come near him. Quivering with excitement again, Rufus sniffed them, standing when a few of the small goats decided that he was something they could hop onto.

Moving into the larger pasture where the adult goats were, Lizzie explained her daily schedule with the animals.

"Do you have to shear them?" he asked.

Shaking her head, she said, "Generally, goats raised for milk or meat do not have the kind of fleece that needs to be shorn. I'll do that for the alpacas."

Once inside the goat pasture, she was pointing out her milking goats when, without warning, Scott was butted from behind and his body flew forward. He barely got his hands up in time to keep his head from smashing on the ground. Lying flat on his stomach on the grass, he gasped as the wind had been knocked out of his lungs. "What the fuck?" he cursed, trying to see what had hit him.

"No! Charlie!" Lizzie yelled.

As Scott gathered his wits, he maneuvered to stand, still trying to figure out what the hell hit him. Lizzie had grabbed one of the larger goats by the horns and was dragging him to the side. Giving the goat a shove, she managed to get Charlie over to the other side of the pasture.

Turning back to him, Lizzie's eyes were wide as she apologized, "Oh, my God, Scott, I'm so sorry. Are you okay? I forgot to warn you that goats will headbutt. I've got most of my goats trained, but Charlie wanted attention."

"Attention? I'll give that fucker attention," Scott said, only half-joking, dusting off his jeans.

She rushed closer, bending to wipe off his jeans as well, but he captured her hands in his. "I'm fine," he assured. Standing, he kept her hands in his and peered down into her eyes. Wanting to kiss her, he watched as concern mixed with horror filled her eyes.

"I can't believe you could've gotten hurt here." She blinked away the gathering tears.

Giving her hands a little shake, he repeated, "Lizzie, I'm fine. Believe me, I fell a lot more and a lot harder when I was learning how to walk again and certainly learning how to run."

She swallowed, her throat working as though it was difficult, and slowly shook her head. "How can I think about having people come and be with the animals if somebody could get hurt?"

Always wearing her emotions out for anyone to see, Scott wanted to erase all of her doubts and worries. "That's why we're going to have insurance and talk to a lawyer. We'll make sure we have everything in place to make everyone safe before we let people come. And if that means the children are only with the baby goats, then that's fine. You can even have feeding stations so that people can feed or pet the adult goats through the fence."

Wide blue eyes looked up at him, and she slowly nodded. "Yeah, that might work."

Determined to lighten the mood, he said, "So, think of it this way. It's good that it happened this morning because now we know of something we need to plan for. So, Charlie deciding to send me on my way was a good thing, even if my pride took a hit."

Mirth slowly took the place of concern in her eyes just before she began to giggle. Like watching a flower bloom, her face was transformed into outer beauty as her laughter took over, and she threw her head back, letting the emotion pour from her.

Wiping her eyes as she tried to control her laughter, she gasped, "I'm… sorry. I shouldn't… laugh, but… you looked so funny… flying through the air."

Her hilarity was so infectious he could not help but laugh as well. Finally gaining control, they stood hand-in-hand, smiling at each other.

Swallowing deeply, she said, "I truly am sorry that Charlie butted you, but it felt so good to laugh. I don't think I've done that in weeks."

Smiling, he lifted her chin with his knuckle. "You can always count on me, even if it's just for a laugh." He began to lean toward her, the idea of kissing her taking over his thoughts, when Rufus began barking, anxious to get in on the action.

Lizzie blushed and stepped back. "Um... I guess we'd better finish our morning chores."

Scott followed as she walked back toward the barn. Bending to rub Rufus' head, he whispered to his dog, "Stop cutting in on my action, boy. And for fuck's sake, stop being a cockblocker."

14

Lizzie tried to still her nerves as Scott drove them in his truck to The Diner. They had continued to work and talk about the farm until lunchtime. She invited him in for lunch, but he insisted that he take her out.

He had followed her into the house where she showed him the downstairs bathroom where he could wash. Leaving him on the first floor, she bounded up the stairs to her bathroom where she quickly washed her hands and face and re-brushed and braided her hair. Pulling off her plaid work shirt, she jerked a clean T-shirt from a drawer and pulled it on.

Trying not to appear as though she were anxious, she slowed her steps as she walked back downstairs. Noticing he had put on a clean T-shirt as well, she lifted an eyebrow in surprise.

He simply shrugged. "I brought an extra one in the truck. I was hoping I could take you out for lunch."

The way he said it made it seem like a date, but she pushed that thought to the side, knowing they were just going as friends. The morning had passed quickly, and she had enjoyed his company. She missed so many things about her grandfather and one of those was his conversation.

Now, pulling into the parking lot of The Diner, she sucked in a deep breath and let it out slowly as he walked around and helped her down from the passenger side. The parking lot was crowded, and she wondered if there would be anybody inside that she knew.

She loved the feel of his hand resting on her lower back as they entered the diner, the bell over the door ringing. Carrie looked up, her gaze jumping between Lizzie and Scott, and a wide smile split her face.

As expected, Joe was in the kitchen and threw his hand up in a wave. Mavis' smile was almost as big as Carrie's as she pointed toward a table and said, "Y'all go ahead and have a seat."

All of the booths were occupied, and it did not pass Lizzie's notice that as they sat down at one of the tables, they were in full view of everyone there. *What if they think this is a date? People are going to wonder why he's out with me.*

Her mind in turmoil, she did not notice when he reached across the table and took her hand until he gave it a shake.

"Hey, what are you thinking?"

She blurted, "We're sitting where everyone can see us. It just feels weird, that's all." A chuckle erupted from deep in his chest, a sound she wanted to memorize and pull from her memory banks when she was lonely.

"Let 'em look. They'll all be envious that I'm here with the prettiest girl around."

She blushed in spite of her best efforts to not take his words to heart. "Hush, Scott. Don't tease me like that." She started to pull her hand back, but he linked his fingers with hers instead.

"Lizzie, I'd never tease you like that. It's the truth. I'm here with you, the prettiest girl in this place."

"If you keep holding my hand, they're going to get the wrong idea," she whispered, leaning forward.

"I don't know how they can get the wrong idea. You, me, lunch… I'd call it a date."

At that, she snapped her mouth shut, knowing that her cheeks were heated but unable to keep her lips from curving. Uncertain what to say to that, she pretended to stare at the menu.

Carrie made her way over, bending to give Lizzie a hug. "Hey, sweetie, it's nice to see you out again. What can I get you?"

Once orders were given, Carrie hurried toward the back. A moment later she returned and poured tall glasses of sweet tea. The bell over the door rang again, and Carrie called out, "Hey, Sheriff. Detectives. Have a seat, and I'll be right over."

Swinging her head around, Lizzie watched as Colt, Hunter, and several others walked to the stools at the end of the counter. Brow furrowed, she looked up at Carrie and asked, "Why do you still call your husband 'Sheriff'?"

Grinning, Carrie said, "We first met when he'd come into the Diner. I always called him 'Sheriff', and even though we're married now, when I'm working, that's still what comes out." Leaning down, she said, "Actually, it drives him a little crazy. So, I just do it to have some fun." She whirled around and headed off to the counter to take care of him and some of his detectives, leaving Lizzie to smile.

"Do you come here often?" Scott asked, drawing her attention back to him.

Shaking her head, she replied, "No, not really. To be honest, there was very little time or extra money for eating out. Plus, as good as Joe's cooking is, my grandmother's was better." Leaning forward, she whispered conspiratorially, "Don't tell Joe that!" Leaning back in her chair, she lifted her shoulders in a little shrug. "But sometimes when we would be out at the feed store or lumberyard, Papa Beau and I would stop in here. That's actually how I met Carrie."

Scott held her gaze, and she dropped her eyes to the table, fiddling with her napkin.

"So, what are we going to do this afternoon?"

Jerking her gaze back to his face, her eyes widened. "Uh… this afternoon?"

"Yeah, we haven't gotten to the alpacas yet. I'm hoping I get to see what you do with them. Plus, don't we have to milk the goats sometime?"

She unsuccessfully tried to keep from grinning at the thought of Scott trying to milk the goats and nodded. "Yes, there's lots to do. Are you sure you want to stay for the afternoon?"

"Absolutely. When I said I came to work today, I planned on working the whole day. Anyway, Rufus is asleep in the barn, I need to make sure he keeps learning how to be a farm dog."

Now laughing aloud, she thought of his dog curled up in the straw, exhausted from playing in the morning. Tilting her head slightly, she asked, "How did he lose his leg?"

"I didn't own him then," Scott answered. "I had gone to a shelter to adopt a dog, and he was there. He was only about six months old, and they told me that he had been in an accident. A vet was able to save his life, but he lost his leg. Animals are resilient and have a strong will to survive. As soon as he could, they said he was up and running around, learning how to balance with three legs. But it made it harder for him to be adopted. As soon as I saw him, we just seemed to bond. I didn't even have to think about it… I wanted him, and he seemed to want me. We've been together for a couple of years now."

"Resilient and a strong will to survive," Lizzie repeated, her voice barely above a whisper.

Silent for a moment, Scott held her gaze. "What are you thinking?"

She swallowed deeply, then sighed. "At first I was going to say that I wish I had Rufus' strength. I seem to have let life knock me down, even knock me sideways." She held his eyes for a few seconds, then dropped them down to the table, her fingers fiddling with the silverware. "Sometimes, I don't even know who I am anymore. I feel like I was one person growing up. Another person after my grandmother passed. And a different person even now. Every time something happens to me, I change and not always for the best. But when I think about everything that you've been through, I can tell that you and Rufus are very alike. So much more than me."

Reaching across the table, Scott took her hand and turned it over, linking his fingers with hers. She held his gaze, staring into his blue eyes, not sure she could look away if she had to.

"I think you're very resilient. You're one of the strongest people I've ever met, and believe me, I've met a lot of people." Still holding her gaze, he added, "And I know what you mean about Rufus. There was something we shared, and as soon as I met him, I knew we were alike. Resilient, with a strong will to survive."

A thread of magnetic emotion seemed to move between them, pulling them closer as her fingers linked tighter. The restaurant's noise swirled around them, but they were cocooned in their own little world.

Not sure why she felt the need to confess, she said, "I know I said this at the fairgrounds, but I feel like I need to say it again. When I met you, I thought you were the type of person who probably had everything handed to you. Family connections. Money. Stepping straight into a good-paying job. I didn't realize you'd been in the military, so I thank you for your service. And I apologize for my previous assumptions."

"Don't you remember, Lizzie? You don't have to say this. We started over."

Warmth passed through Scott's eyes, and before she had a chance to delve deeper, Carrie set their lunch plates in front of them, breaking the connection. She pulled her hand from Scott's as they began to eat, keeping the conversation lighter as they talked about the afternoon chores.

As they finished, Scott asked, "Would you excuse me for a moment, Lizzie? I see that Colt and Hunter are about to leave, and I need to ask them a question."

"Not at all." She stood and tilted her head toward the back. "Actually, I need to run to the ladies' room."

Quickly taking care of her business, she washed her hands before stepping out into the hall leading back into the restaurant. Carrie came out of the kitchen and moved close, saying, "Lizzie, I'm glad I saw you before you left. This week is an American Legion Auxiliary meeting. I really want you to come."

Sighing, she hated that her mind jumped back to high school and the many cliques that existed. She had never been one of the cool kids, the popular ones. Instead, she made her way through high school enjoying learning but never taking the time to make real friends. She said, "It's not that I don't want to... In fact, I think I'd like to. It's just that, well... I hate walking into places where I haven't been before. It makes me really nervous."

Giving her a one-armed hug, Carrie said, "Oh, I know how you feel. Don't worry, lots of people feel that way when they first try something new. Tell you what. I'll come pick you up, and that way we'll walk in together. I know once you get there and realize how many people you know it'll be much easier."

"Are you sure you wouldn't mind?" she asked, a touch of excitement replacing the anxiety.

"Not at all." Grinning, Carrie added, "Anyway, I have a feeling by then, you'll know lots of people." With a cryptic wink, she headed back into the kitchen, leaving Lizzie staring in her wake.

Hurrying back into the Diner, she looked toward the counter and saw Scott still conversing with Colt, Hunter, and several other men. He appeared relaxed, but when his gaze moved past Colt's shoulder and met hers, his smile widened even more. She watched as he shook their hands and made his way straight to her.

Not stopping until he was directly in front of her, he wrapped his arm around her shoulder and leaned down. "Gotta say, I told you earlier that you were the prettiest girl here. But seeing you beam at me from across the restaurant, I'd say you were the prettiest girl I've ever seen."

Not giving her a chance to retort, he tossed up one hand in a wave to the others while keeping his other arm around her shoulders as he led her back to his truck.

It had been a long time since she had been on a date, and while all they did was have lunch at a crowded diner, she loved every moment of it.

The afternoon was spent with the alpacas, discussing the upcoming shearing, bringing the goats into the barn, learning how to milk the goats, and then Scott reveled in the evening walk around the farm, checking fence lines and assuring that the animals were secure.

As the hours clicked by, he was more and more impressed with Lizzie. She was not physically large but handled the animals with a calm ease. There was no task she did not attempt and certainly did not shy away from hard work. She was smart and articulate, and by the end of the day, he had a much clearer idea of how the farm ran and what her goals were.

And he could not wait to help her meet those goals and give her new ones... hopefully, ones that included him.

She led him back into the house, Rufus following with his tongue lolling, and Scott once again made his way into the downstairs bathroom to wash his hands and face. He knew he needed to leave but hesitated in the kitchen as they stood, an awkward silence filling the room.

"Thank you for your help today," she began, her eyes searching his. "And for lunch. It was nice to have company. Well, *your* company today."

Stepping closer, he placed his hands on her shoulders, gently massaging the tight muscles underneath his fingers. "The pleasure was all mine, Lizzie."

He was surprised when she shook her head vigorously back and forth and said, "No, Scott, it wasn't. I don't think I realized how isolated I've become since Papa Beau's death. I generally spend my days talking to the animals." Snorting, she continued, "They're good company, but aren't good conversationalists."

He chuckled. "Then I'm glad I rank higher than a goat for company."

She playfully slapped his chest, rolling her eyes, and

he quickly added, "I just want you to know that today meant a lot to me, too. I feel like I now know so much more about you and the farm. We can make this farm become just what you envision, Lizzie." He stared at her pink lips, itching to kiss her but unsure if she wanted that also. Leaning forward, he felt her body pull toward his.

Their lips touched and it was just as sweet as he imagined. Her lips were soft and smooth, and her body melted toward his. He angled his head to take the kiss deeper.

"Woof!"

Jumping apart, they looked down as Rufus stood next to them, his baleful eyes staring up at Scott. Shooting his dog a glare, he sighed. "I guess I better get him home."

Lizzie laughed, and they walked to the door. "Make sure you lock up when I leave." He bent and kissed her again, the barest touch of lips, now knowing there would be others. Just before he stepped outside, he turned and asked, "What time do you get up in the mornings?"

Scrunching her nose, she shrugged. "I'm an early riser. I'll be up with the sun. Why?"

Tapping his forefinger on the end of her nose, he grinned. "I just like learning everything about you that I can."

Stepping outside, he waited until he heard the lock click in place and then he looked down at Rufus as they walked to his SUV. "Boy, if you don't stop being a cockblocker… hell, even a kiss-blocker, you're going to have to stay at home."

"Woof."

Laughing, he held the door open, giving Rufus a boost into the passenger seat before he walked around and climbed behind the steering wheel. Driving home, he thought about his day. He had not had so much exercise since his days in the military and his rehabilitation when he got out. His muscles were sore but from activity that produced a real result and filled a real need.

Now, thinking about the beautiful woman he had just left behind, he grinned at the thought of tomorrow and spending it with her again.

15

Waking the next morning, Lizzie could tell by the shadows in her bedroom that the day was going to be overcast. The forecast did not predict rain, but the clouds would make the temperature cooler, for which she was glad. The previous day had been bright with sunshine as well as bright with Scott's company. She lifted her hand to her lips and could swear she still felt the press of his against hers.

Uncertain why he kissed her if they were just friends, she refused to give any headspace to doubt. It had been a while since she had been kissed, and she was willing to take his brand of friendship even with the possibility of losing her heart.

Stretching, she climbed from bed and hurried through her morning routine. Ravenous, she grabbed a piece of buttered toast, munching as she walked to the barn. Letting the animals out into their pastures, she began the morning feeding.

She had just made it back inside for a proper breakfast when she heard the rumble of engines outside. There was the distinct sound of a few motorcycles, but they were much closer than passing by on the road. Standing, she walked to the front of the house and peered out the living room window. Eyes wide, she watched as a parade of pickup trucks, SUVs, and motorcycles drove up to her house. She would have been afraid except for the first man who climbed down from the familiar SUV leading the pack... *Scott?*

Breakfast forgotten, she rushed outside to see what was happening. Scott looked over and grinned widely, tossing his hand up in a wave. Stalking to her, he did not give her a chance to ask what was happening before he wrapped his arms around her, picked her up, and twirled. "I hope you don't mind, but I called in a little help."

Stunned at his greeting, she looked over to see a group of men walking toward her barn, some with wooden planks in their hands and others with paint buckets. Blinking, she stared dumbly, recognizing Colt, Hunter, Mitch, and Grant. There were many others that she did not recognize and turned her gob-smacked expression back to Scott. "Who are all these people?"

Grinning, Scott replied, "Friends. They belong to the American Legion, and we're always looking for projects in the community that we can do to help others. But, to be honest, they're really just friends of mine who knew and respected your grandfather. I sent out the word yesterday that we could use a little help and asked if anyone had a couple of hours free to let me know." He glanced around at the large group and chuckled, "Looks like a lot of them had some free time."

Her breath left her lungs in a rush, and she slowly shook her head. "I don't even know what to say." She dragged her gaze from the men heading to the barn back to Scott's face. "I hate being a charity case, but I know I need the help. And I should be pissed at you for being so high-handed, but… well, I need the help."

He bent slightly so that his face was directly in front of hers. "Lizzie, I would never do anything to hurt you or embarrass you. Don't think about this as charity. Believe me, every one of these men would step up for each other. And in turn, at some time, you'll be able to pay them back by doing the same when one of them has a need."

Nibbling on her bottom lip, she turned his words over and over in her mind as they snagged a memory of something her grandmother used to say when she was fixing a meal for a neighbor in need. *"Lizzie, remember that helping others is a gift. And when you allow someone to help you, you're giving them a gift as well."*

Offering a jerky nod, she blinked back the tears. "Well, I guess we'd better show them what needs to be done."

Before letting her go, he bent and took her lips in a quick kiss. She startled, realizing he kissed her in front of his friends. Blush hit her cheeks as she grinned, walking hand-in-hand with him toward the barn.

Two hours later, Lizzie stood rooted to the ground as her heart pounded in her chest, and she looked at her barn. Her grandfather had kept the barn in good repair, but in recent years his ability to climb a ladder and reach certain places had diminished. Now, in front of her stood a perfectly-repaired barn, freshly painted red with white trim.

In addition, several fence posts that were showing signs of rot had been replaced along the pastures and pens. There was nothing she could do that would ever repay their generosity, but she vowed to start making pies, determined to deliver them to each man who had helped.

Formally introduced to Mitch and Grant, she could not help but smile, thinking of her teenage crush on most of the Baytown Boys there, including the two McFarlane brothers, Aiden and Brogan, Callan Ward, and Zac Hamilton. Gareth Harrison and Lance Greene were new to her, but Jason Boswell, owner of an auto shop, had once worked on her car. Along with Colt came Hunter and two more detectives, Mark Robbins and Elizabeth Perez. Finally, she met Joseph, someone working with Jason.

The group made her nervous simply because she had never been around that many handsome men at one time and was sure the testosterone level at her farm just raised a million percent.

Now, she wondered if they were staying for lunch and how she would feed them all. Before she had time to worry about their empty stomachs, she heard more cars pulling into her lane. Thoughts reeling, she turned to see a large group of women, platters in their hands, coming around the side of the house, led by a smiling Carrie.

Before a sense of panic descended, she felt Scott's hands on her shoulders and his breath brushing across her ear as he whispered, "Relax, babe. Everybody here just wants to be your friend."

There was no time to process his words before he wrapped his arm around her shoulder, and they met the women together. The other men came forward, taking dishes from the women's hands and heading toward the kitchen.

She greeted Carrie as her son Jack bounded toward the men. She hugged Belle, Jillian, and Tori, then met Scott's accounting partner, Lia, and her daughter, Emily. Tori's son was toddling next to her, pulling on her hand as soon as he saw the goats in the distance. Emily was bouncing up and down with excitement, barely listening as Lia admonished her to wait before going to see the animals.

Aiden lifted Emily into his arms, and Mitch grabbed his son, both men walking the children over to the fence where they could see the baby goats. At that moment, she decided there was nothing sexier than a hot man holding their child. Glancing to the side toward Scott, her vision filled with him doing the same with their child. Blinking, she jerked, forcing that thought from her mind and turned back toward the women.

Katelyn's baby was big but not able to toddle yet, seeming content to stay in his mother's arms, shoving his fist into his drooling mouth. Introduced to Brogan's wife, she smiled at the baby tucked sleepily in Ginny's arms.

Carrie continued the rounds, and besides a very

pregnant Jillian, she met three other pregnant women, Maddie Hamilton, Jade Greene, and Rose Boswell. Last was a beautiful blonde who rushed to her and said, "I'm Sophia Bayles. I can't wait to talk to you about some logo designs for your farm and your goat milk products!"

Once more overwhelmed, Lizzie realized it was not with anxiety or fear, but a warm rush of delight moved over her.

Grateful that Carrie seemed to be taking over the group instructions when she ushered the women into the house, she observed the men setting planks of wood on sawhorses in the backyard. Looking around for Scott, she caught his eye and he hustled over.

"You okay?" he asked.

"Well, I had been worried about how to feed all of the men, but now that's not a problem. But I don't have enough chairs for everyone!"

"No worries, babe. I think some of the women brought blankets for us to spread on the ground. We'll put the food on the table and just have a big picnic."

Faster than she thought possible, the makeshift table in the backyard was loaded with salads, casseroles, platters of fried chicken, sandwiches, fruit, and chips of all varieties. Pies, cakes, and cookies filled one end of the table. Sodas and beer were pulled from icy tubs.

Tori must have seen Lizzie's shocked expression because she laughed and said, "We're pretty used to throwing together a party very quickly. Mitch and I have a small cabin on the beach, and we often have impromptu get-togethers there." Looking around, Tori added, "Pretty soon, we're going to need more playpens!"

It had not escaped Lizzie's attention that Scott claimed the spot next to her, his body leaning close as they munched on their food. She felt him hover and assured, "I'm fine. It's a little overwhelming, but everyone is so nice."

The conversation drifted to her plans for the farm, and she was thrilled that it was met with such enthusiasm.

"Mama, I want to have my birthday party with the baby goats!" Emily exclaimed.

Looking at their daughter, Lia and Aiden grinned. Turning their attention back to Lizzie, Lia asked, "Her birthday is in a month. Do you think she could have her party here?"

About to burst with excitement, she nodded. "I should have all my licenses by then. That would be amazing!"

Jack looked over, his expression much more serious than most preteens, and said, "I really would like to help out here, Ms. Weston. If you ever need me, please let me know."

She watched Carrie beam at her son, Colt smiling with pride as well. Now that she had seen Jack with the animals, she realized he could be an enthusiastic addition and would be able to help. Nodding, she said, "We'll get together with your mom and dad and talk about what would work with your schedule." She knew she had said the right thing when Jack's smile widened, and a bit of childish enthusiasm spilled forth as he fist-pumped the air.

After eating, she gave everyone a quick tour of the farm, letting the children pet the baby goats as Scott warned the adults about the head-butting older goats. Everyone was charmed by the alpacas, and Tori and Mitch's son, Eddie, screamed with delight at the chickens scratching in the dirt in their pens.

As she glanced toward the barn, repaired, painted and beautiful, she said, "I just hope I can make my ideas for the farm work so the men trying to get me to sell will leave me alone." The large gathering grew quiet, and her feet stuttered to a stop as Scott's hand on hers jerked.

"I know that Giardano Farms was interested. Is he still bothering you?" Scott asked.

"He came by a week after my grandfather passed away. But it was Paul Dugan of PD Development who came by the other day, trying to tell me that Papa Beau had planned on selling the farm to him so that he could build a neighborhood—"

The grumbling from all around and whispered curses halted her explanation, and she glanced at the angry faces before turning her face up toward Scott's.

"I've heard about him," Colt said, "and none of it good."

That proclamation caught her attention, and she felt Scott stiffen beside her.

"He snaps up land for a song, then builds sub-par houses and sells them for more than they're worth," Colt continued.

"And he's a horrible tipper when he comes into the diner," Carrie grumbled.

Colt chuckled. "Don't think that's a crime, darlin'."

"Hmph, well, it should be!" Carrie continued to complain.

Scott's grip on her shoulder tightened, and he said, "Lizzie, you don't need to be harassed by these men. You tell anyone who's on your property that they're trespassing, and they need to leave. If they don't, you call the Sheriff's office and me."

Seeing Scott's tight jaw and icy gaze, she rushed to assure, "That's exactly what I told him." It was her turn to give Scott's hand a little shake to gain his attention. "I'm not some scared little girl. I shy away from crowds, but that's not because I'm scared. This is my land, and I'm going to hold onto it."

"Damn straight," Scott huffed, the others quickly agreeing.

Wanting to keep the mood light, she finished the tour of her farm, and most of the gathering left after goodbyes and hugs. Sophia walked over and pulled a drawing pad from her large bag.

"I hope you don't mind, but I've done a few sketches of a possible logo," Sophia said. Flipping open the notebook, she showed Lizzie drawings of adorable baby goats with the alpacas in the background and the Weston Farm sign overhead. "I thought something like this would be wonderful for your farm logo." Flipping a few pages further, she showed a drawing of two goats with the words *'Weston Farm Goat Milk Lotion'*. "And I thought something like this would be perfect for your labels."

Tears hit her eyes as she was beginning to see her dream taken further than she could have taken it alone. "Oh, my God, I love these!"

Sophia smiled brightly. "These are just the beginning. I'll email some more to you and you can choose. Once you decide, it will be easy to have labels made that you can put on your bottles."

Pulling Sophia into a warm hug, her mind was reeling with the events of the day. Waving goodbye to her, she looked around, seeing that Scott was the only one left.

He stood near the barn, and on impulse, she pulled out her phone and took a picture of him, devilishly handsome standing in front of the red building.

"What are you doing?" he laughed, walking over.

"I wanted a picture to remember this day." Her arms slid around his waist as he pulled her in for a hug and kissed the top of her head. "It's been a long time since I've felt as though I could breathe without the worry of everything pressing down on me." Tilting her head back so that she could stare up into his eyes, she added, "I owe it all to you, Scott. I don't know why you're doing this for me, but thank you for everything."

Bending, he kissed her lightly before pulling her tightly into his body. "You work harder than just about anybody I know, Lizzie. I want to help make your dreams come true."

"I've felt so alone since Papa Beau died." She blinked at the sting of tears and the tight feeling in her chest.

He slid his hands upward to cup her cheeks, his thumb smoothing over her skin. They were so close that when he spoke, his breath puffed over her face, warming her deep inside. "You're not alone anymore. Believe me when I tell you—you can count on me."

16

Wanting to kiss her once again in the late afternoon sunlight, Scott felt Lizzie's hesitation. With his arm still around her, he leaned backward, just enough to peer into her face. "What's wrong?"

She hesitated and he waited, getting the feeling that she was trying to make a decision. He wanted her to believe in the words that he had just said but had no idea if she would trust him.

She sucked in her lips but held his gaze steadily as she said, "There is something I need help with, Scott. But it's a really big deal, and I don't know who else to ask."

Thrilled that she was opening herself up to him, he cupped her face with his hands and said, "Lizzie, you name it, and I'll help with it."

"I haven't gone through Papa Beau's room yet."

Understanding flooded him and he was filled with the realization that she had probably been avoiding her grandfather's room. He was sure that Beau would not want her to agonize over his possessions but knew how hard it was for her to deal with them alone.

"There's no time like the present."

Her eyes shot open wide, and he wondered if he had overstepped his bounds or pushed her further than she wanted him to go. Pressing forward, he explained, "Honey, your grandfather would want you to hold on to all of your good memories but not become mired in the past. You have no idea how thrilled I am that you asked me for this help, and I want to give it. If now is not the right time for you, then let me know. But I'm here, I've got the time, and I want to help."

She slowly released a huge breath. Her head jerked in a nod. "Yeah. At least, I'd like us to get started."

Wrapping his arm around her, they walked into the house together. He turned and asked, "What do you think we should do first?"

"Honestly? I haven't been in his bedroom since he died. I don't even know where to start in there."

"Do you think there will be some items that you want to throw away? And others to give away?"

Her face scrunched in concentration, and she began to nod slowly, her gaze cast toward the side. "I'm sure the answer to both is 'yes.'"

"Then let's take some large garbage bags to his room, and we can determine which items to give away and what would be trash."

Lizzie appeared to be satisfied with having a specific chore to do and went to the pantry, taking out a box of trash bags. She then rummaged in a kitchen drawer and grabbed two permanent markers, saying, "I suppose we might need to label the bags so we don't get them confused."

Taking the items from her, he said, "Good thinking." Lifting his free hand, he was pleased that she immediately linked her fingers with his, and they walked toward the front of the house and up the stairs.

He was not surprised to discover a wide landing and hall at the top of the stairs with multiple doors on either side. From the outside, it was easy to see the house was large, one built for a family. On the second floor, he had no doubt that was the builder's intent.

"There are four bedrooms up here," Lizzie began, pointing toward the front of the house. "The two in the front were a guest room and my mom's room. Mine is over there." She twisted slightly and pointed to the back left of the hallway. "My grandparents had the room across the hall from me. Papa Beau had been lonely ever since my grandma died, but he always said he wanted to sleep in the same bed where she had laid her head."

"That sounds like a good marriage to me," he said, drawing a smile from Lizzie.

"They were very happy."

He watched and remained quiet as she approached Beau's closed bedroom door, giving her a chance to pull herself together and gain her courage. Stepping close to her back, he wanted Lizzie to feel his presence without rushing her. Finally, she grasped the doorknob, gave it a short twist, and pushed it open.

The placement of Beau's room allowed the evening sun to pour through the windows, sending dust motes over an otherwise clean room. An antique bed covered with a handmade quilt was the showcase of the room. The bed linens were not perfectly made but appeared as though someone had jerked the covers up and gave them a pat before heading out to work.

Scott cast his gaze around the room, seeing a well-worn cushioned chair in one corner next to a brass floor lamp. The only other furniture in the room was a nightstand and a wide dresser with a mirror hanging over it. Several pictures adorned the walls, and upon further investigation, he recognized a much younger Beau, dressed in his overalls, with his arm around a beautiful young woman. In another picture, he was sitting on top of a tractor with a young boy perched nearby, a wide smile on both of their faces.

Setting on the nightstand were two framed photographs. One of an older woman, her gentle smile lighting her face, and Scott assumed that was Lizzie's grandmother. The other photograph showed Beau and Lizzie standing side-by-side in front of the barn with an alpaca directly behind them. It was easy for Scott to see that in Beau's world, his wife and his granddaughter meant everything to him.

Movement to the side caught his eye, and he turned to see Lizzie standing close by, the fingers of one hand pressed against her lips as her other hand still clutched his. He tossed the garbage bags to the bed and turned so they were facing each other, pulling her close. With her face resting against his chest, he said, "Remember, honey, we're only doing what you want to do. I'm here to help, and I'll take charge of anything you want me to, but mostly I'm just here for you to lean on."

She tilted her head backward and her lips curved slightly. "Thank you," she whispered. She dragged in a shaky breath, then let it out slowly and squared her shoulders. "Okay. Let's get to this."

They agreed to start with the dresser, and he filled the bags with the clothes from the drawers, determining which could be given away and which should be tossed. Once they had accomplished that, they moved to the closet. Beau did not have a wide assortment of clothing, mostly pairs of overalls, heavy denim jeans, and a variety of work shirts.

"Papa Beau only had one good suit, and that was what I had him buried in," Lizzie explained. "Almost everything else was what he wore on the farm."

As they examined the articles of clothing together, they determined that the work clothes were serviceable enough to be given away. Once the closet was finally cleaned out, he looked down and asked, "Is there anything you want to save out of his clothing?"

Lizzie looked at the bags they had filled and shook her head. "No. I want to keep pictures, and I want to keep my memories. But there are other people who can use this clothing and Papa Beau would want anything he had to be used for someone less fortunate."

While she continued to walk around the room, her fingers trailing over the furniture and the bedspread, Scott set the bags out into the hall. He considered taking them downstairs but did not want to be unavailable if she needed him. He kept his eyes on her, wondering if their activities were taking too much of an emotional toll. She picked up the picture frames that were on Beau's nightstand and walked across the hall to her room, placing them next to her bed. He followed her, watching from her doorway.

She turned, her eyes holding his, emotion swirling between them, and smiled. Moving to him, she lifted her hands and placed them gently on his arms. "I've been so afraid of coming into Papa Beau's room but having you with me has made all the difference."

Much to his surprise but to his absolute delight, she lifted on her toes and gently pressed a kiss onto his lips. His arms banded around her back, pressing her body tightly to his. She melted into him, and he captured her moan as he took the kiss deeper.

Lizzie was stunned at her bold move initiating the kiss but had assumed it would be a simple expression of gratitude. Seeing him stand at the doorway to her bedroom after giving so much of himself over the past two days, she was grateful but was lying to herself to think that was all it was. Slowly but surely, Scott had settled into a place in her heart, and while it was a risk to kiss him, she was willing to throw caution out the window.

Now, with her body pressed tightly to his, her breasts crushed against his chest, he angled his mouth to cover her lips with his own. As his tongue gently swept into her mouth, she was glad he held her so tightly, uncertain her legs would hold her upright. A moan met her ears, but she had no idea if it was his or hers.

Lost in the sensations of the kiss, she wondered how Scott could make her feel so good after an activity that could have gutted her. He pulled back slightly, and she instantly felt cool where she had only felt the heat. Opening her eyes slowly, her gaze met his. Wondering why he stopped, her stomach clenched at the idea that he did not like the kiss.

It was not as though she had never kissed anyone before, but her experience was limited. The same went for sex. Not a virgin but also not sure that real life matched her romance novels. Swallowing deeply, she pressed her hands against his chest to move away, finding them trapped between their bodies. Tilting her head slightly in question, she stared, not knowing what he expected.

Dragging in a ragged breath, he said, "I'm trying to do the right thing here, Lizzie. All I want to do is kiss you, but the last thing I want to do is take advantage of you."

His words poured over her, soothing the jagged cracks that had been exposed by her grandfather's death. Instead of pressing against his chest, her fingers curled inward, clutching his shirt, drawing him nearer. "You're not taking advantage of me," she whispered, wondering if he could hear the desperation in her voice. "I want you to kiss me."

"To forget?" he asked, his voice still rough.

Her lips curved ever-so-slowly as she recognized his own insecurity. Her head moved back and forth in slow motion. "No, to remember. To remember what it's like to feel wanted and desired. To remember what it's like to be a woman." Seeing the fire flame through his eyes, she added, "And, because I want to be kissed by *you*."

A squeak emitted from her lips as he squeezed tighter, lifting her into his arms. Freeing her hands from between their chests, she clutched his shoulders as he walked over to her bed. Bending, he gently laid her on the mattress, her head on a pillow, then twisted his body to lie next to her. Sliding one of his arms under her neck, he grasped her hips with his free hand and pulled her toward him.

Facing each other, she slid her arm around his back, her fingers trailing over the soft material of his T-shirt, feeling the muscles underneath. Closing the slight distance, his mouth settled over hers. His lips, both soft and strong, commanded and teased all at the same time. As his tongue swept inside her mouth, she once again felt the sensations jolt through her. Her breasts felt heavy as her nipples tingled, and she felt a spasm in her womb.

Clutching him tighter, she wanted to erase any space between their bodies. Swept away by the waves of passion just from his kiss, she wanted nothing more than this man, right now, right here, in her bed.

His kiss was claiming, and yet giving. She allowed him to take control, gently moving her head so that he could delve his tongue deeper. The fingers at her hip clenched and she felt each one as though branded. Their kiss became more urgent, heads moving back and forth, noses bumping, each swallowing the other's groans.

Wanting to be closer, her hips began to undulate, desperately seeking friction. Sliding her leg over his, she jolted, breaking apart with a gasp. "I'm sorry," she rushed, eyes wide. "I don't want to do anything to hurt you."

He chuckled and slid one hand from her hip to pat his leg. "Baby, there's nothing you could do to hurt this."

The last thing she had meant to do was break the kiss and ruin the mood, but she watched as he slid his hand back to her, up her side to cup her cheek. As his thumb moved over her face, he sighed.

"I want you to be comfortable, Lizzie. So we can take this as slow as you need." Bending forward to place a soft kiss on her lips, once again he leaned back and said, "We can talk. You can ask me anything."

She licked her lips, staring at his handsome face. She had so many questions. Questions about his injury. Questions about his rehabilitation. Questions about his life before and after the military. He was strong and courageous, but right now, in that moment, she saw a flash of vulnerability move through his eyes, and she wondered about his own fears.

"Is it scary?" she whispered. From the slight jolt of his head, she could tell that he was not expecting that question. Hurrying to explain, she continued, "Is it scary to start a new relationship?"

Understanding dawned, and he gave a mournful smile. Before answering, he shifted in the bed, rearranging them so that his back was against the pillows at the headboard, and she was tucked next to him, her face

171

turned up toward so that they could hold each other's eyes.

"I had a girlfriend," he began. "I met her when I was stationed in the States before doing a tour overseas. I didn't like to hang out in bars, not interested in women who just wanted to bang a soldier. She was a civilian who worked in one of the offices on the base. We dated for six months and were very serious about each other. We talked about getting engaged before I had to leave but decided to wait until I got back. I suppose I thought it was a way to bind her to me, but I respected her wish to wait."

Wanting to see his face clearly, Lizzie shifted again on the bed so that she was facing him, one hand on his thigh and the other linked with his.

"We wrote to each other. Skyped with each other. She even told me that she regretted our not being engaged because she wanted to get married as soon as I came home."

Her heart pounding, Lizzie spoke softly. "I take it that didn't happen since you're obviously not married now."

A rueful snort emitted. "No, it didn't happen. She came to see me in the hospital when I finally got back to the States. She tried, but in the end, she just could not see herself being happy with me. I had several surgeries, long rehabilitation, and had to learn to walk again. Multiple fittings with various prosthetics to see which one would work the best." Shrugging, he said, "I could tell she wasn't happy but was just staying out of guilt. We had a long talk, and she admitted that she could not see being married to me, even though she knew that made her look bad."

"You think?" Lizzie bit out, her back now ramrod-straight. Throwing her hands out to the side, she said, "She was never ready for better or for worse, in sickness and in health. If she was, then she would never have needed to bail! And she was worried about looking bad? Jesus, Scott… as sorry as I am that you had to go through that, she didn't have the strength it takes to weather whatever storms come!"

Furious for him, she let out a huff then lifted her gaze back to his, seeing his wide-eyed surprise. Pressing her lips together, she dropped her chin to her chest, mortified that she had just blasted the woman he had once been in love with.

She felt his knuckle on her chin and he lifted, now surprised to see his wide smile. Before she had a chance to apologize, he chuckled.

"Damn, woman. I've been on the end of your fire, but it's a lot more fun when your fire is directed at someone else on my behalf."

Shoulders slumping, she said, "Don't tease me, Scott. I should've kept my mouth shut, but I just hate that you were going through so much and then had to take on the burden of losing her at the same time."

Leaning forward, he kissed her lightly before settling back against the pillows, a smug smile resting on his face. "It was tough at the time, babe, but I realized pretty quickly that she wasn't the right person for me. Since then, I've dated some but no one special… no one who has the kind of strength to handle what life throws at them. Something, by the way, you have in spades."

Coming from him, the words meant so much, gliding over her and filling the empty spaces deep inside.

17

From Lizzie's questions and the fact that they were laying on her bed, Scott knew they had moved to the part of the relationship that most people never have to face. The amputation. He wished, with the hope of intimacy, the subject could be as easy as talking with one of his friends. But that had never proven to be so.

He held her gaze and waited for the questions that would now inevitably come since he had thrown open the doors to his past. He watched as she rolled her lips in, pressing down, her gaze not leaving his face. Finally, unable to wait any longer, he asked, "What are you thinking? What's on your mind?"

"I was just wondering… well, I was hoping…"

"Lizzie, it's okay. Ask whatever questions you want."

Tilting her head to the side, she jutted out her chin slightly and blurted, "I was wondering when you were going to kiss me again."

He blinked. Slowly. Twice. Her response was not what he expected, although he could not deny it was what he hoped for. Grinning, he replied, "If you're ready, there's no time like the present."

Her lips curved into a beautiful smile, and she nodded as she shifted her body closer, almost laying across his chest as she brought her face toward his. "I'm ready."

His arms banded around her body, pulling her close. He wanted to share his life with her but was thrilled he did not have to dissect everything with her all at one time.

Their lips met, and just like before, he felt the electricity move through his entire being. There was a hesitancy in her kisses, but he now felt it was more innocence than concern. He had no idea what her sexual experience was and did not care. All he wanted was the drug-inducing, lust-flaming headiness that filled his entire being when her lips met his and she moaned slightly into his mouth.

She shifted, throwing one leg over his thighs, straddling him. His cock swelled painfully, swearing he could feel her heat through their clothes. His fingers gripped her ass, digging into the softness. Noses bumped, tongues tangled, and their breathing came in pants.

Lizzie finally leaned back, and he stared at her lips, swollen with his kisses, and her hooded eyes as her gaze stayed on his mouth.

Both trying to catch their breath, he said the only intelligent thing that came into his mind. "Wow."

Her eyes jumped to his, and her grin widened as a giggle slipped out. "Yeah, wow."

They stared at each other for a long moment, but

just as she was about to lean in for another kiss, his fingers squeezed on her ass once more. "It's killing me to say this, babe, but I really should be leaving."

Seeing the wide-eyed shock on her face, he rushed, "All I want to do is strip you naked, lay you on this bed, and plunge myself deep inside." He hesitated, waiting to see what her reaction to his words would be.

"Then why don't you?" she asked, her voice raspy as her fingers dug into his shoulders, her gaze full of pleading.

His heart soared at her words, but he drew upon all of his strength to shake his head slowly. "Because I want to do the right thing, Lizzie. It's been a long day and an emotional evening clearing out Beau's room. When we make love, I want you to be sure. Not only sure of what we're doing, but when we're doing it."

She looked as though she were going to object, then snapped her mouth shut, thoughts working behind her eyes. Slowly, she nodded. "While I admit I want to have you stay with me and be with me in every sense of the word, what you're saying makes sense. I don't want you to do anything that you would regret either."

She leaned forward and kissed him lightly, and he was sure he had never tasted anything so sweet in his life. Climbing from her bed, they stood and kissed once more. Linking fingers, they walked out into the hall, and he saw the bags that had been left there.

"Make sure to leave them, and I'll come tomorrow and haul them off for you." Tapping her nose with his finger, he said, "Promise you won't try to lug them downstairs yourself?"

Rolling her eyes, she nodded. "I promise. But are you sure you have time tomorrow?"

"My day usually finishes about four p.m., so I can come then, if that's all right."

"How about I fix you dinner?"

Grinning, he nodded. "Can't think of a better way to start out my week than with your home cooking."

Hand in hand, they walked downstairs and through the house to the kitchen door. Giving her promise that she would lock up after him, he called to Rufus and they headed out to his truck. Driving away this time was one of the hardest things he had done. The pull to have stayed with her in her bed was strong. But so was the desire for self-preservation as well as caring for Lizzie.

Sighing heavily, he leaned his hand over and scratched Rufus' head. "You like the farm, don't you, boy?" A moment passed, and he added, "Yeah, me too. The farm and Lizzie."

Later, his hand was pressed against the wet shower bench, the water sluicing over him as his other hand worked his cock. Eyes closed, he imagined the feel of gliding deep inside the warmth of Lizzie's sex.

With his head thrown back, he roared through his orgasm. He had grown used to using his hand, finding it too exhausting to seek out a willing woman and not finding anyone he wanted to have a relationship with. But this time was different. With the vision of Lizzie in his mind, this orgasm had rocked his body, and he could not imagine what it would be like when he could finally lay with her. And as he finally caught his breath, he smiled.

The day was dragging. With no clouds in the sky, the hot sun was relentless as it beat down on Lizzie. She made sure to keep the animals in the pastures that had the most trees where there was plenty of shade.

Having spent the afternoon replenishing her supplies of goat milk lotion and soap, she continually looked at the clock, willing the time to move faster so that she could see Scott again. The chicken was marinating in buttermilk, the apple pie was cooling, and the fresh vegetables were ready to be cooked.

She closed her eyes as she wrapped her arms tightly around her waist, imagining the feel of his body pressed to hers. When she had straddled him last night, she'd felt his erection and if he had agreed, she would have slept with him easily. She could still feel the touch of his lips on hers, and her breasts ached for the same.

Soon, please let it be soon. She respected his desire to take things slow, knowing that he did not want her to feel rushed or pressured. It was true, she had only gotten to know the real Scott in the past couple of weeks, but what she knew coincided with everything Papa Beau had told her. Kind and caring. Strong and capable.

And now, she knew what his hands felt like on her ass and his tongue in her mouth and could not wait for more. Hearing the goats bleating, her eyes jerked open and she glanced at the clock on the wall.

Washing her hands in the kitchen sink, she looked out toward the pastures but did not see the alpacas.

Grabbing a dish towel, she dried her hands as she hurried toward the door. Sliding her feet into her work boots, she hustled outside and hurried to the pasture. Still not finding the alpacas, she opened the gate and walked into the field, closing the gate behind her. The pasture was large, but there was nowhere for the alpacas to hide other than the shade of the trees.

Turning in a circle, her heart stuttered as her feet did the same, seeing part of the fence knocked over. "Shit!" she cried out, running toward the opening, her feet pounding across the dirt and grass. She spied Caesar standing in the road and tried to still her unsteady heartbeat as she climbed through the broken fence and slid down the short gravel hill toward him.

A vehicle was coming over the crest of the hill just as she saw Cleopatra ambling toward the road from the other side. She was sure the driver would see the large alpacas, but fear had her rushing to them, waving her hands wildly.

As the vehicle neared, it stopped, and her breath left her lungs in a rush as she observed Scott's wide-eyed expression peering back at her. He climbed from the SUV and she began screaming, "Help me! Help me get them back in!"

Cleopatra made her way to Caesar, both animals standing nearby, staring at her as though they did not have a care in the world.

"Will they follow you?" Scott called out.

Shaking her head, she replied, "I don't think so." Jolting, she added, "Wait! Let me go get some food! See if you can find Mark Antony, but if anyone else comes down the road, keep the other vehicles away from them!"

Without giving Scott a chance to agree, she turned and scrambled back up the gravel incline, climbed through the broken fence once again, and raced toward the barn. She grabbed a metal bucket off a hanger on the inside of the barn and filled it with feed. Seeing a rope, she slipped it around her shoulders, not knowing if it would be needed.

Turning, she ran, retracing her steps. She ignored the burning in her lungs as she skidded back down the gravel on her ass, nearly dumping the bucket of feed.

"Be careful, Lizzie," Scott called out as he hurried to her. With his hands underneath her armpits, he lifted her up, taking the rope from her shoulder. "I don't see Mark Antony but try to get Cleopatra and Caesar to follow you."

She did not have to worry because the two alpacas had already captured the scent of the feed in the bucket and trotted over to where she stood. Looking up, she said, "Scott, take the bucket and lead them back into the pasture." The thought hit her that he might not be able to maneuver the gravel incline with his prosthetic limb, but before she had a chance to voice her concern, he took the bucket from her.

"Don't worry about us. I've got them." With the two hungry alpacas following the feed, Scott managed to climb up to the broken fence, leading Caesar and Cleopatra.

Knowing he would take them all the way to the barn, she raced to the other side of the road and up the incline. She had no idea where Mark Antony may have wandered, but he must have known his friends were being fed because he came trotting out from a grove of trees nearby.

Seeing him safe, she had to lock her knees to keep them from buckling. Calling out to him, she had no trouble looping the rope around Mark Antony's neck, leading him back down to the road and across before making the climb back up into her pasture. By then Scott had the others secure in the barn and was hustling back toward her.

"I'll get my SUV and bring it into your drive," he said, cupping her face and leaning forward to kiss her forehead before he headed back to the road again.

Grumbling all the way, she managed to get the third alpaca into their pen, securing them carefully before giving them their evening feed. Walking from the barn, she met Scott by the pasture. "I need to see what happened."

Retracing her steps for what felt like the hundredth time, she approached the broken fence post and knelt to examine the wood.

"Did they push against it and knock it over?" Scott asked, coming up behind her, Rufus on his heels.

Staring in abject horror, Lizzie's blood began to race through her body at the sight of the cut fence post. *It wasn't old. It wasn't rotten. It was cut... on purpose.*

18

Scott glanced toward the farmhouse, knowing that Lizzie was safely ensconced in the kitchen with Carrie, Belle, and Katelyn. Jack was in the barn, mucking out the stalls and keeping an eye on the animals in the pasture.

Swinging his gaze back to the men in the field, he watched as Colt and Hunter carefully looked over the cut fence and surrounding area as Deputy Robbins took pictures.

Gareth, standing next to him, said, "Luca Giardano has been in the news a lot, so I'll give you the abbreviated version. Large agriculture on the Eastern Shore had been mostly potatoes until the Great Depression. Slowly, by the middle of the 1900s, vegetable farming became the most profitable crop, and after that, it was tomatoes. By 2000, there were over 3200 acres of tomatoes being grown. Luca's grandfather bought his first farm not long after he came over from Italy. It appears he had some family money, and during the depression snapped up more and more small farms. He passed everything on to his son, and Luca's father continued buying more land for more crops. He finagled contracts with some of the big national food processing chains, commanding prices that none of the small farmers around could compete with."

Nodding, Scott met Gareth's eyes and said, "So far, I'm not hearing anything untoward."

"Oh, he's not a shining star, but what I'm finding doesn't seem too unusual. I don't know anything about agriculture, but I've been learning. The reason tomatoes grow so well out here was because of something called plastic ground mulch, called plasticulture. It appears as a powerful tool to increase vegetable yields. I won't go into all the shit I've been learning about tomato growing—"

Scott's snort interrupted Gareth, and both men laughed.

"Oh, yeah," Gareth admitted. "I learned a lot more than I ever needed to know about fuckin' tomatoes!"

They allowed the moment of mirth to settle, easing the tension Scott had felt since arriving at Lizzie's. Sighing, he nodded for Gareth to continue.

"It appears that environmentally, plasticulture has been vilified even though it actually increases the flavor of the tomatoes and the hardiness of the crop. By 2009, environmentalists were complaining because the runoff of the herbicides was affecting the clams and oyster farmers in the area. The problem is, tomatoes are a big business... at a tune of almost a hundred million dollars, and out here, Giardano Farms controls a lot of that."

Whistling through his teeth, Scott said, "With that much money, why does he want to continue buying up more farms?"

Shaking his head, Gareth said, "I don't know. I know that the Weston Farm lies between two of Luca's plots of land. I'm sure it would be easier if he has all of this as well."

"What about the ecologists? Did farms have to make any changes?"

"Yeah, laws were finally passed in Virginia to regulate plasticulture farming, which, of course, gave a hit to Luca. By then, he had taken over from his own father. About the same time, there was a huge lawsuit when it was discovered that some of Luca's farms had illegal wells that were irrigating his crops. He ended up having to pay about four hundred thousand dollars in fines and rework his wells so that they were within guidelines."

"So, he's hardly a Boy Scout," Scott commented, watching Colt stand and begin walking toward him.

"Honestly, he's no different than many other big farms. That's why it's hard to see him doing anything illegal to get this farm. He's got a lot of money and a lot of acreage. He's had some trouble in the past, but so have the other farmers and has always paid his fines and then met regulations."

Strangely, Scott was irritated that Luca was not turning out to be a more nefarious individual. If he had been, it would have been easier to see someone working for Luca wanting to force Lizzie to give up the farm.

"Luca is in his fifties. Are there any sons of his that are wanting to become the next tomato king?"

Laughing, Gareth replied, "He's got one son that's finishing graduate school in agriculture business and a daughter that's an accountant working for her dad." Looking at Scott, he suggested, "Hey, with you being an accountant also, maybe you can get together with her and find out more."

He had to admit the idea held merit, but right now, the only thought he had was the look on Colt's face as he approached.

"What have you got?"

Colt growled, "Two of the fence posts were definitely cut. This road has little traffic so there probably was no one coming by last night to see anyone at the fence. Once the fence posts were cut, it took little to pull it down."

"When was the last time she checked the fence?" Hunter asked.

"She goes around every evening," Scott explained. "That was something that her grandfather always did, and she does it as well. So, this morning, she had no reason to think that the alpacas would not be safe in that pasture."

"There's no distinctive footprints in the area, but the animals as well as the two of you probably would have obliterated them if they were there. The wooden posts appear to be sawed roughly, so I would assume someone had a handsaw, not a chainsaw," Colt added.

Everyone swung their gazes toward Gareth, and Colt asked, "You're here, so I'm assuming you're doing some digging for Lizzie?"

Dipping his head toward Scott, Gareth replied,

"Actually, Scott's got me on this. He was concerned about Luca Giardano trying to buy out Lizzie. On top of that, I'm taking a look at Paul Dugan."

Getting nods from the others, Gareth continued. "Yeah, he's a slick shit, for sure. From what I've been able to dig up on him, he gets his hands on cheap land, builds crap neighborhoods with crap houses, and then, when owners complain, he just lets things go into drawn out litigation until the homeowners can't afford to keep paying so they give up the lawsuit—or he coun-tersues. Found out that his lawyer is his brother, Yancey."

Colt added, "Yeah, I've heard of him. I've taken several complaints, usually from elderly widows who feel like they were manipulated into selling their land very cheap. He was investigated about a year ago but manages to skate just on the side of the law to keep from doing anything illegal."

Blowing out a breath, Scott shook his head. "I can't believe that with everything she's going through, Lizzie has to deal with this shit."

"Could it just be kids?" Gareth asked. "Are we missing the obvious and making this more than just teens looking to play a prank?"

Pondering, Scott said, "I don't know. I just know I'm going to keep a better eye on this place and on Lizzie. It's what Beau would've wanted, and it's what I want, too."

Colt chuckled. "I wanted to keep Carrie safe, and she ended up in my house pretty damn quick."

"Don't think I'll be moving Lizzie out anytime soon,"

Scott said. Staring at the barn for a moment, his gaze searched the area. "I'm going to add some lights out here. I can't secure the entire farm, but I can at least make sure that there is plenty of illumination around the barn where the animals are at night."

Gareth grinned and asked, "Would you be interested in a security camera, as well?"

Eyebrows lifted, Scott replied, "Absolutely."

Colt promised that he would add Lizzie's road on the night rotation for a sheriff's car to drive by. Offering his thanks, Scott shook their hands before they walked back to Colt's SUV.

Gareth clapped him on the shoulder. "I'll get a camera set up and keep digging to see what I can find out. In the meantime, take care of Lizzie."

Walking back to the house, he watched as Katelyn gave a heartfelt hug to Lizzie before climbing into the car with Gareth. Carrie and Belle had driven together, and with Lizzie assuring them that she was okay, they left as well.

He walked over and immediately enveloped her into his arms, noting Rufus had not left her side. Kissing the top of her head, he asked, "How was your visit with the girls?"

With her arms banded around his waist, she leaned back and peered up. "I'd hardly call it a visit, Scott. I know they just came with their husbands to keep me from going out there and poking my nose into the investigation. Honestly, I'm so mad, I barely registered anything they were saying." Shoulders slumping, she sighed. "But it was nice that they came. I've never had a group of girlfriends before, so it's cool that they wanted to check on me."

They stood silent for a moment, their arms still wrapped around each other, then she mumbled against his chest, "I need to fix dinner."

"Oh, no, Lizzie. We'll go out—"

"Nope, not on your life," she said, narrowing her eyes as she looked up again. "I've been planning this dinner all day and looking forward to it. The chicken has been marinating and it will take me very little time to throw together the vegetables. I'm not letting the asshole who tore down my fence ruin the rest of my day!"

Chuckling, he gave her a squeeze and nodded. "Let me wash my hands and then I'll help."

"That sounds perfect."

He watched with interest as she boiled then mashed potatoes, adding crunchy bits of bacon, butter and sour cream, and chives. They chatted while she rolled out homemade biscuits and put them in the oven, then battered and fried the chicken. Quickly boiling corn on the cob, she soon plated full meals for them, and they sat down at the table with glasses of sweet tea.

Throughout the process, she did not talk a lot, but then, Lizzie was not someone who chattered endlessly. She spoke when she had something to say and appeared to be comfortable with silence. He kept a pulse on her, but the events from earlier, while upsetting, no longer had her rattled.

He almost brought it up, asking if she was okay with everything, but did not want to push. So, instead, he sat close to her at the family table and enjoyed the meal, giving Rufus a few bites of chicken and gravy. She shared a few stories of growing up on the farm, including a few memories from Baytown High School.

"I rarely went to social events," she admitted. "There was always work to be done on the farm after school, so, like most agriculture kids, I got off the bus and went to work. I did belong to the FFA." Grinning, she said, "I raised a few prize-winning pigs, I'll have you know."

"Prize-winning?"

"I've got the blue ribbons to prove it," she laughed. After a moment she sobered. "We sold off most of our pigs, except for the two that I have behind the barn. I'm raising them to be fat and sassy and will have someone butcher them for me this fall. Someone local does that, and I'll get the meat wrapped to go into the freezer."

They were ready to dig into apple pie for dessert, and his spoon halted on its path to his mouth. Eyebrows lifted, he repeated, "Butchered?"

"It's a working farm, Scott. I know it's hard to imagine growing up this way, but when Papa Beau had some cows as well as pigs, that was how we got a lot of our meat. The extra we had, the butcher would pay us for so that he could sell it to others."

"I feel rather foolish," he admitted. "That makes perfect sense, and yet, I just had not thought about it."

She lifted her shoulders in a delicate shrug. "I sometimes imagine what it must've been like for my great-grandparents. Certainly, they could have gone into Baytown to a mercantile store, but their vegetables were grown in the garden, their dairy came from the couple of dairy cows they kept, and their meat came from the cows and pigs they raised."

"Are you going to get more pigs?"

Nibbling on her bottom lip for a moment, she shook her head slowly. "No, I don't think so. To be honest, I don't eat enough meat to warrant having a whole pig butchered for me. Certainly, I could just sell the meat, but then I'd have to spend money on the feed. I think when the last two are gone, I won't buy anymore. The goats I'll keep raising for the milk, and while alpacas are not big money makers, I can get about two thousand dollars a year on their fleece. That's not a lot, but if I can learn to clean it and spin it, then I would get a lot more."

"And don't forget about your farm plans. Parties. Soap and lotion-making classes. Animal petting days. And even goat yoga!"

Throwing her head back, she laughed. "Oh, I haven't forgotten any of that. And I know that goat yoga made a big impression on you."

"I know we just went over a rudimentary business plan, but how are things going?"

Pushing her now-empty plate away, she leaned back in her chair, pulled one leg up and wrapped her arms around it, rested her chin on her knee, and held his gaze. "I'm trying to keep my costs down as much as possible like you suggested. Graphic design isn't Sophia's career, but she created a beautiful logo for my products, and I've been able to print them on sticky labels here at home. They're not in color, but I think they're adorable. I have been working to make more lotion and soap, trying to replenish the depleted stock from after the sale at the fairgrounds."

"I think that's great," he said.

"Jack has come over twice after school, and he's going to work out great. He's able to do a late afternoon feeding and get the animals into the barn, giving me a chance to make more products. I created a flyer for hosting children's birthday parties with the baby goats and women's parties for product making. I gave them to Katelyn, Carrie, and Belle today and they're going to distribute them around town." Shrugging, she said, "We'll see how it goes, but with Lia and Aiden's daughter having her birthday party here, I think word-of-mouth will help."

Shifting forward in his seat, Scott leaned toward her, resting one hand on her leg and the other cupping her cheek. "Have I told you lately that I think you're amazing?" With her cheek in his hand, he could feel the heat of blush as it rose over her delicate features. "It's the truth, Lizzie. You have strength and tenacity in you that I've rarely seen before. But, having met Beau, I can imagine that it came from your family."

Closing the space between them, he angled his head and kissed her. She immediately dropped her leg down and reached out, clutching his shirt in her hands.

If he had any doubt of her desire, she obliterated it when she shifted forward, straddling his thighs and pressing her body close to his. Throughout that maneuver, their mouths remain sealed, tongues vying for dominance, sharing each other's moans.

He had wanted to give her more time, wanted her to

be sure. With his hands on her shoulders, he gently pulled back a scant inch, opening his mouth to suggest they slow down.

As though reading his mind, she scrunched her fingers in his shirt even tighter and said, "Scott, I want you now. I'm not looking for a balm for grief. I'm not looking for a way to forget what's going on with the farm. I just know what I feel for you and what I want. And I want. You. Now."

A slow smile curved his lips, and he stood, giving her room to wrap her legs around his waist. Carrying her to the bottom of the stairs, he hefted her slightly before allowing her feet to slide to the floor. She smiled, linking her fingers with his, and led him up the staircase.

19

When they arrived at the top of the stairs, Lizzie's feet did not falter as she led him straight into her bedroom. A quick glance around assured her that the room was picked up and no underwear was lying about. She sucked in her lips as she recognized what a ridiculous notion that had been considering she hoped Scott would soon be seeing a lot more than just her underwear.

A combination of excitement and nerves shot through her but, refusing to give into them, she stopped at the bed before turning and facing him. She stared up, hoping he was not going to put the brakes on them again. She had no idea what the morning would bring but so wanted this night with this man.

Their fingers unlinked as he lifted his hands and cupped her face, his thumbs gliding over her cheeks. Her hands moved to his waist, her fingers digging in slightly before he pulled her closer and she clutched his back.

Bending slightly, he kissed her again, this time soft and slow. His lips were strong and supple, and as a moan erupted from deep inside her, he slipped his tongue into her mouth, capturing the sound. Just as before, her nipples tightened with need.

They were pressed together from knees to chest, and the evidence of his desire was overwhelmingly pressed against her stomach.

His hands slid from her face, down her back, and slipped under her T-shirt. As his fingers skimmed over her skin and moved upward, the material was dragged as well, snagging on the underside of her breasts.

His thumbs caressed the sides before moving over her nipples. Air left her lungs as she fought to breathe, the sensations causing a swirl of electricity moving to her core.

Forcing her feet backward a step, she lifted her hands above her head, giving silent permission for him to remove her shirt. He wasted no time in doing just that, dropping it to the floor as his gaze landed on her breasts, barely contained in her simple white cotton bra. The sight of his heated gaze on her body gave her courage, and she reached behind her and unsnapped the bra, letting it slide down her arms, exposing her to his view.

His hands moved back over her breasts, now able to tweak her nipples with no material hindering the sensation. She battled between wanting to revel in the feel of his firm hands and wanting to feel his naked chest pressed against hers. The desire to see him won out, and as he continued to mold her breasts, she tugged at the bottom of his T-shirt, pulling it upward.

"I'm too short," she complained in a soft voice, unable to get the shirt completely over his head.

Grinning, he disagreed. "I think you're perfect." He reached behind his head and grabbed onto the T-shirt, pulling it off and tossing it to the floor.

Her fingers followed her gaze as they trailed over the ridges of his muscular chest and tight abs. They found several scars, puckered skin snagging her fingers, making her ache for his past pain. Leaning closer, her breasts touched his upper abdomen as she kissed the scars on his shoulder. She had noticed a small scar on his upper lip, wondering how he had been injured while thinking it gave his face such character.

Now, she looked at his naked upper body, thinking all of him had such character. Capturing his gaze, she whispered, "You're the most beautiful man I've ever seen."

Moving faster than she could have imagined, he picked her up, sealing his mouth over hers in a deep kiss before laying her on the bed. Bending, he pulled off her socks and then divested her of her jeans and panties.

It had been several years since she had been naked with a man. Hoping her romance novels were not completely wrong, she had only had sex with one other partner, and that event could have easily been classified as more fumbling in the bed of a pickup truck than anything else. He had delivered feed to the farm, flirted with her, and asked her on a date. She agreed, but the date turned out to be more of a drive in the country and sex in his truck. Once again, not the stuff of romance novels.

But now, with Scott looming over her, his intense gaze appearing to appreciate every nuance of her body, she could not help but smile. In a short time, he had proven his worth and had come to mean more to her than anyone else.

He stood, his hands on his belt, and said, "I'm comfortable with what's going to happen, Lizzie, but I want you to be comfortable, too."

Sitting up quickly, she reached out and placed her hand over his, saying, "I assure you, I'm comfortable. I'll let you take the lead, but no matter what, you'll need to tell me if there's anything I need to do."

Grinning, he shook his head. "There's nothing you need to do, darlin', except keep staring at me the way you are. Right now, my dick's so hard, it's not easy to slow things down."

She watched as he shoved his pants and boxers over his hips, freeing his impressive cock. Turning, he sat on the edge of the bed next to her and slid his pants and boxers all the way off. She had seen his prosthetic as he walked around the fairgrounds after the race and knew that he was a below the knee amputee. But, other than that, she'd never spent much time thinking about him being an amputee. He had proven himself capable on the farm and obviously capable as a runner and athlete. But now, naked as well, he turned to look at her, uncertainty in his eyes.

Lizzie scooted closer, placing gentle kisses on his shoulder. Not wanting him to be self-conscious about taking his prosthetic off, she continued to shift on the bed until she was directly behind him. With her legs on either side of his hips and thighs, she pressed her breasts against his back, wrapping her arms around his waist, continuing to move her lips over his back and shoulders.

He groaned, "Jesus, babe, I'm not going to last at this rate."

She continued to hold him tight as he bent forward, unfastening his prosthesis. She was curious about it but knew that now was not the time for a lesson in how it worked. Now was the time for touching and feeling, getting to know each other's bodies.

He leaned forward a little more, and she knew that he had laid the prosthetic leg carefully on the floor. She gasped as he twisted quickly, his arms now banded around her, and pulled them both down on the bed, facing each other.

She gave no thought to anything other than his mouth on her lips, his tongue gliding over hers, and his hands roving over her breasts. Their legs tangled as he pressed his hips into hers and she gave over completely to the desire firing her blood.

Sliding his hand between her legs, she opened herself up to him, allowing him to slip his fingers through her slick folds and deep into her sex while sucking on her nipple. Scissoring his fingers, he used his thumb to press on her clit, and as primed as she was, she quickly cried out her release. He continued to stroke her slowly as she came down, her chest hitching as she sucked air into her lungs.

As his hands slowly glided over her mound and soft belly on its way between her breasts and up to cup her cheek, she blushed, confessing, "I knew that was going to be fast. It's been a while for me."

He grinned, dimples appearing on both sides of his cheeks. "Don't be embarrassed about that, Lizzie. First of all, it was fuckin' hot. Second of all, it's been a while for me too, so I knew I needed to make sure to get you ready, hoping I don't go off too soon once I get in there."

She loved his honesty and smiled in return. He shifted to his back, grabbing a condom that she had not noticed he had pulled from his jeans. Once sheathed, he settled his hips between her thighs, and with one hand planted beside her holding his weight, he guided the tip of his cock to the entrance of her sex. Hesitating, he lifted an eyebrow in silent question, seeking her permission.

Heart full, she clutched his shoulders and brought him forward, whispering, "Yes."

He entered slowly, his thrust measured as he allowed her body the chance to become accustomed to his girth. Her tight, warm channel almost had him orgasm immediately, but he forced his thoughts to making it pleasurable for her, wanting to draw out the desire for both of them.

Her pale blonde hair was thrown across the pillow, her blue eyes holding his gaze. Intrigued by the smattering of freckles that ran across her cheeks and nose, he kissed them before sliding his nose past hers and latching onto her lips.

Chest to chest, hips to hips, he thrust over and over, loving the way her sex held tight to his cock. Sliding his tongue into her mouth, he moved in rhythm with his hips, swallowing her groan while feeling it against his chest.

His balls began to tighten, and he knew he could not hold off for long but wanted her to come again. Her breathing came in pants and he shifted his weight off her slightly, not wanting to crush her. Her fingers dug into the muscles in his upper back, and she widened her thighs, bringing her knees up. His pelvis rubbed against her clit, and she began to shake.

"Are you close, babe?"

Not answering aloud, her body began to quiver, and her fingers dug deeper. Soon, she cried out her orgasm, and he felt her inner muscles clench against his cock. Unable to hold back any longer, every muscle in his body tightened as he roared out his release. Continuing to thrust until he was emptied, he dropped his forehead onto the mattress next to her head, knowing he needed to lift his heaviness from her but uncertain that any muscle in his body would actually obey his command.

Moving his hips back gently, he slid his cock from her body and shifted to the side just enough to give her enough room to breathe. Still craving her body against his, he wrapped his arms around her and rolled so that she was now partially on top of him.

Sure that that was the extent that his body could

move, he held her close as they lay, breaths slowing and heartbeats calming. Her long hair lay in damp tendrils across his sweaty body and he pushed it back from her face.

They lay in silence for several moments, and as his consciousness slowly settled in, he was filled with two thoughts. One, that was the most electric sexual encounter he could ever remember. And two, he could only pray that it was as good for her. As if on cue, she lifted her head and peered into his face, smiling.

"That was amazing, Scott."

Wanting to beat his chest in male pride, he kissed her instead. "I've never felt anything like that, babe. I came harder than I've ever remembered, and it's all because of you. Beautiful, sweet, strong you."

Her grin spread wider, and as her finger traced over his face, she admitted, "I've never had that happen to me before. I mean, not with someone else. I've been able to make myself come, but never... well, just never before. I was beginning to think my romance novels lied to me."

He hated that she had never experienced an orgasm during sex before, and yet was thrilled that he was the first one to be able to give that to her. Especially since the sex with her had been the best for him.

"I don't know how you feel about this, babe, and I need you to be honest with me. But I'd love to stay the night."

Her eyes sparkled as she replied, "I think if you tried to leave, I'd have to tackle you."

Laughing, he said, "Never underestimate an amputee. I might be able to get away from you."

Eyes wide, she blushed deeply. "Oh, my God! Scott, I didn't mean anything by that." Giving her head a little shake, she added, "I sometimes forget that you are missing the lower half of your leg. I don't even think about it."

"You have no idea how good that makes me feel, Lizzie. Yes, I am an amputee, but I don't want that to be the only thing that defines me. I'm thrilled that you see me as a whole man."

Pressing her breasts against his chest, she cupped his face and leaned close, her breath a whisper over his skin. "You are very much a whole man."

He hated to leave the bed but needed to take care of the condom. Wondering how she would feel, he threw caution to the wind and suggested, "How about we take a shower together?"

Each smile of hers grew wider and brighter as she replied, "Absolutely."

It took a little maneuvering since he did not have his crutch, but with some help and no embarrassment, they made it work together.

Later, snuggled together in her small bed after checking on Rufus sleeping downstairs, he kissed her forehead and tucked her tightly against him.

"Tell me about your family," she whispered, her request surprising him.

He sucked in a deep breath before letting it out slowly. "You know my grandfather had the accounting office in Baytown. My father followed in his footsteps but settled in a small town in Maryland. Dad worked and Mom enjoyed the social standing his job afforded her. You were right when you said I had been given things. I played sports in high school, not having to have an afterschool job. My parents were already picking out my college by the time I was in middle school. I was expected to major in accounting and my grandfather talked about me taking over his business when he retired."

She shifted up on one elbow to stare down at him, her gaze holding his steadily. Interest, not condemnation, in her eyes.

"But the closer I got to graduation, the less interested I was in going straight to college. Everything seemed so planned. I felt choked. I craved adventure. I craved traveling beyond my hometown in Maryland. I craved setting my own course and not simply following the course my parents had set out for me."

He scrubbed his hand over his face and continued. "A recruiter was at our school, and talking to him, I felt called to join. To serve. To do something besides just let my family dictate what my life was going to be like. I knew it was a risk, but it was one I was willing to take."

"How did your parents react?"

Snorting, he replied, "About as good as you can imagine. Mom cried and Dad ranted, but I was over eighteen years old, so it was a done deal. Surprisingly, my grandfather said very little at the time, but at the bus station when I was leaving, he shook my hand firmly, told me to take care of myself, then added that he was proud of me. That meant a lot to me."

Lizzie's fingers trailed along his shoulder and back

as she held him close, and he reveled in the calming touch. "And when you were injured?"

"My parents were great. They flew to Germany and spent time with me when I was in the hospital there. Once I came home, they visited often when I was in rehab. I noticed my mom added veteran's hospitals and rehabilitation centers to some of her community service focus, getting several of her clubs and organizations to help."

Her breath puffed warmly over his chest. "I'm glad you had that."

"Yeah, me too."

They remained quiet, arms banded around each other. As her weight settled and he knew she had found sleep, he lay awake for a little while, knowing that, at least for him, their friendship has grown into much more.

And as sleep claimed him, he vowed to take care of her and do everything he could to keep the farm safe.

20

Driving into Baytown in Papa Beau's old truck with the windows down, Lizzie sang to a country tune on the radio. She felt better than she had in a long time and knew it was from finally getting a good night's sleep. Well, two orgasms while making love to the man she was falling for had a lot to do with a good night's sleep.

Morning chores finished, she had re-walked the pastures but kept the animals close to the barn, not wanting to take a chance until Scott was able to get up security lights. Now, on her way to the accounting firm to see Lia about Emily's birthday party, she hoped she could talk Scott into having lunch with her. Lunch out was such a treat, but she was in the mood to celebrate the new change in their relationship.

There was a parking space almost in front of the accounting office, but she would have had to parallel park next to a Mercedes. *No way! Not in Papa Beau's big old truck.* Driving just down the street, she was able to park with ease.

Climbing from the truck, Lizzie stood on the sidewalk and glanced down at her clothes. She had changed after her morning chores and shower and smoothed her hands over her clean jeans and tugged slightly at a light pink T-shirt with little cap sleeves. Her feet were encased in her favorite cowboy boots, not new, but not scuffed. Taking her hair out of its braid, it fell down her back in waves.

Stepping into the outer office, she smiled at Mrs. Markham.

"Good morning, Elizabeth," came the greeting. As usual, Mrs. Markham's smile was warm and inviting. "I'm afraid Scott has a client right now."

"That's all right, I'm actually here to see Lia about her daughter's birthday party at the farm."

At this, Mrs. Markham's face brightened. "Oh, how delightful." Checking with Lia, she said, "Please, follow me."

As she walked down the hall, Lizzie noted that Scott's door was closed and hoped his appointment would be finished by the time she was ready for lunch. Moving into Lia's office, she was greeted warmly once again. Taking the seat offered, the two women chatted for a moment before getting down to business.

"I've taken out new insurance to cover visitors to the farm," Lizzie began. "Since I'm not serving food there, I'm not required to have any other license. The animals are all seen by Sam Collins, the veterinarian, and they are safe and clean. Of course, the children will only be with the baby goats. They will be able to feed and pet the adult goats, but only through the fence. And they can see the alpacas as well."

Lia clapped her hands with glee. "Emily is so excited about this party. It's all she can talk about. Thank you so much for letting us have it at your farm."

Shaking her head, she lifted her hand and waved it dismissively. "Lia, you and Aiden are the ones I need to thank. With you having the party at the farm, that will go a long way to getting others to want to do the same."

Leaning forward, she pulled a small notebook from her purse and said, "I just need a few things from you. How many children and adults will be coming, and you can just give me an approximate number. I can set up a picnic table... well, it's a folding table that I can set up in the yard for whatever food you're bringing."

"Right now, there are thirteen children and probably about eight adults coming. Is that okay?"

Scribbling in her notepad, she looked up and smiled. "Absolutely."

"Aiden said that he can bring some folding tables and chairs from the American Legion."

Breathing a sigh of relief, Lizzie enthused, "That would be wonderful. I have a few, but probably not enough." After jotting a few more notes, she looked up and said, "Okay, Lia, here comes the tough part. I'm not exactly sure what to charge, especially since this is my first party."

Her voice full of determination, Lia said, "You need to charge the full amount, Lizzie. I know we're friends now and this is your first party, but remember, you're working on increasing your business." Turning her laptop around, she continued, "Let's take a look and see what some of the other places are charging for this, and then we can go from there."

"Thank you so much for this. Scott and I were going to look at prices later, but when I decided to come into town and talk to you, we hadn't had a chance."

Lia stood and walked around her desk, taking a seat next to Lizzie so they could both look at the computer screen at the same time. "Well, I know he's with a client right now, so we've got time. And I'd love to help."

The two women began scrolling through various farms in Virginia that offered events Lizzie wanted Weston Farms to host. Smiling and talking, her heart felt lighter knowing she was moving closer to her dream.

Scott tried not to stare at the woman sitting across from him, but it was hard. Not because she was beautiful, although she was. Her clothes were immaculate, her makeup perfect, and her hair obviously cared for by a stylist. He had seen a picture of her online but still had been surprised when she walked in. Careena Giardano was not what he expected.

He stared because he wanted to have a better understanding of the woman who might be able to help Lizzie or at least give him some clues as to what Luca's intentions were for Weston Farms.

"I'm so glad you agreed to meet with me," he said. "As I told you on the phone, I'm working with Elizabeth

Weston and know that your father is interested in buying her farm."

Lifting a perfectly manicured hand to glide her fingers through her hair, pushing the strands over her shoulder, Careena smiled. "I was thrilled when you called, Scott. I so rarely get into Baytown and had no idea that Ms. Smith had taken over your grandfather's business or that you had joined her."

"It's Mrs. McFarlane now," he corrected. "She married Aiden McFarlane."

Arching a shaped eyebrow, she reacted with surprise. "She married the man from the bar?"

"Aiden is co-owner of Finn's Pub, if that's what you mean."

Giving a little shake of her head, she said, "Oh, I didn't mean anything by that. It just surprised me, that's all. I remember seeing him as a teenager, although I went to a private school so we didn't run in the same circles, as you can imagine."

Scott forced a smile onto his face, although her meaning was insulting to his friends. Getting down to business, he said, "Your father has approached Ms. Weston, hoping to buy her farm. I'm afraid I don't understand the value for the Giordano Farms. The Weston Farm had already sold quite a few acres to your family. What's left is pastureland, the family home, a garden, a barn, and several outbuildings. I can't imagine that would be very important to the Giordano Farms."

"My father did business with Mr. Weston. I know buying smaller farms can have a negative connotation to people who don't understand agriculture. You see, small farms simply cannot compete with larger farms. It causes stress, heartache, money problems, and even family problems for the smaller farms. My father offered very good prices to Mr. Weston years ago for those acres, certainly not trying to take advantage of him. That's all he wants to do now, is to help Ms. Weston."

"So, your father's hoping to be a benefactor of smaller farms? That seems rather altruistic of him."

Careena threw her head back and laughed, the sound delicate, and yet practiced. Her hand pressed against her chest as her mirth slowed, and she once again pinned him with her dark eyes. "You would be right. He's not trying to be altruistic, nor does he consider himself to be the patron saint of small farms and farmers." Leaning forward, she placed her hand on his desk and said, "There's really no mystery here, Scott. Giordano Farms owns land on either side of the Weston farm. It would be much more convenient for us to own the entire tract of land. My father tried for years to get Mr. Weston to sell, but he wouldn't. Now that he's gone, I cannot imagine that Ms. Weston is having an easy time of it. We are more than willing to pay an excellent price for her land. With that money, she would be able to buy a house in town or in the county, wherever she wanted to live."

Cocking his head to the side, he said, "Farming is all that Ms. Weston has ever done. If she no longer has the farm, what do you suggest she do?"

Careena shifted back in her chair, a confused look on her face. "I'm not sure what you're getting at, but she would be free to do anything. There are many restaurants that are popping up in Baytown that she could work in. I'm sure there are stores that need seasonal sales help. I know many of the beach houses in The Dunes Resort need housekeepers. I would think a woman of her resources would have plenty of opportunities for employment."

Shocked at Careena's easy dismissal of Lizzie's employment desires, he pressed, "May I be so impertinent as to ask what *you* would get out of this? I know you're an accountant for your family's farm, but you seemed particularly interested in meeting with me when I called you. I'm just curious to see if there's something I'm missing."

Careena looked down at her hands, a slight sigh leaving her lips. From what Scott had observed, she maintained control over all her mannerisms, and he wondered if the sigh had slipped out unexpectedly.

Lifting her head, she held his gaze. "Scott, I don't expect you to understand this, but I'm going to do something very rare and give you my honest reasons. I'm the oldest child, and I have worked hard all my life. I was expected to go to college and earn a degree in something that would help the family business. Accounting was fascinating to me and my father was thrilled. I knew that I had a place with our business as soon as I graduated. My younger brother will soon graduate with a business degree specializing in agriculture, and he'll join us as well. May I emphasize my *younger* brother. I am the oldest by several years, and yet, to my father, still seen as just a female. My father is ready to place my brother at the helm of Giordano Farms when it's the right time. Not me. I still feel as though every day I have to prove myself."

Lifting her shoulders in a delicate shrugged. "There it is, plain and simple. No matter how old I am, I still seem to be trying to please my father. If I can get Ms. Weston to agree to sell Weston Farms, that will go a long way in raising me in my father's eyes."

Scott continued to stare at the beautiful woman sitting across from him, and while her words may have been practiced, he believed they were true. She really wanted Weston Farms and hoped that would give her an edge over her brother as her father looked at who would be best to lead the company.

Before he had a chance to speak, she leaned forward and reached into the slim, leather briefcase sitting at her feet. Pulling out a thin file, she placed it on his desk and flipped it open. Tapping on the top page, she said, "Please take a look at this. I think you'll find the offer we are willing to make to be more than generous. It truly would set up Ms. Weston very well for the next phase of her life."

Promising to look over the offer, knowing he would never work to convince Lizzie to sell her farm, he stood and escorted Careena to his door. Opening it, he said, "Thank you for coming in today, Ms. Giordano. It was very nice to meet you."

Careena shook his hand, giving it a slight squeeze and holding it for longer than expected. Smiling up at him, she said, "It will be a pleasure working with you, Scott. I'm so thrilled that you will help convince Ms.

Weston to sell her farm to us." With her hands still in his, she leaned closer and said, "I believe this could be the start of a wonderful partnership."

With a final squeeze of his hand, she turned to walk down the hall. Something must have caught her eye because he watched as her gaze moved up and down before seeming dismissive. He watched as she left, his mind no longer on her, but wondering how he was going to deal with the overzealous woman who wanted Lizzie's farm.

Turning, he jolted as he saw Lizzie and Lia standing in the hall, Lia's eyes large and round and Lizzie's full of hurt. Realizing how the situation appeared, he threw up his hands and said, "Lizzie, it's not what you think."

Her chest heaved and she blinked back tears, starting to walk past him toward the front door of the office. He reached out and snagged her shoulders, halting her steps. Trying to turn her toward him, he said, "I met her to see what their intentions were. I'm not working with her."

He felt her body quiver as she lifted her head and pinned him with a glare. "That's not what it sounded like to me. She was quite clear as to what she thought your *partnership* was in relation to *my* farm!"

"No, no, please listen—"

"Mr. Redding, your next appointment is here," Mrs. Markham interrupted, her gaze shooting between everyone in the hall.

Twisting his head, he said, "Lia… can you take the meeting?"

Before she could answer, Mrs. Markham said, "I'm

sorry, but Ms. McFarlane, your next appointment is here as well." Leaning closer, she continued, "Scott, your appointment is Mrs. Bailey... newly widowed and already in tears about the taxes."

Knowing he needed to see Mrs. Bailey, he looked back down at Lizzie and said, "I'll be out at the farm just as soon as I can. Please, please, know that what you heard is not what you think is happening."

Lizzie wiped her tears with her hand, then squared her shoulders as she stepped backward out of his grip. Lifting her chin, she said, "Don't bother. I was right when I said that I can only count on me."

He watched as she walked out the door, and all he wanted to do was run after her, begging her to listen. But before he could take a step, Mrs. Markham ushered the elderly Mrs. Bailey toward him, the widow already dabbing at her eyes and saying, "Oh, Mr. Redding, you have to help me. I don't have any idea what Walter did when it came to our taxes."

Forcing a professionally pleasant expression on his face, he took Mrs. Bailey's hand and led her into his office. Sighing heavily, he sat behind his desk and prayed that Lizzie would give him a chance to explain. Having her angry with him cut straight into his gut. Having her think that she could not count on him cut straight into his heart.

21

Lizzie stomped around the pasture, now in her work clothes, having almost ripped off her cute T-shirt in anger. Her hair was once again braided down her back and her feet in heavy work boots. She had skipped lunch, afraid if she tried to eat she might choke.

The drive home had been very different from the drive into town. No music. No singing. No happy expectations of a lunch out with Scott. Instead, she had turned the events in the office over and over in her head.

As her anger burned, she thought of the beautiful woman who had left Scott's office and climbed into the Mercedes. The woman whose gaze raked over Lizzie, easily dismissing her as no competition even though she had no idea who Lizzie was. It was not the first time she had seen that before... women and men who looked to see if her nails were manicured, her hair was colored and highlighted, or her clothes were fashionable. And when they determined they were not, the rejection came.

Lizzie could have cared less what the woman from Giordano Farms thought about her, except her hand had been in Scott's when she had so easily dismissed Lizzie. And hearing the woman say that Scott was going to help with the acquisition of Weston Farms rocked her, completely throwing her off balance.

The animals scattered away from Lizzie as she stomped around as she finished her chores. As she continued to turn the events over in her mind, she knew in her heart that Scott would not betray her. That, she was sure of. *But what if he thinks that he's helping me by encouraging me to get rid of the farm?*

Dropping her chin to her chest, the heavy weight that had been on her after Papa Beau died came back in full force.

Desperately needing something to take her mind off her troubles, she looked up at Caesar and said, "It's time, buddy. Let's get you shorn."

She knew it would be difficult to shear the large animal by herself, but she had watched others do it and had a plan. Leading him into the barn, she tied a rope around him and secured it to one of the stalls inside. Taking the large, clean plastic sheet that she had purchased just for the fleece, she lay it on the straw.

Caesar eyed her warily as she finished her preparations. Once he was securely fastened, she covered his face with a special bag that would keep him from being able to nip at her. He shook his head slightly, but she was gentle and talked to him the whole time. Pushing his body closer to the gate, she had to use her weight to keep him in place and wondered if her slight stature would be enough to finish the job. So far, Caesar was cooperating, although she imagined he was not pleased.

Taking the heavy, electric shears, she started at the back of his upper neck and began shearing downward. The long, heavy fleece fell away from Caesar's neck in a giant clump. Making a pass as close to his neck as she thought she could, the fleece rolled away, exposing more, and she was able to make several passes to obtain all the fleece in a section.

Grabbing handfuls, she tossed it to the tarp at her side. As soon as she finished the neck, her arms already ached, but she had to laugh at the skinny neck now exposed. "Caesar, I knew you were bushy, but now I can see you really were all fleece!"

She praised him for cooperating as she stopped her shears, grabbing the oil. Making sure to keep the blades lubricated, she turned back to her task. Already sweating in the hot barn, it dawned on her that with the heavy fleece gone Caesar would be much more comfortable.

Now it was time to begin shearing his body, this fleece being much thicker and heavier than what was on his neck. Making long, even passes with the shears, the fleece once again rolled together, and she grabbed handfuls with her free hand to toss it to the tarp, using her body to keep Caesar as still as possible.

Sweat trickled down her back and between her breasts, and she wanted to wipe her brow but did not have a free hand. She had planned on shearing all three alpacas today, but it became apparent that would not happen.

"Why the hell are you doing this by yourself?"

The familiar, deep voice sounded to her side, and she jumped. Swinging her head around, she pinned Scott with a glare. "Jesus, Scott! I could've cut Caesar by you scaring me like that!"

She turned off the shears and continued to glare toward him. It did not miss her notice that he was no longer dressed for the office but had on jeans, boots, and a T-shirt that showed off more of his muscles than she wanted to focus on. "Why are you here?"

"I'm sorry I scared you. But I told you that I was coming over, and I don't break my promises."

Her lips pinched tightly together as she continued to glare. "We don't have time for this now. I'm busy."

"And I'm helping."

Needing to focus on the job at hand and keep Caesar safe and comfortable, she turned back toward her alpaca. Scott stepped closer, and with his much larger body was able to hold Caesar in place as she continued to run the shears over his back, sides, and belly. By now, the fleece was clumped together, rolling backward over Caesar's flanks.

Her arm began to ache from the weight of the shears and the time it was taking. Concentrating to make sure she was doing the best job she could, she almost did not hear Scott speak.

"Are you okay? Do you need me to take over?"

It was on the tip of her tongue to snap at him, but she knew he was simply trying to help. Shaking her head, she replied softly, "No, thank you. This is the first time I've ever done this, but I've watched others."

"Is it always done this way?"

Shaking her head as she squatted to get under Caesar's belly and around his legs, she said, "No, many farms have a way to tie the animal in a lying position. That makes it much easier."

"We'll look into that for here," he stated in a soft voice as he rubbed Caesar's head. "We can get whatever you need to make this easier on both you and the animals."

Scott's words seared right through her. It was not lost on her that if he had plans to encourage her to sell her farm, he would not be making future plans. The weight on her chest lifted ever-so-slightly.

Lizzie did not look up at Scott but continued to carefully run the shears over Caesar's body, rolling the fleece into great bundles before tossing it to the tarp. Now that his neck and body were shorn, she needed to focus on his legs. Caesar quivered, and she hesitated, wondering if he was going to buck. Scott anticipated the animal's movements, and, using his body against Caesar, pressed him gently but firmly against the wall.

"I'm trying to get this done, but I'm afraid to go too fast," she admitted.

"Don't worry about it. You just do what you need to do, and I'll try to keep Caesar still."

Mumbling her thanks, she knelt on the ground as she carefully maneuvered the shears over the legs. Twisting, she looked at the massive mountain of fleece that was now collected on the tarp and could not help but grin. Looking up, she caught Scott's eyes on hers, the same sparkle of excitement staring back.

"It's hard to imagine that that's about seven hundred dollars sitting right there, isn't it?" she whispered.

His grin widened into a smile as he nodded. "I'm amazed, babe. Absolutely amazed."

Standing, she looked over Caesar and noticed where some small patches had been missed. Going back over with the shears, she tried to even him out as much as possible. "I know it looks a little messy, but as soon as it starts growing, he'll look fluffy again."

Moving to Caesar's head, she said, "If you can hold him a little bit longer, I'm going to trim his head just a little bit. I won't do it as much as some people might because I'm afraid."

Scott nodded silently while she got a smaller set of shears. Moving ever-so-gently, she sheared around his ears and throat, then over his forehead and cheeks.

Standing back, she heaved a great sigh of relief. "I think that's it."

Scott efficiently untied Caesar, talking to him in a soothing voice. Letting him go, Caesar bolted from the barn into his pasture, and Lizzie and Scott followed, standing by the fence, watching the newly-shorn alpaca frolic. With their arms propped on top of the gate leading to the pasture, they stood side-by-side, close but not touching. They remained quiet for several minutes, staring at Caesar looking rather ridiculous as a skinny alpaca being sniffed by Cleopatra and Mark Antony.

Exhaustion pulled at the core of her being. Her arms, shoulders, and back were tired from the exertion.

Her head ached from thinking too much about the farm. And her heart hurt at the idea of losing Scott in any way.

She jolted as he bumped her shoulder and turned to see him peering carefully at her. She shoulder bumped him as well, adding a little extra *umph* for good measure.

He chuckled and turned to face her fully. "I hope with everything that you hold dearly you believe that I would never do anything to harm your dreams. I would never betray Beau or you that way."

Her chest deflated as her sigh left her body, and she nodded. "I know. I believe you." Looking up, she said, "I'm ready to listen if you'll tell me what's going on."

"How about we go inside, get washed off, get comfortable, and I'll tell you everything?"

She could not argue with his suggestion but simply nodded and turned to walk toward the house. He fell in step beside her, and her fingers itched to reach out and link with his. But the emotions of the day still crashed over her, and she simply remained by his side as they walked into the kitchen.

As had become their habit when they came in from working, Scott walked directly to the downstairs bathroom, pulling his shirt off as he went. Trying to ignore the sight of his muscular torso, she hurried past him and ran up the stairs. A quick wash, a change of clothes, and brushing and re-braiding her hair was all she took the time to do.

Downstairs, she found that he had poured tall glasses of iced tea, and she reached for one eagerly.

Quenching her thirst, she set the almost empty glass down, and he refilled it.

"Shearing is hard work," she began. "Thank you for your help. I think I could've done it by myself, but it certainly made it a lot easier with you there as well."

Standing on the other side of the counter, he leaned forward, his weight resting on his forearms planted near their glasses. Holding her gaze, he replied, "Lizzie, I have no doubt that you would have been able to accomplish the shearing all by yourself. But I'm grateful you let me help. I'm also grateful that you're letting me be part of your world."

Uncertain what to say to that, she was glad when he took the initiative and picked up their glasses, saying, "Let's get comfortable and then we can talk."

She followed him into the living room, and it dawned on her that she was completely comfortable with him in her house and her life.

And utterly terrified of the day when he might leave.

Scott was relieved that Lizzie was calm and ready to hear what he had to say. Of course, the fact that she was exhausted probably had something to do with her willingness to acquiesce. Whatever the reason, he wanted to press his advantage.

Settling onto the comfortable sofa, he patted the cushion next to him and breathed a sigh of relief when she sat down close. They both shifted toward each other, setting their glasses of iced tea on the coffee table.

Wanting to relieve her anxiety quickly, he jumped into his explanation.

"I've had Gareth investigating Giordano Farms just to see if I could figure out what was Luca's motivation for wanting to buy out your small farm. During that, Gareth told me the history of tomato farming on the Eastern Shore, which was not particularly fascinating to me, and a little history of the Giordano family, which was."

Glad to have her full attention, he continued. "Luca has two children, a daughter that is an accountant for their business and a son that's finishing a degree in agricultural business. I decided to call the daughter, Careena, to see if I could ascertain why they are so keen to get your property."

"Do you think they're the ones who had my fence cut?"

Shaking his head, he replied, "Babe, I've got no idea. I'm sure it wasn't the Giordano's themselves, but I wanted to have an idea of how much they wanted this property."

"So, that was her today?" When he offered his nod, she asked, "What did you find out?"

"I pushed as to why they would be so interested in a small farm and got the reply that this farm was right between two parcels of their land and it would be advantageous for them to have the whole tract. She implied that her father was somewhat of a benefactor by alleviating the stress on smaller farmers who were no longer able to compete. She could not understand why you would want to refuse their offer since you are now alone and implied that your life would be much better if you would take the money."

Jerking back as though slapped, Lizzie repeated, "Better? How would my life be better?"

"The amount they are willing to pay would allow you to purchase a house, either in town or in the county. She seemed to think that without the heavy work and stress of the farm, you would be happier." Watching her face grow red, he threw his hands up in front of him and said, "Obviously, she doesn't know anything about you. What you want. What makes you happy. What your dreams are. She's looking at this purely from her optic."

Lizzie snapped her mouth shut and looked away. He observed the flare of her nose and tight muscles in her jaw. Reaching over, he did what he had been wanting to do since he arrived on the farm... he took her hand in his and held it tightly.

"Sweetheart, I believe in you. I believe in your dreams. I believe in your vision for this farm, which is your heritage. All I was trying to do is see if I could find out what the Giordanos were thinking. What I finally discerned was that she thinks by pressing forward, she'll win her dad's approval."

At that, Lizzie jerked, her gaze searching his as her brow scrunched in confusion. "I don't understand, Scott. She's got everything. You just have to look at her and see that. She's beautiful and has enough money to be well-dressed and well-manicured and well put together. She drives a Mercedes and has a college degree. She could probably snap her fingers and get any man she wanted. I'm not saying she doesn't work hard, but she's probably had a lot of things handed to her."

Rubbing his thumb over her fingers, he said, "It's true, she may have all of those things, but she made it very obvious that trying to gain her dad's approval was extremely important to her. She implied it's because she's a daughter and not the son." Shrugging, he added, "Quite frankly, I don't know, and I don't care. But I am going to have Gareth keep an eye on her. Maybe she, more than her father, wants you to sell. And right now, I don't trust anyone who wants you to sell."

Snorting, she bit out, "A daddy's girl trying to get his attention when it's obvious she has his attention. I mean… at least he's there. He cares. She works for him."

It slammed into him that she never talked about the father who abandoned her. "Oh, fuck, Lizzie, I'm sorry."

Her gaze jumped to his and she gave a little shake. "It's not like I give my dad much thought. I was lucky. I was surrounded by love with Mom, Papa Beau, and Grandma. Even my stepdad is wonderful. But Ms. Giordano is trying such grand gestures to make her dad thinks she's the bee's knees when he probably already does. My dad could care less about me or this farm."

"Do you have any good memories of him?"

She sighed heavily, her attention on her lap. "He liked to go fishing in the bay. He took me a couple of times when I was little. Even then, I knew he was goofing off when Papa Beau was working so hard. It didn't take me long to refuse to go because I wanted to help on the farm."

"It really is your dream life, isn't it?"

He gave Lizzie a moment to let his words settle over her, and, as usual, she hid nothing. She looked at him and smiled, scooting closer until he could wrap his arms around her and kiss her forehead. Holding her tightly, he said, "Your dream for this farm is my dream, too. I'm in this with you, baby. I promise you can count on me."

She relaxed into him and they sat closely as the minutes ticked by, both reveling in the intimacy of the moment.

22

On top of everything else Lizzie was trying to do, she added walking the pastures to check on the fence to her early morning routine before letting the goats and alpacas out. Scott had spent the night again, and her lips curved slightly at the memory of their lovemaking. Strong and caring, he made her feel cherished.

She had just let the animals out when she heard a car approach and turned to see Lia parking next to the house. By the time she had made it to her, Lia was holding onto Emily's hand, the little girl straining to see the animals.

"What brings you out today?"

"I should've thought of this yesterday," Lia replied. "It's a teacher workday, and so I have the day off to be with Emily. I thought perhaps I would come over and we could finish up the details about the party."

Before she had a chance to continue her greeting, another car came into sight. This time it was Carrie and Jack who alighted from their vehicle.

Waving, Carrie said, "I forgot to tell you that Jack has today off since it's a teacher workday. I thought I'd let him help more."

"Fabulous! He can start by watching Emily if she'd like to pet the goats from outside the fence," Lizzie said.

Jack grinned and took Emily by the hand, carefully watching over the little girl as she squealed with delight. Looking at her two friends, Lizzie invited them into the house. "We can have some coffee while chatting."

Once inside, coffee cups filled and the three women sitting at the table, Lia and Lizzie finalized the plans for Emily's party with Carrie excitedly throwing out commentary.

After taking time in Lia's office the previous day to look at the prices other similar farms charged for various events, they had agreed on the price for Emily's party.

Grinning, Lizzie said, "I've already had several more bookings for children's birthday parties, and I sheared one of my alpacas last night. I've had offers for the fleece, and the buyer is willing to pay top price. I'll never make a lot of money at my endeavor, but since I have few expenses other than just the farm, as long as I can save a little bit each year, I'll feel like I'm coming out ahead."

Soon, Carrie hugged her goodbye. "I'll come pick Jack up in a little bit. Make sure to put him to work. He's strong and needs something to do."

Lizzie walked outside with Lia and the two sat in chairs underneath the shade of a tree while Emily finished petting the goats.

"I hope you and Scott were able to work things out," Lia said. "I know him, and he would never do anything to sabotage your relationship or the farm."

Nodding, she smiled. "We did. I was so upset yesterday when I heard what Ms. Giordano said. Plus, seeing her hand holding tightly to his and all that she is and all that I'm not just crashed down upon me."

Lia's brow furrowed as she turned from gazing toward the pasture and looked at Lizzie. "All that she is and all that you're not?"

Lizzie was silent for a moment, then said, "Lia, I'm not running myself down just to look for someone to give me compliments. I like who I am. I like working on a farm. I like owning my own business. But I'm not blind. Ms. Giordano looked very well-tended, not like someone who works outside all the time. She drove a Mercedes, not an old clunker truck that barely runs. I try not to let those distinctions bother me, but I've been fighting so hard to keep my head above water, even when Papa Beau was alive, that I couldn't help but wonder."

"Wonder what, sweetie?"

"Wonder what Scott was doing with a mess like me he could have someone so put together."

Lia did not rush to offer assurances, but as Lizzie watched her, she appeared to be thinking carefully before speaking. Finally, Lia said, "I was so uncertain of Aiden at first. He had a reputation for being more of a love 'em and leave 'em kind of man, and I was a woman with a daughter who needed stability."

New to having girlfriends that she could simply chat

with, Lizzie was fascinated as she heard stories from her new friends, learning that when it came to relationships, everyone struggled with something. "What did you do?"

"I watched and waited. I watched to see how he treated me and Emily and discovered that he treated us with love and kindness. And I waited to see if it would last. And it did. And once he had my love, I never looked back. I knew what I had and wanted to hold onto that. And he's proven that I made the right choice every single day."

The two women held each other's gaze for a moment, both slowly smiling with understanding.

"Mama!" screamed Emily, standing near the gate with Jack. "Come and see the goats!"

The heavy conversation over, Lizzie and Lia walked toward the pastures, enjoying the beautiful day. After Lia and Emily left, she put Jack to work mucking the stalls and doing general cleanup in the barn while she worked in the kitchen making her goat milk products.

That evening, she and Scott, along with Jack's help, sheared Cleopatra. They were almost finished when Carrie and Colt drove up, observing the procedure when Jack begged to help finish. She felt more confident this time, having learned a few tricks shearing Caesar the night before. By the time they finished, there was another massive pile of beautiful fleece on the tarp and another very skinny alpaca.

"I can't believe what they look like without all that fur!" Carrie cried out as Cleopatra headed into the pen with the other two.

Scott wrapped his arm around Lizzie, and they walked the others toward their SUV. She smiled at the sight of Colt with one arm around Carrie and his other hand affectionately wrapped around the back of Jack's neck. Her mind was suddenly filled with the vision of Scott always on the farm, his hand on the neck of their child. Her breath catching in her throat, she was glad the sun was setting and no one could see her blush. She and Scott were so new in their relationship, but the idea that he might be her forever stayed strong.

Once their visitors left, she and Scott took care of the animals, putting them up for the night. He had flipped on the lights around the barn and she was grateful for the added security. "I'm really glad it's illuminated out here. I have to admit that I feel more secure."

"Gareth had a friend in security that lives in Richmond. He gave them a call and they made it a priority to come out here and put the lights and... uh... in."

Her smile faltered slightly at his little verbal misstep, and she asked, "Lights and what?"

Scrubbing his hand over his face, Scott replied, "I didn't want you worried about the cost, but I also had a couple of security cameras installed at the same time. They don't run all the time, but they are motion-sensored. They're set for higher than a small animal, so if a fox or raccoon goes by the barn, they won't turn on. It's just an added precaution in case someone is skulking around."

Narrowing her eyes, she asked, "And when were you going to tell me this?"

"Well, I was hoping never unless we needed the information that was on the cameras."

Huffing, she threw up her hands. "Why do I get the feeling you're going to tell me that you paid for this?"

Turning so that she was facing him, he drew her closer and held her gaze. "Lizzie, I don't know how to make it any plainer to you that you mean something to me. And that something is growing more every day. I can't predict the future, but right now, I see this relationship continuing. And I hope to God you see the same thing."

His words soothed her ire, and she sighed as she melted into him, wrapping her arms tightly around his waist and placing her cheek next to his heartbeat.

"Good, I see that we're on the same page," he said. She leaned back and looked up at him, but he continued, "I want you safe and I want this farm safe. And right now, I'm suspicious that all these things are tied together to sabotage you. The goats getting out of the barn. The fence that was cut. These things worry me, and I'm gonna do what I have to to keep you safe."

Swallowing deeply, she felt tears prick her eyes. Barely whispering, she said, "I think I'm falling for you."

His smile widened as he leaned down, taking her lips in a deep, wet kiss. "Good, babe. Then we're going to fall together."

A light fog clung to the ground in the early morning as Lizzie walked toward the barn, munching on a piece of toast. Her thoughts were swirling ever since she had woken from a restless sleep. Mark Antony needed to be shorn today, and she needed to gather all the fleece from the three alpacas and call her buyer. She needed to return several phone calls to confirm dates for two more children's birthday parties. And she needed to find time to make a run to the feed store.

Scott had not spent the night, having rushed to her place after work and leaving Rufus at his house. It had been on the tip of her tongue to suggest that he bring Rufus over and just leave him with her during the day. The dog would get more exercise, and she knew he would love being at the farm. She had hesitated, though, uncertain if it was too soon. *Maybe if I'm brave, I'll ask him today to let Rufus spend his days with me.*

It normally did not take her long to do a quick scan of the pasture fences to determine that they were intact, but with the fog, she had no choice but to walk closer to the perimeter, a task that added several more minutes to her already-busy day.

Stepping inside the barn, she was met with the humming of the alpacas, their heads peering over the gate of their stall. Calling them by name, she laughed aloud at the sight of the two skinny necks of Caesar and Cleopatra next to the still full-fleeced neck of Mark Antony. Rubbing their heads, she said, "You might think your roommates look funny, but by the end of today, you'll look just like them."

Leading them out of the barn, she let them into their pasture and hauled feed to put in their trough. Moving back to the barn, she let the goat kids out into their smaller field, petting them as she put their feed down as well.

Returning to the back of the barn where the sheds were for the goats, she noticed a small hole in the fence near the shelter. Hurrying toward them, she was relieved to see her goats still contained in the pen. Rushing through the gate, she stood as they came to her, gently butting against her legs. She began counting and her heart pounded as she discovered she was missing two. Stalking toward the small hole in the fence, she could see where several wires had been cut and goat hair was stuck to the ragged edges of wire. Shooting her gaze out into the pasture, a sick feeling began to sneak through her stomach. Her heart pounded as she looked toward the distance and spied two lumps on the ground.

The goats scattered as she hopped the fence and began running, each step bringing her closer to the nightmare. Two of her goats were lying on their sides, and it was easy to see they were not breathing. A small pile of plants lay nearby that had not been there the evening before. Unsure of the plants, she knew they had been placed there for a nefarious purpose. *Some fucking person poisoned my goats!*

Jerking her phone from her back pocket, she dialed 9-1-1, and with a shaky voice reported what happened, telling them that Sheriff Hudson and Detective Sims had been investigating problems at her farm. Once assured that someone was on their way, tears began falling as she dialed Scott. Barely able to speak, she once again managed to explain what she found. "Please come. I need you."

"Baby, I'm on my way," he promised.

Disconnecting, her whole body shook as she looked down and saw the foam around her goats' mouths. Forcing her mind to one more task, she called Sam Collins, gaining the promise that the vet would be right out.

Legs finally giving out, she dropped onto the grass next to the goats, her hands resting on either one as she sobbed.

23

That was how he found her. After racing to the farm, coming to a stop with gravel shooting behind his vehicle next to the house and running out to the field, Scott spied Lizzie sitting on the ground between two of her beloved goats, tears running down her face. He knelt down next to her, pulling her body into his, enveloping her in his embrace. Rocking her gently back and forth, he smoothed her hair away from her face.

She burrowed in close to him as though trying to dig her way inside to protect herself from the pain raging all around.

It only took a few minutes for Colt, Hunter, and two deputies to arrive. Right on their heels came Gareth and Katelyn, having been called by Scott as soon as he got off the phone with Lizzie. Scott looked up at Colt, uncertain what he should do.

Speaking softly, Colt said, "Lizzie, I know this is hard, but I'm gonna need you to walk me through what's happened here."

Before Lizzie had a chance to speak, an old truck pulled into the driveway but continued past the house, not stopping until it got to the gate. The sputtering noise from the engine had everyone swing their gazes around. Spying the veterinarian moving toward them, Colt muttered, "Jesus, Sam needs to get a new vehicle or get that one fixed."

Scott had met the pretty, petite veterinarian when he first adopted Rufus and took him in to be checked. Samantha Collins was a dedicated veterinarian who would take care of any animal even if the owner could not pay. He had no doubt her vehicle was due to working in a rural area in the poorest counties in Virginia. But Colt was right, she definitely needed her truck checked out. He made a mental note to talk with Jason when he went back to town.

He watched Sam approach, her intelligent gaze settled on the scene in front of her before she sighed heavily. "Oh, fuck, Lizzie. I'm so sorry."

Lizzie looked up through watery eyes and begged, "Please, Sam, tell me they didn't suffer."

It was easy for everyone to see that Sam struggled with Lizzie's question, but Scott appreciated her reply. "Lizzie, honey, why don't you let Scott take you back to the house. The Sheriff has to take a look around and so do I. As soon as we know what we're dealing with, honey, I promise, I'll come talk to you."

Scott, knowing that Lizzie was in no shape to make a decision on her own, stood and assisted Lizzie to her feet. With his arm wrapped around her, he sent a pointed look toward Gareth and Colt, letting them know that he wanted to be involved in anything they found.

Katelyn stepped forward and said, "Lizzie, let's go into the kitchen. You look like you could use a cup of tea, and we'll make some coffee for everyone here."

Scott was afraid that Lizzie would protest, demanding to stay in the field, but was grateful when she did not. Barely nodding at everyone, she took Katelyn's hand and started to walk toward the house. Stopping, she turned back. "Don't do anything with… them. At least not without me."

His heart breaking for her, Scott watched as Katelyn wrapped an arm around Lizzie and led her back to the house, where they disappeared inside.

Whirling around, rage searing through him, he growled, "Colt, we gotta do something. This shit can't keep going. First the property. Next the animals. When the fuck is somebody going to come after her?"

Sam's gaze jerked from the goats on the ground to the men standing around. "Obviously, there's things going on here that I had no idea about. Colt? I'm going to let you tell me what you need from me."

Colt's jaw ticked as he looked from Scott to the veterinarian. "Sam, I need to know the cause of death. Accidental or intentional." Looking at Hunter, he said, "Get the deputies on the cut wire at their pen."

Scott watched as Sam snapped on a pair of gloves before kneeling next to the goats. On her knees, she bent forward and examined their faces, pulling her phone out of her pocket to snap pictures. There appeared to be vomit on the ground nearby, and she scooped small samples, placing them into plastic bags. Moving to the other goat, she also took samples of fecal matter. Finally, she looked at the remains of cut plant limbs nearby, her mouth tight as she stood and turned toward the others.

"Azaleas are the standard flowering bush of the South but well-known to be poisonous to many animals, including goats. I remember Lizzie taking out all of the azalea bushes around the house when she decided to raise goats. Her grandfather hated to lose the pretty bushes that her grandmother had planted and loved, but he understood Lizzie's need to make the entire area safe. Obviously, the goats don't get to the house, but she didn't want to take a chance." Inclining her head downward to the clump of cut, half-eaten plants, she said, "That's the source of the poison, right there."

One of the deputies nearby scrunched his brow and asked, "So, the goats just got into the poisoned plant by accident and that's all?"

Colt whipped his head around and bit out, "I hardly think the goats cut their own plants and brought them into their pasture to munch on. She just said that Lizzie got rid of all the azaleas. That would indicate somebody brought the plants in!"

The deputy blushed but continued to take pictures of the area. Scott, barely trusting his voice to hold with the anger coursing through him, asked, "Why would the culprit put the plants out here when the goats were in the pen near the barn? He would have done more damage to the whole herd if he'd toss the azalea bushes into that pen."

Shaking her head, Sam said, "I'm afraid that's for you all to figure out. I can't begin to imagine what kind of person would poison defenseless animals." Shifting her gaze toward Colt, she added, "I'm going to head to the barn and check out the rest of the animals to make sure there's nothing else going on. Once you're finished out here, let me know. I'll take care of disposing of the goats after I talk to Lizzie." With a nod from Colt, she collected her sample bags and headed toward the barn, and Scott was grateful that Sam had dropped everything to come out immediately.

Another deputy came from the barn and said, "The wire was definitely cut. Not a huge hole, but obviously enough that a couple of goats got out."

Colt scrubbed his hand over his face. "That's probably what they wanted. Someone is out to make things difficult for Lizzie but not necessarily try to destroy her whole farm."

Scott looked at Colt and Gareth, saying, "I had the security camera feed into an app on my computer. I can also pull it up with my phone, but it may be too small for us to tell anything from here."

"Let's see it anyway," Colt said.

The men moved into the shade so they could view his phone screen while Scott quickly opened the app. Scrolling along with his finger, they finally spied a shadow moving along next to the barn. Cursing, Scott said, "Fuck! I didn't get the right camera angles. Fuckin' hell, I don't know if we can see any better than this."

"Send all that information to me," Gareth said. "I've got some programs that will be able to sharpen the image on this."

"Whatever you get, send it to me," Colt said.

Colt headed back to his deputies to finish searching the area while Scott and Gareth headed toward the house. Once there, Gareth collected Katelyn, who offered Lizzie a heartfelt hug. After seeing them drive away, Scott pulled an emotionally exhausted Lizzie into his arms.

Lizzie turned her red-rimmed eyes toward Scott, her heart aching but her brain still scrambling to understand the events of the morning. His eyes held pain as well, but try as she might to want him to feel better, the weight on her chest simply intensified. His arms held her tightly, and she clung to him for dear life, dark emotions clawing at her.

She tried to speak but it came out as little more than a croak. "I don't know how much more I can take."

His arms spasmed, squeezing her even more. With his lips pressed to her forehead, he replied, "We're going to get through this, baby. I know you're hurting, but just let it out. Give it all to me, and I'll carry it. I swear to you, I'll carry your pain."

As her tears slowly subsided, she heard his steady heartbeat as her face pressed against his chest. It never wavered. It just remained steady. She thought about his words, and it dawned on her that he had not promised that nothing bad would ever happen to her again. But that when it did, he would be there for her, carrying her pain. She could not imagine a more beautiful declaration of love.

Tilting her head back, she held his gaze and said, "I love you." Swallowing past the lump in her throat, she whispered, "It may not be the right time to say that, but it's what I feel right now."

He pressed his lips against her forehead once again, taking her weight and giving his strength to her. "There's never a wrong time to tell someone you love them, Lizzie. Just know that I love you, too."

Tucked together, they stood in her kitchen for several more minutes until she finally felt as though she could stand on her own. Pushing back slightly, her hands clutched his arms as she said, "I didn't get anyone fed this morning. I've got to go out and do that."

"I've already called Lia and told her what's going on. I'm going to repair the fence in the pen and help you get everything done. We'll wait and shear Mark Antony tomorrow. He'll be fine to wait another day."

"But that means I'll have to put the buyer off another day."

"Will that keep them from buying the fleece at all?"

Shaking her head, she replied, "No. I suppose the next day will be fine."

"That's what you need to do, baby. Prioritize what has to be done, and then we'll take care of it."

Just as they stepped apart, a knock on the back door had them turn to see Sam standing outside. Calling out, "Come on in," Lizzie quickly swiped her hands over her cheeks to wipe away the remnants of her remaining tears.

Stepping inside, Sam accepted the cup of coffee that Scott handed to her. "Thanks," she said, taking a sip of the hot brew before accepting Lizzie's offer for them to sit down at the table. Once settled, Lizzie waited for Sam to speak, noting the fatigue around the veterinarian's eyes. She was so grateful that Sam had come quickly and yet realized that she probably pulled her away from other clients.

"Before you tell us what happened, I just need to let you know how much it means to me that you dropped everything to come out here," Lizzie said. "I'm sure this is an imposition."

Shaking her head, Sam smiled wearily. "Oh, Lizzie, I'm glad I could be here for you. I'm just sorry for the reason." Taking another sip of coffee, she cleared her throat. "Okay, let's get this done, and I'll take care of the goats for you." She sat up straight and tucked a few wayward strands of dark brown curls behind her ears. Sucking in a fortifying breath, she began. "From my preliminary investigation, it appears the goats ingested azalea clippings, which are poisonous, as you know."

"Azalea clippings?" Lizzie gasped. Her gaze shot between Sam and Scott, and she said, "There were no azaleas here!"

Scott reached over and grasped her hand, giving it a squeeze, saying, "We know, honey. Just listen, please."

"There was a clump of azalea branches, most of the leaves stripped and the branches chewed on," Sam explained. "I even found a bit of string that seemed to have tied them together. My guess? Someone threw them into the field, knowing that when the goats got out, they would eat them and become sick. I've taken blood samples from both goats as well as samples from the vomit and feces nearby. That will let me know for sure if the azaleas were the culprit."

"But why?" Lizzie cried.

"I'm afraid that's for the Sheriff to discern," Sam said. "I know they were looking at the cut fence of the pen near the barn. I'm afraid that's all I can tell you for now."

The realization that someone was willing to kill an animal just to get rid of Lizzie slammed into her, having the effect of drying her tears and filling her with anger. Forcing her words to remain steady while her body shook, she thanked Sam profusely.

Sam stood to leave and then said, "I hope you don't mind, but I fed your animals. I knew you would get to them but wanted you to take care of yourself first."

Scott stood and turned toward Lizzie, offering his hand as she moved next to him. "Dr. Collins, we appreciate what you've done more than you can know."

"I can't say it was my pleasure, but it was my job. I'm glad that I can be here for you. Oh, and by the way, call me Sam... everyone does," she replied. She turned and started for the door, saying, "Of course, the animals are not in the field where the two goats are. I'm going to open the gate and back my truck close by. Scott, I'll need some help loading them into the back of my pickup."

Lizzie and Scott nodded their agreement, but a few minutes later heard Sam's engine grinding and clunking but not starting. Shoulders slumping, Lizzie shook her head and said, "Is this day just cursed?"

Giving her hand a squeeze, he kissed her forehead. "I'll call Jason and have him send out a tow truck. Why don't you fix some breakfast, sweetheart? I'll help Sam, and since the animals are already fed, that saves us some time."

She doubted she could eat a bite without choking but knew that Scott was trying to give her something to do to keep her mind as well as her body busy. Nodding, she moved over to the refrigerator as he headed outside to help Sam.

"Jason is sending someone with a tow truck, and they should be here soon." Scott was standing next to Sam's truck, hoping to alleviate some of her frustration but knowing he had little chance of doing so. The rumble of a diesel engine and the crunch of gravel had them look up to see the tow truck pulling into Lizzie's drive.

When the driver climbed out, he recognized Joseph. Walking forward to greet him with his hand stuck out, he said, "Has Jason got you working in the garage as well as the tattoo shop?"

"Yep."

Scott knew that Joseph was a man of few words and had his day not already been shot to hell, he probably would have grinned. As it was, he simply stated, "We've had problems here this morning. I don't know if Jason filled you in, but Dr. Collins, the veterinarian, needs to deal with two of Lizzie's goats that were poisoned and died."

He watched as Joseph's jaw ticked as though tight

with anger, but the large man simply nodded.

"I wasn't sure if one of Jason's mechanics could see if he could get Sam's truck started now or if it was going to have to be towed. Since you're here, I'm assuming all the mechanics were busy." Another nod from Joseph was the only response. "Well, since it's going to have to be towed into the shop, I'll follow so that I can take Sam back to the vet's practice to get another vehicle. We'll still have to dispose of the goats."

"Don't worry about following," Joseph said. "I can get the vet to the office and can also deal with the goats."

Joseph walked over to Sam's truck and called out to Scott, "Keys?"

Sam stepped forward and, pulling the keys out of her pocket, handed them to Joseph.

The large man's gaze raked over her before asking, "Where's the vet?"

Arching an eyebrow, Sam straightened and firmly stated, "I am."

Scott had the feeling that Joseph was rarely shocked, but the look on the other man's face gave evidence that Joseph was surprised.

"You're Sam? The veterinarian?"

With her hands on her hips, Sam cocked her head to the side and asked, "Which stuns you more? That my name is Sam? Or that a female can be a veterinarian?"

Joseph scowled and turned without answering, walking back to the tow truck. Once inside, he maneuvered it so that he would be able to hook up her truck.

Glancing toward Scott, Sam snorted. "The man

doesn't say much, does he? And what little he does say, he manages to put his foot into his mouth."

Scott considered himself to be a peacemaker, and under better circumstances might have tried to smooth things over between the taciturn tattoo artist and the irritated veterinarian. But as shitty as the morning had been for Lizzie, all he wanted to do was make sure things were right with her.

"You can trust him, that's all you need to know. I'm going to head back inside to check on Lizzie. Let me know if you need anything else from me."

A few minutes later, in the kitchen with Lizzie, he looked up as she called to him. She was standing at the kitchen sink, staring out the window, her fingers pressed to her lips as another tear slid down her cheek. Hurrying over, he stood behind her and wrapped his arms around her, looking out the window to see what had caught her attention.

Joseph had walked to the field and had picked up one of the goats in his arms, cradling its lifeless body carefully, giving evidence that he understood the precious burden. He laid it gently into the back of Sam's pickup truck before going back into the field and, with just as much care, bringing the second goat's body.

"Sam's clinic is between here and Baytown," Scott began. "They must be planning to stop at her clinic so that she'll have the proper way to dispose of them before towing her truck into town."

Nodding, her head bumped into his chin. "That's really nice of them to do that for me."

"They're both nice people. Maybe they'll recognize

that in each other." Turning Lizzie in his arms, he pulled her against his chest and held her tightly. Glancing over her head, he saw that she had fixed a little breakfast and was determined to see if she would eat. Nudging her toward the table, he said, "Come on, sweetheart." Thrilled she did not resist, he vowed to not only take care of her but find out who was threatening her and the farm.

Lizzie went through the motions of her day, glad that most of her tasks were so rote she could have done them with her eyes closed. And yet, today more than other days, she spent more time with her animals. Rubbing their heads. Giving little treats. Snapping pictures with her phone. She was anxious to shear Mark Antony but knew that Scott was right to wait another day. She was weary down to her very bones and feared she did not have the strength for a strenuous endeavor.

By mid-afternoon, Sam had called to tell her that she had sent off blood samples, and while it would be several weeks before a definitive answer was in, her examination of the goats indicated plant toxicity.

"I want to thank you for everything you did today," Lizzie said, once more standing at her kitchen window, looking out over the farm.

"You know it's part of my job," Sam replied. "A sad part, but I'm willing to help in any way I can."

"Did you get your truck fixed?" A little snort came from the other woman, and Lizzie's ears perked up.

"Yes, the grumpy bear got my truck to Jason's, and he's already got it working. I should get it back tomorrow."

"Grumpy bear?"

"I know I shouldn't call Joseph that because he really was very kind this morning." Sam began. "But throughout the entire ordeal, he barely said a word to me. I think if he could talk only in single words or grunts, he would."

"I'll be sure to thank him when I see him again," Lizzie said. "Let me know as soon as you hear anything else." Gaining Sam's assurance, she disconnected, and for a moment thought of Joseph. Shaking her head, she had to admit that Sam had given an apt description. While she might not have called Joseph 'grumpy', he certainly was a bear of a man. And the sight of him standing next to the tiny veterinarian now caused her lips to curve ever-so-slightly.

Soon afterward, Scott came through the back door, having completed a preliminary check around the barn, Rufus bounding ahead of him. Kneeling to rub the excited dog's quivering body, she allowed him to lick her face as she wrapped her arms around his neck.

"Hey, boy, let me have some of that."

She looked up at Scott and placed her hand in his as he gently assisted her to stand. With his arms wrapped around her, she reveled in his embrace, deciding that her face buried against his chest was one of her favorite places to be.

"You've got to be exhausted, babe," he said. "Go upstairs and fill the bathtub. I'm going to lock up down here and get Rufus settled." Kissing the top of her head, he added, "I'll be up in a few minutes."

She could not think of anything she would rather do at the moment, so she nodded against his chest before leaning back, peering up, and asking, "You'll come as soon as you can?"

He leaned forward and pressed his lips against her forehead and she closed her eyes, loving his gentle touch.

"I promise, I'll be right up."

She gave his waist a squeeze, then let him go and stepped backward. He pulled out his phone, and she knew he was checking the security cameras. No longer wanting to face the evidence of her property needing to be watched, she headed upstairs.

At the top of the stairs, she stood for a moment and pondered the rooms. Years ago, her grandparents had renovated the two bathrooms. The one in the hall that she and her mother had used was nicely appointed with the shower and bathtub together. Papa Beau had the bathroom attached to the master bedroom enlarged, and because her grandmother so loved to take a bath at night, he had installed a large, deep garden tub as well as the shower stall that he always used.

After Scott had helped her clean out Papa Beau's room, she had scrubbed the master bedroom and bathroom thoroughly, keeping a few mementos of her grandparents. Clean sheets adorned the bed, and fresh towels hung in the pristine bathroom. And yet, she still had rarely gone into the room. The nights that Scott stayed, they slept in her small bed.

Now, halted in the hallway, it struck her that the house was hers, and hers alone. Her grandparents would never need their space again, and she knew in her heart that they would want her to claim it and be happy there. Inhaling deeply, she let the air slowly leave her lungs as she turned and stalked toward the master bathroom. Turning on the water, she let the tub fill as she went back to her bathroom and gathered her toiletries.

As soon as the tub filled, she stripped and stepped into the hot water, settling down so the water came to her neck. Enveloped in the warmth, she understood the simple indulgence her grandmother craved. Leaning back, she closed her eyes, and for the first time that day relaxed.

She startled when a soft kiss was placed on her lips, then settled again as she remembered where she was and who she was with. Scott was sitting on the floor next to the tub, his fingertips dangling in the water, gently soothing over her shoulder.

"I was about to head into the hall bathroom when I saw the light on in here."

His words may have been spoken in a statement, but she heard the unasked question. Rolling her head to the side, she held his gaze and said, "Grandma loved to soak in a tub after a hard day's work. When Papa Beau updated the bathroom and kitchen years ago, he had this garden tub installed."

The water was still warm, and Scott appeared perfectly content to sit by her and listen. "I cleaned everything after you and I went through his room, but I still couldn't bring myself to come in here. The master bedroom and this bathroom still felt like it was theirs. But tonight, it was as though they gave me permission to finally call this mine."

He linked fingers with her and gave a little squeeze. "I know you miss them. I know after a day like today you miss them even more."

She nodded and swallowed past the lump in her throat, refusing to give into tears. "Katelyn reminded me earlier that loss reminds us of past grief. She was right. Losing the goats today just made me think of losing my grandparents."

She lifted her hand and ran it through his thick hair, sweeping it to the side before cupping his jaw and running her thumb lightly over the scar on his upper lip. No longer wanting to talk about her own loss, she said, "Talk to me."

While she really wanted to know about his own loss from his time in the military, she left her command open-ended, wanting him to choose his time and place to open up to her. Holding her breath, she waited to see what he would say.

"Because of my scores on the ASVAB, after boot camp, I became a Financial Management Technician and worked in the accounting offices. I was enlisted, not an officer, but found that I enjoyed the work, and it probably helped solidify that my parents and grandparents were right—accounting was a career I could enjoy. I even began to take college classes while in the Army."

"So, you never thought about making the Army your career?"

Shaking his head, he replied, "No, not really. Don't get me wrong, the Army was good for me. But I just wasn't cut out for the regimented lifestyle as a career. I figured that I would do one or two tours, get out, and finish my degree."

His fingers continued drifting through the water, now gliding lightly over her leg. Tingles began to move throughout her, and she itched to lean forward and press her lips against his. Shifting slightly in the tub, she placed her forearms on the edge and held his gaze, fascinated with every word he was uttering. Remaining quiet, she focused her attention on him, hoping he would continue. He did not disappoint.

"When I got the orders to serve a tour at Kandahar in Afghanistan, I wasn't worried or afraid. The conditions were rough, but essentially, every day I worked in an office." Snorting, he elaborated, "Sure, the office was a tent, but we had air conditioning that worked sometimes. Same with the heat. Everyone had to be battle-ready over there, but I loved the PT and weapons training. It broke up the monotony of staring at papers all day. To be honest, every time I passed by the hospital, I thought of the people inside. Sometimes I felt guilty that my job was so safe, and other times I just felt fucking thankful."

He grew silent, and it was now her turn to run her hand over his shoulder. The water was beginning to cool, but she did not want to move, wanting Scott to continue to tell his story, giving that part of his past to her. "So, what happened?"

"It was actually near the end of my tour if you can

believe that. I was assigned to a smaller base, agreeing to fill in for a shortage they had. I did that for a month, and then was in a convoy heading back to Kandahar."

She watched as his eyes drifted to the side, knowing that he was no longer with her but had shifted to a place years before. Her breath caught in her lungs as she waited.

"Same old story, like a lot of other people," he said, his voice now soft and raspy. "IED. I don't remember much, other than heat and smoke and screaming. Fuck, for all I know, the screaming was coming from me. It's all fuzzy now. I remember waking up for a few minutes in the hospital and then the next thing I remember was waking up and being told I was in Germany. It took several days for them to wean me off the major painkillers, enough for me to even be able to look down and see that there was only one foot underneath the sheet."

Her fingers that had been drifting over his skin clenched as her breath left her lungs in a rush. "Oh, Scott, I'm so sorry."

His gaze moved back to hers and his lips curved into a sad smile. "Baby, don't feel sorry for me. I'm alive. I came back. I won't say it was easy, but it only took a few days in the hospital and rehab to know that I was a fuck of a lot luckier than many. Even my amputation was easier. They were able to save my knee, so I only lost my leg below the knee. Rehab was a bitch, and it took several prosthetic fittings and quite a few prostheses to get the right one. But once I had that and learned to walk again, I was good."

Shifting in the water so that her face was directly in front of his, she whispered, "I'd say you were a lot more than good, Scott. I think you're amazing."

Closing the distance, they kissed, soft and gentle before flaming hot. As his arms banded around her, his hands dipping back into the water, he jerked away. "Jesus, baby, your water is cool!"

"Yes, but you can keep me warm."

With a growl, he stood and lifted her effortlessly from the tub. Grabbing a thick towel, he dried her briskly before scooping her up and stalking toward the bedroom. Seeing that he was heading toward her room, she said, "Scott, here."

His brow furrowed as he looked down at her, and she quickly explained. "Everything in here is clean, right down to the new mattress pad and sheets." Seeing him still stare in question, she added, "This bed is bigger."

"Lizzie, babe, I want you to be comfortable. I'm perfectly happy in your old room."

Shaking her head, she cupped his face and said, "I'm ready, Scott. Ready for you to be here with me. Ready to hold onto my memories of my grandparents while making this house mine. *Ours*, if you want."

His arms banded tightly as he gently laid her on the bed after whipping the covers back. "Are you sure? It's been a crazy-ass day."

She clung to him and agreed, "You're right. It has been a crazy day. But what I know with all my heart is that at the end of a crazy day, I want you and me together in every way. We can make our crazy-ass days better."

25

With Lizzie already naked, Scott wasted no time in divesting himself of his clothes and sitting on the edge of the bed to slip off his prosthesis. Whirling around, he lay his heated body over hers, not wanting her to be chilled more from having been in the cool water. As his lips found hers, his hands roved freely over her soft skin, the delicate scent of her bodywash filling the air.

She immediately opened her legs, allowing his hips to settle between her thighs, his cock eager and ready. He had no doubt she felt the same as she lifted her hips, pressing their bodies tightly.

Not wanting their lovemaking to go too quickly, he began kissing his way downward, past her jaw to suckle at the pulse point between her neck and shoulder, grinning as her fingers dug deeper into his back. Continuing his path, he kissed between her breasts before moving back and forth, sucking her nipples deeply into his mouth. Her hips continued to undulate, and pleas slipped from her lips.

Shimmying downward, he knelt between her legs and lifted her calves to his shoulders. He captured her gaze and offered a wicked smile before diving in to taste her essence. She was more exquisite than he could have imagined, and he had imagined a lot. His world was filled with thoughts of Lizzie, all other women falling into oblivion. Sex had become rare in recent years, but she brought back the magic of loving another being.

Sucking on her clit, her hips bucked upward, and he pressed his hand on the slight curve of her belly to hold her in place. Inserting a finger into her warmth as he continued to suck, she cried out as her fingers grasped his head, tangling in his hair. He continued to lick, feeling her juices spread over his tongue. He felt her vibrations against his mouth, and as they slowly subsided, he lifted his head and stared down at her beauty. Her eyes were closed but her lips were curved into a wide smile, and he wanted to shout. In spite of her crazy-ass, grief-filled day, he had placed a smile on her lips.

Crawling back up her body, kissing as he went, he finally grabbed the condom he had tossed to the bed and rolled it onto his eager cock. He held her gaze when she opened her eyes, and her hands slid from his hair to around his neck, holding him close.

"Make love to me," she whispered, her voice husky with need.

"There's nothing I'd rather do more in the world than always make love to you."

True to his vow, he slid the tip of his cock through

her slick folds and entered her slowly. With his weight held off her by his arms propped on either side of her head, he leaned down to kiss her once more. Plunging his tongue deep inside, he shifted his hips forward inch by inch until he was balls deep into her tight channel.

Thrusting slowly, he hastened his pace as her feet dug into his ass and her fingers clutched his shoulders. Soon he was mindless to anything but the feel of her body welcoming his. With a slight shift in his angle of penetration, his pelvis rubbed against her clit, and she cried out as her orgasm rushed over her. Quickly following, he roared his own release, feeling her inner muscles clench against his cock.

His roar turned into a groan as he poured himself into her, slowly pumping until he was drained. Arms giving out, he shifted to the side before crashing onto the bed, pulling her body into his. Perhaps it was because they had just talked about the Army, but he wondered how he could have hiked for miles carrying a full rucksack and lifted weights on a daily basis, and yet sex with Lizzie depleted his strength.

Barely able to breathe, much less speak, he managed to gasp, "Jesus, babe, you wear me out."

A light giggle slipped from her lips as she cupped his jaw. "I don't know how. All I did was lay here."

"That's all it takes. You naked, a bed, and sex. Best thing in the world to have."

He hated to move but hobbled to the bathroom to dispose of the condom before coming back to bed and pulling her close again. They lay silent for a while, and he found with her breasts pressed against his chest and his hand curved around her ass, his cock twitched in excitement.

Lizzie pushed against his shoulders and he fell to his back, her lips landing on his. She licked his mouth before kissing the hard curve of his jaw. Now, it was her time to kiss her way down his body. Her mouth felt amazing on his heated skin, and he lay spread out for her continued ministrations. She suckled and licked each of his nipples, causing his cock to rise again.

She slid past his hips, and he wondered what her intentions were. His heart began to pound as she continued to kiss down his thighs and then moved her lips to the tattoo near the end of his stump. The names of his friends that did not come back were inked into a pattern that appeared to be a chain. He closed his eyes as the feel of her lips skimmed over his leg, smoothing the jagged edges deep inside.

She kissed her way back up toward his hips, and it was soon evident the direction of her mouth. She straddled his legs, bending to take his erection into her mouth.

Wondering if he had died and gone to heaven, his fingers clenched her long hair, and he forced himself to loosen their tight grip, not wanting to cause her pain.

She bobbed up and down, sucked and licked, fisting the base of his cock with her hand. Just when he was sure he could not last, he reached down and grabbed her under her arms, pulling her forward. She shifted her knees to his hips and settled over his cock, resting her hands on his shoulders for leverage. With her hair falling in a pale, glowing curtain around them and her tantalizing breasts bouncing just above his face, she settled downward, sheathing his cock. Rocking back and forth, they matched each other's motions, perfectly in sync.

He lifted his hands and palmed her breasts, rubbing his thumbs around and over her taut nipples. Feeling her inner core tightened again, he lightly pinched the rosy flesh, and she threw her head back, crying out as he mirrored her actions, pouring his own orgasm deep inside her.

This time, she was the one who crashed down, eliciting an *'umph'* from his chest. Mumbling, "Sorry," she lay on top of him, both of them breathing heavily.

"I'm not, babe."

Continuing to lay wordlessly for several long minutes until their bodies began to cool and their breaths evened, she slid to the side. Suddenly jerking, eyes wide, she said, "Condom! We forgot to use a condom!"

Now it was his turn to throw open his eyes, and his arms banded tightly around her. "I'm clean, Lizzie. I get tested every year at my physical, and there's been no one for a while before you. And honest to God, I've always used condoms." He held her gaze, desperate for her to believe that he would never hurt her.

"I trust you, Scott. I wasn't even thinking about that. But please, believe me, I'm clean too. You know it's been a long time since I was with someone before you, and

I've been tested since then also." She rolled her lips inward. "But I'm not on the pill."

A flash of Lizzie standing next to the farmhouse, a child next to her and her belly rounded while carrying another shot through Scott's mind. Knowing he would love that to be a reality, he also did not want to scare her. Brushing the hair away from her face, he said, "Sweetheart, if you get pregnant, I can't think of anything better than to have a child with you. So, if that happens, we'll just move our timeline together up a little. But if it doesn't happen, we'll keep taking precautions until we're ready."

She held his gaze, her chest heaving as she breathed heavily. Her lips quivered slightly as she questioned, "Ready?"

Smiling, he kissed her lightly and said, "Ready for us to become permanent."

He watched as her eyes widened, and not wanting there to be any misunderstanding, he continued, "We've already declared our love for each other, Lizzie. When the time is right, no matter when that is, we'll take it to the next step. Engagement. Marriage. Babies. And if that happens to be slightly out of order, my love for you will be the same."

A tear slid out of the corner of her eye, landing on the pillow. Capturing her lips again, he kissed her until she smiled. Tucking her in, he felt her body give way to sleep. Exhausted, he soon followed her.

The dawn cast lines of shadows across the room as Scott turned to see the early morning sunlight slipping through the blinds. As his gaze drifted around the room, it bore little likeness to the room he had seen previously. A few pictures still hung on the walls, but the old curtains had been replaced as well as the bed linens. A new rug now graced the floor, and while Lizzie's things were not on the dresser or shelves, it was easy to imagine them settling into this room, making it their own.

He remembered the first time he saw this farmhouse when he stopped to chat with Beau by the fence near the street. He loved that it looked like a home and not just a house. And now, knowing and loving the woman inside, it felt even more like home.

Glancing down at Lizzie still sleeping in his arms, he smiled at how she claimed him even when unconscious. Her head rested on his chest, her arm snaked across his waist, and her leg was thrown over his thighs.

Thinking back to the previous evening, he was amazed at how freeing it was to talk to Lizzie about the injury where he lost his leg. Her gentle acceptance, while both showing concern but not overt curiosity, was like a balm to his soul. He had not found that with any other woman. And their lovemaking afterward had been explosive, reaching a new level of intimacy.

She stirred slightly, her breath puffing warm against his chest as she settled back into slumber.

His mind now moved from the more pleasant memories of the evening to the horror of the events of the day. His heart ached for the grief she felt over the loss of her two goats and the frustration that someone was trying to sabotage her farm and her dream.

He had no doubt that Careena Giordano was involved and wondered if she did the bidding of her father, Luca.

Scott intended to find out.

26

A week. A week where nothing untoward happened on the farm. A week where Lizzie still worked from sunup to sundown but now did so with a heart more at peace. And each night lay in bed, limbs tangled after making love with Scott.

She always cared for her animals, but now found that she showered them with even more affection. They managed to get Mark Antony sheared, and her alpaca fleece buyer had come several days ago, thrilled with the quality of the fleece and leaving Lizzie with a check for over two thousand dollars in her hand.

She thought that Emily's birthday party would be her first event, but Belle had asked if they could bring a small group of seniors from the nursing home to her farm. Lizzie was thrilled and when the seniors arrived in their van, she greeted them with glasses of iced tea and gave them a tour of her barn, let them pet the alpacas and goats through the fence, and allowed them into the pen with the baby goat kids. A number of the seniors had been raised on farms and excitedly talked about their memories. Others had never been around goats or alpacas and were equally excited for the new experience.

Belle had taken Lizzie to the side and said, "We wanted to keep the group small so that we could fit them into this van. If you're interested, we'd love to be able to bring out a different group each month. When the weather is nice, we can even do more than one trip per month. I know you said you wanted to host this one for free to get used to having people around, but Lizzie, we have a stipend for trips." She handed Lizzie a check from the nursing home and asked, "Is this amount per visit acceptable?"

Her mouth dropped open, and she shook her head forcefully back and forth. "Belle, there's no way I'm gonna take this money from you!"

Grinning, Belle just shrugged. "Believe me, the nursing home has an entire fund set up for trips. You have to accept it."

The older men and women hugged her before getting back on their van, and she waved as it pulled back down her lane.

Heading back inside, she quickly calculated that if she only hosted a couple of gatherings or parties each month plus the sales of her goat milk products and alpaca fleece sales once a year, she would be able to keep her farm. The idea that she could hand it down to her own children ran through her mind, and her feet stumbled. *Children... children with Scott.* Walking down the hall, she passed a picture of her grandparents hanging on the wall and stopped to admire the twinkle in Papa Beau's eyes. *I wonder if he had any idea what he was setting up?*

Lizzie was walking back from the barn, her arms full of containers of fresh goat milk. Looking over her shoulder, she called out to Scott, "How much longer will you be?"

He wiped the sweat from his brow before hefting another bag of seed on his shoulder. "This is the last one."

"Good. I've got barbecue chicken in the crockpot, so we can eat as soon as you're ready."

Turning back toward the house, she halted, stunned to find a well-dressed man and woman standing in her drive. The man was tall, his pants neatly pressed with a perfect crease down the front. His dark brown hair was sprinkled with silver, neatly trimmed. The woman at his side was also tall, perfectly coiffed, wearing classy pumps with a knee-length skirt and silk blouse.

Staring dumbly, she did not think they looked as though they wanted to have an event with her animals but could not imagine any other reason why they were there. Setting the milk containers on the ground, she stepped forward, a smile on her face. "Hello. Welcome to Weston Farms. May I help you?"

The woman glanced toward the man, then said, "We're looking for Scott Redding and were told he was *here?*"

The woman's voice raised at the end, making her statement more of a question as though she could not believe Scott was actually here. Lizzie wondered if they were accounting clients of his but could not imagine Lia sending them to the farm. "Yes, um... he's in the barn right now."

Before she had a chance to say anything else, Scott came out of the barn, his hands slapping against his dust-covered jeans. She turned to look at him and watched his eyes widen when they landed on the couple.

"Mom? Dad? What are you doing here?"

Lizzie watched in stunned silence as Scott jogged past her, bending to kiss his mother's cheek and shaking his dad's hand. Staring open-mouthed at the three of them, she tried to wrap her mind around the fact that she was meeting his parents without warning. She was wearing her oldest jeans, a T-shirt that had seen better days, and as she glanced down at her apparel, she was certain there was a little manure smeared on the side of her work boots. *Oh, no!! Now? They have to come now?*

Scott turned, immediately grabbing Lizzie's hand and pulling her forward. His smile wide, he introduced, "Mom, Dad, I'd like you to meet Lizzie Weston, owner of this beautiful farm. Lizzie, these are my parents, Clara and Stanley Redding."

Wishing a hole would open up allowing her to disappear, she wiped her hand on her pants, uncertain that the act had made her hand any cleaner, and stuck it out in greeting. "Mr. and Mrs. Redding. It's nice to meet you." She cast a sideways glance up toward Scott, but he seemed oblivious to her discomfort.

"Why didn't you guys call?" he asked.

Lifting a brow, his father replied, "We were on our way back home from a trip to Virginia Beach and did try to call. But for the last hour, you haven't answered your phone."

His mother finished by saying, "We finally called Lia, and she said she was sure that you would be here working."

His father's gaze moved past Lizzie's shoulder to the barn and pastures behind her. "We were going to stop by to see if you'd like to have dinner. We didn't realize what kind of *work* you'd be doing."

His parent's gazes now moved to where Scott's arm was wrapped around Lizzie's shoulders, firmly tucking her into his side. Lizzie tried to smile but could feel her mouth's tightness as it was hard to ignore the incredulous looks they were giving her.

Looking up at Scott, she said softly, "Scott, why don't you head out with your parents and have a nice dinner—"

"No way, sweetheart. You've got barbecue chicken, and I know you fixed plenty. We can all have dinner here."

Unable to discern how to kick him in the shin without his parents seeing it, her tight smile remained on her face.

"We wouldn't want to put you out," his mother began, but Scott jumped in.

"It's no trouble at all. It'll give you a chance to get to know Lizzie."

Unable to figure a way out, Lizzie tried to channel her grandparents' always-welcoming demeanor. "Scott is right. I've got plenty. I just need to go in and wash up and then supper will be ready."

"Mom, Dad, let me show you the animals while Lizzie takes a few minutes to deal with the goat milk." Looking down at her, he said, "I'll be in shortly and help get dinner on the table."

Shaking her head, she said, "Take your time. Really, take your time." Keeping the smile plastered on her face until the three of them walked toward the barn, she grabbed the milk containers and raced into the kitchen. Her mind whirling, she placed the milk in her refrigerator, checked the chicken in the crockpot, and grabbed several more buns from her breadbasket.

Glancing through the kitchen window, she could see the three of them disappear into the barn and she raced upstairs. Staring at her image in the mirror, she groaned in frustration. How could this be the way she met his parents? *Dropping in and Scott invites them to dinner when I'm not prepared!* In truth, she had not considered meeting his parents. It was one of those *out-there* events that she just had given no head space to as she and Scott evolved into a couple.

With no time to take a shower, she stripped her clothes and washed her face after scrubbing her hands. Jumping into clean jeans and a cotton blouse, she pulled her hair from its braid, running a brush through her long tresses.

Hurrying back downstairs, she completed a quick swipe over the dining table, making sure it was clean. There was a pile of mail on the end of the kitchen counter, several boxes of empty bottles and molds for making her milk products sitting in the corner, and Rufus' dog bed was against one wall. Hearing voices approach, she knew there was no time to clean further.

Insecurities rushed back as she imagined what his parents were thinking. Swallowing deeply, she stomped toward the refrigerator then halted as her gaze landed on the magnet-backed calendar in front of her. There was a circle around today's date, and she stared, not knowing how she had forgotten. Papa Beau's birthday. Closing her eyes, she smiled even as her heart ached. Papa Beau always invited a friend over for his birthday. Sometimes it was Preston. Sometimes it was a neighbor. Sometimes it was someone down on their luck. He used to say the only birthday present he wanted was to celebrate another year alive with a friend.

Her cheek felt damp and she quickly swiped at the errant tear that escaped. *Well, Papa Beau, this is not how I wanted to meet Scott's parents. But this is how I'll celebrate your birthday since I can't be with you.*

Scott's eyes met hers as soon as he and his parents walked through the back door. Hurrying over, he looked down and whispered, "Are you okay? I'm so sorry they just dropped in on us. Mom let me know that I should never have invited them to dinner without checking with you first. I just wasn't thinking, babe—"

Reaching up she pressed her fingers to his lips and smiled. "Shh," she said. "I was caught off guard and confess I wish I didn't look quite so bedraggled the first time I met your parents." Shrugging, she added, "But this is me. This is my farm. This is my life. And it was Papa Beau's birthday today, so we'll have company for dinner just like he would like."

Without giving Scott a chance to apologize further, she hurried him off to the bathroom, saying, "Go clean up, and we'll eat as soon as you're ready."

He leaned down, kissing her gently, his hand cupping her face, his thumb smoothing over her cheek. Passing his parents on the way to the bathroom, he said, "I'll be right back."

"How can I help?" Clara asked, stepping around the counter and into the kitchen.

It was on the tip of her tongue to politely refuse any assistance, but seeing the open expression on his mother's face, she said, "If you would like, you can set the table." While his mother placed the plates and silverware on the table, she spooned the slow-cooked chicken barbecue into a large bowl and placed it on the counter. Next came the warm rolls, ready to be piled high with barbecue and slaw. Fresh carrots, cooked with brown sugar and cinnamon, completed the meal.

Stanley began questioning her about the farm as soon as they began to eat, and she wondered if she would have to choke her meal down. But it soon became obvious that he was curious about the workings of the farm, not denigrating farm life.

His mother was interested in the alpacas, admitting she had never seen one before. The conversation flowed, and she began telling amusing stories of her grandparents and the farm. By the time they were devouring slices of peach pie, Scott had slid his chair next to hers, his arm draping around her shoulders, his fingertips teasing over the skin at her upper arm.

As they stood from dinner, Stanley looked at Scott. "Take a walk outside with me?"

Lizzie watched as the two men stepped into the backyard, and her heart began to pound, not knowing what his father might be saying. A hand on her shoulder caused her to jump, and she jerked her head around, seeing Clara standing right beside her.

"I'd like to thank you for dinner, Lizzie," Clara said. "It was terribly rude of us to just drop by and so sweet of you to offer to feed us."

She smiled, this time her mouth relaxed as she stared at his mother. "You're welcome here anytime."

Clara opened her mouth as though to respond, then simply smiled in return. "Thank you. That would be lovely."

They continued to work side-by-side, but Lizzie's mind was firmly on the two men outside, wondering what they were discussing.

Scott looked over at his father as they walked through the yard. The evening sun had passed beyond the tree line, causing the shadows to deepen around them. They stopped and stood, side-by-side, staring out over the pastures. A light breeze blew, the fresh smell of farmland all around.

"She's not at all like the woman I figured you would end up with."

His father's words startled him, but he could not say that they surprised him. Sighing, he had hoped they would see Lizzie for what she was… a warm, beautiful, hard-working woman. "Look, Dad—"

"Oh, don't get me wrong. I think she's wonderful. Just not what I expected."

Scott knew that his father had something on his mind, so he remained quiet but determined to stand his ground about Lizzie.

His father sucked in a deep breath, then let it out slowly. "I couldn't believe it when you told me you had joined the Army."

Blinking, Scott was shocked at his father's opening. Uncertain where this was going, he turned his head to see a painful wince cross his father's face.

"I thought it was just a rebellion. I figured you'd put in a tour, come home, and settle down." Shaking his head, Stanley said, "I never in a million years thought you'd be injured like you were. Foolish, I know, to not realize that was a possibility. No parent wants to see their child injured like that. No one should have to go through that."

Not knowing what to say, he reached out and placed his hand on his father's shoulder. "Dad, I appreciate what you're saying, but I'm okay. That's not to say that there aren't days I hate that I lost part of my leg. But I'm alive, and I got to come home. Had some friends that didn't get that, so I figure I'm lucky."

Stanley's head nodded up and down slowly as he

swallowed deeply and looked over Scott's shoulder toward the farmhouse. "Is it serious?"

"I knew her grandfather long before I ever met her, and looking back, I think I started falling in love with Lizzie just from listening to the way he talked about her."

"I would have never believed it if I hadn't seen it with my own eyes, but you, here with her and at this farm, look happy."

His lips curved into a wide smile. "Dad, I've never been this happy in my life."

Stanley held his gaze for a long, silent moment, then his lips curved as well. "The only thing a parent ever wants is for their child to be happy and healthy. Seeing you here with Lizzie was a surprise, but you've now given me everything I could want. I'm happy for you, son."

Pulling his father in for a heartfelt, backslapping hug, Scott breathed easier. Leaning back, he said, "Let's get inside, Dad. I'm sure Lizzie's a nervous wreck wondering what we're talking about out here."

Walking back inside, Scott knew that he was right by the tense lines around Lizzie's smile. Immediately stepping over to her, he enveloped her in his embrace, kissing the top of her head. Mumbling against her hair, he whispered, "It's all good, babe." He felt the air rush from her lungs as her arms tightened around his waist.

Soon, they were all standing outside saying goodbye, more heartfelt hugs being given, this time including Lizzie. Scott held her against his side as they waved his parents away. Looking down, he asked, "Are you okay?"

She was quiet for a moment, then replied, "Yeah. I am. I confess that I was absolutely freaked when they first showed up and you invited them to dinner. All I could think about was how they might look down on me being a simple farm girl and not good enough for you."

"They loved you, sweetheart," he assured, "and love me being with you."

"I wish they could have met Papa Beau. He always liked having company on his birthday."

"Well, now that I know that, we'll make sure to always have company on this day." He hoped he had made the right suggestion, but when she turned her beautiful smile up toward him, he knew it was perfect.

Locking up downstairs, they headed up to the bedroom, where she showed him just how perfect his suggestion had been.

27

Scott scrubbed his hand over his face, thrilled with the phone call he just received from Lizzie, and yet frustrated with the pile of work on his desk. She had hosted another group of seniors with Belle, excited over the money the farm would make, but he did not trust that the threat was over.

They had made it through a week with nothing else untoward happening, but he feared it was possibly the calm before the storm. A knock on his door had him looking up, seeing Mrs. Markham escorting Gareth into his office. Thanking her, he watched as Gareth sat down in the seat across from his desk, and his stomach clenched, wondering what his friend had to say.

"I know I'm grabbing at straws," Gareth began, "but I came across something that was interesting." Opening the envelope in his hand, he pulled out a picture and handed it to Scott. "I found this in a local newspaper a few months ago. It was an Eastern Shore business meeting, and look who's standing together, front and center."

Scott looked at the newspaper clipping and spied Careena Giardano and Paul Dugan standing next to each other, wide smiles on their faces. Looking back up at Gareth, he tilted his head slightly to the side as he said, "Okay... I see that they know each other, but this is nothing more than a group of businesspeople at a luncheon having their picture taken."

Nodding, Gareth said, "I agree. Now, look at the next picture that was taken at the same luncheon."

Scott looked at the next picture, which showed several other people standing close together smiling at the camera. He recognized a few but still did not see any connection. Scrunching his brow, he shook his head. "I'm sorry, Gareth, maybe I'm just tired or being thick, but I'm not seeing anything."

Chuckling, Gareth leaned over and tapped the picture with his forefinger. "Took me a while to see it, too. Look at the bottom left corner."

In the background of the picture, easily ignored by anyone not looking, was a picture of a couple sitting at a table, their heads bent close in conversation. Careena and Paul.

Shaking his head slightly, he said, "I don't get it. Granted, it's too much of a coincidence that the two people that are after Lizzie's farm look like they're in cahoots. But I don't see how they can be working together. Careena wants the farm to prove to her father that she can bring the deal to closure and should have more say in the running of the business. Paul wants the farm so that he can pop up cheap houses."

Nodding, Gareth said, "I agree, Scott. It doesn't make sense. But I've been looking into the Giordanos and Paul Dugan individually, and this is the first time I've found a connection between the two."

Possibilities began to slam into Scott, but for each consideration, he could not see why Careena and Paul would be able to work against Lizzie in a way that would be advantageous for both of them. "This is why you're in the private investigation business and I'm an accountant," he said. "I want everything to add up, and this is just as confusing as ever."

"I'm still checking, but I have to tell you, Scott, I'm not coming up with anything suspicious on Luca, and so far, while I don't care for Paul's construction short-cuts, he's stayed on the right side of the law. Whoever's been threatening Lizzie's farm is getting desperate. That's why they've escalated their actions."

Shoving back into his chair, Scott threw his hands up to his side and grumbled, "That's why this whole mess is killing me. I don't want someone to escalate to the extent of harming her."

"Maybe with the security lights and cameras up we scared someone off."

"I hope so, but I'm not going to take that chance. I think it's time I paid a visit to Paul Dugan."

Eyebrows lifted, Gareth said, "You need to be careful, Scott. You can't start threatening someone without proof."

"I'm not going to threaten him. But I'd like him to know that I'm there now and plan on staying. So, if someone is messing with Lizzie, they're messing with me."

A grin slipped across Gareth's face. "I know the situation is fucked up, man, but I'm happy for you. She's a great girl."

The two men stood and shook hands, and Scott walked Gareth out. Glancing at the clock on the wall behind Mrs. Markham, he thought about cutting out early when Lia rushed from the back.

"Oh, Scott, I'm glad you're here. I just got a call from the school, and Emily's got a little fever so I have to pick her up. I was supposed to meet our new clients at the Sunset Restaurant for a late lunch. It's the Whitley family. They're new to town and live in one of those million-dollar homes at The Dunes Resort. I've called them to let them know that you will be meeting them instead." She stopped at the door and turned quickly, her nose slightly scrunched. "I hope that's okay. You didn't have any other plans, did you?"

Shaking his head, he smiled. "No, it's fine. Go on and get Emily. I'll take care of the Whitleys. I know it's just an initial meeting anyway, but I can find out who their former accountant was." He waved as she rushed out the door and sighed slightly. Turning toward Mrs. Markham, he offered her a rueful smile. "Guess I better get to lunch."

Walking into the Sunset Restaurant, Scott caught a

glimpse of Careena standing next to her Mercedes, talking to a man. From the back, the man looked like Paul, and it appeared the two were arguing. Wishing he could get closer, he scooted around a tall clump of ornamental grass.

"If you'll just be patient, we can make this happen," he heard Careena say. Unable to discern the man's answer, he heard car doors slam shut. Stepping from behind the bush, he observed the two of them now in her vehicle. Careena wasted no time in speeding out of the parking lot. Desperate to follow them, he watched them leave, knowing there was nothing he could do right now.

Two hours later, Scott was grateful the lunch with the Whitleys had come to an end. They were a pleasant couple, having retired from Chicago, delighted with their large home on the Eastern Shore. They had filled the conversation with pictures of their grandchildren, pets, and vacations. He found there was very little that the couple talked about that their accounting firm needed to know but knew that sometimes business lunches were the best way to get to know clients informally.

Shaking their hands goodbye, he waved as they walked away before he hustled to his car. *Time to pay Paul Dugan a little visit.*

PD Development was in a small, nondescript brick

building just off of Highway 13 in North Heron County. Parking in the front, Scott spied the large black pickup truck with the company's logo on the side. Glad that it appeared Paul was in, he parked in the front of the building and walked in.

Not certain what he expected, he was a little surprised to see a neat reception area, not unlike Mrs. Markham's. A young woman sat behind a desk, and as soon as her eyes lit upon him, her smile widened broadly as her gaze moved from his head to his toes and back again.

"Hi! Welcome to PD Development, where houses are built to fit your needs and dreams come true!"

He blinked at her enthusiastic greeting, and the consideration that he might have to punch Paul to make his point to leave Lizzie alone dimmed with the young receptionist's presence.

"I'm here to see Paul Dugan."

Her smile remained although a crinkle formed between her eyebrows as she continued to look up at him. "Did you have an appointment?"

Shaking his head, he replied, "No. But I think he'll want to see me. Tell him that Scott Redding is here to talk to him about the Weston Farm."

She offered a little shrug as she stood and moved toward the back, her mannerisms indicating that she did not recognize the significance of the Weston farm. A moment later, she popped her head out of an office in the back and said, "Mr. Redding, you can come on in."

As he passed her in the hall, she looked up and whispered, "I get off at four, if you want to get drinks some-time." She winked and headed back to her desk, leaving him to shake his head slightly in surprise. Quickly forgetting her, he headed into Paul's office, shutting the door behind him.

He recognized Paul from the pictures he had seen. Medium height, brown hair that was shot with gray. Not a large man, he definitely had some weight around his middle. What struck Scott the most was his eyes. His ruddy cheeks made his eyes appear small, but they darted around as though taking in everything quickly. Dressed in jeans with a denim shirt with his company's logo embroidered over the pocket, he looked exactly as Scott expected, and yet, not at all like the type of man Careena Giordano would have for a partner... unless he was simply a means to an end.

He shook Paul's hand and took the seat that was offered. Having no desire to mince words, he began, "Mr. Dugan, I'm a personal friend of Elizabeth Weston and considered it an honor to be a friend to her grand-father as well—"

"A better man I've never met in my life," Paul inter-jected, his head nodding up and down rapidly.

Tilting his head, he held Paul's stare until the other man shifted slightly in his seat. "If that's true, then I find it strange that you would attempt to coerce Ms. Weston into selling her farm when surely, you know that it's the last thing her grandfather would've wanted."

Paul pinched his lips together which only served to puff his cheeks out further, giving him a somewhat comical expression. "Now, now, coerce is not the right word," he protested. "That girl has got more than she can handle out there, and I don't mind taking that property off her hands."

Brows lifted, he countered, "Well, how neighborly of you. Seems like several people are wanting to help Ms. Weston. But from what she tells me, you lied to her face about what Beau wanted her to do."

Throwing his hands up, Paul defended himself. "Now, that's just business, Mr. Redding. Good business. A businessman who wants to make it in this day and time should know who they're dealing with and use that to their advantage. I figured if she thought her granddaddy and I had come to an understanding, it would help her make the right decision. That's all I was doing."

"I don't care for your business tactics, nor do I care for your threats against Ms. Weston."

Paul reared back in his seat, his small eyes wide and said, "Threats? I never once made a threat against Ms. Weston. You might not like my business tactics, but I assure you I've never resorted to threats!"

Leaning forward, his voice barely above a growl, Scott bit out, "I know what you and Careena Giordano are doing. I don't understand why, but I'm here to tell you right now—it's going to stop."

Paul blinked, his mouth opening and closing several times before snapping shut as his head quickly shook back and forth. "Careena Giordano?" His eyes narrowed as he huffed, "Mr. Redding, you've got hold of the wrong end of the stick. I can't tell you what Careena is up to, but I can assure you I'm not in cahoots with her on anything. If there's something going on with Ms. Weston, it doesn't have anything to do with me."

"So, you know nothing about the incidences that have been happening at Weston Farms? Fence lines cut? Animals poisoned—"

"Animals poisoned!" Paul all but roared. Shaking his head so quickly his jowls shook, he reiterated, "I'm telling you right now, that's got nothing to do with me!"

Leaning back in his seat, he considered the other man carefully. "Tell me about your relationship with Careena." He knew it was a push since, obviously, Paul was under no obligation to answer any questions Scott might put to him, but since the man appeared genuinely rattled, he wanted to press his advantage.

"Relationship? Hell, I barely know the woman. We don't exactly hang out in the same social circle, if you get my meaning. About the only time I've ever seen her is at the Eastern Shore Business meetings." He glanced down at his fists resting on the desk and grumbled, "She's a tough bitch, I'll give you that." Lifting his head, he pinned Scott with his glare. "If there's something going on with Weston Farm, I'd bet my business she's got something to do with it."

"There was a picture in the newspaper recently of you and her together at a recent meeting. The two of you were sitting rather closely, appearing to have an intimate conversation."

Paul's brow furrowed for a moment as he appeared to search his memory banks before his eyes opened wide. "I remember that. She had some cockamamie plan about me building a bunch of small, one-bedroom houses that Giardano Farms could rent out to migrant workers. Hell, I can build cheap, but she wanted them for practically nothing. Honest to God, that was the last conversation I've had with her."

"What about lunch today at the Sunset Restaurant?"

"What the hell are you talking about Mr. Redding? I was at The Diner for lunch today. You can ask anybody who was there."

Even though it was late afternoon, the sun was still beaming down on Lizzie as she finished her afternoon milking. Jack had been over earlier and cleaned out the stalls and fed the animals. Carrie had just picked him up, and Lizzie grinned at the memory of Jack showing his appreciation when she'd handed him his first paycheck. It was not much, but she was so pleased with the extra help, she was glad he was excited.

It was too early to put most of the animals in their pens near the barn, but with a couple of pregnant goats, she decided to move them inside. Once they were secure, she walked to the house with the goat milk. She wanted to get it into the refrigerator to keep it fresh, deciding she would make lotion the next day.

She had not received a text from Scott, which was unusual. Recently, he had been checking with her often throughout the day. Sometimes the messages were detailed notes of his activities or asking about hers, and sometimes they were simple heart emojis. Both brought smiles every time she looked at one.

Glancing at the clock, she moved to the refrigerator and peered inside, deciding on what to fix for supper. The pork chops she had taken from the freezer yesterday looked enticing. Looking down at Rufus, she asked, "What do you think? Would you and Scott like pork chops tonight?" Rufus' dark, soulful eyes looked up at her, and she laughed. "I get the feeling that you would like anything for dinner." Rubbing his head, she went back to her preparations.

Once the chops were unwrapped, she placed them in a bowl to marinate and set them back into the refrigerator. Mashed potatoes and a salad would complete the meal, so she grabbed those ingredients and began chopping.

Rufus suddenly came to his feet, barking at the back door. Leaning around the counter so that she could see if someone was standing there, she saw nothing. Looking down, she asked, "Hey, Rufus. What is it?"

He continued barking so she stepped to the kitchen sink to wash her hands before going outside to see if there was a fox near the henhouse or another dog in the yard. Staring through the window in front of her, her heart jumped as she spied a man slipping into her barn, a red gasoline can in his hand.

Grabbing her phone, she dialed 9-1-1. "There's a man going into my barn with a gas can," she cried out as the dispatcher answered. "I'm Lizzie Weston at the Weston Farm on Route 231, south of Easton. He's wearing blue jeans and a blue shirt. Darkish gray hair. That's all I can see, but it looks like Paul Dugan. Please, let Sheriff Hudson or Detective Sims know. They're aware of what's going on!"

She knew she should stay on the line but disconnected, trying to get to her work boots near the door while battling Rufus who was still barking and jumping around. Heedless of the possible danger, her mind was filled with getting to the barn to save her goats.

28

Standing, Scott speared Paul with a pointed glare and said, "As of right now, Elizabeth Weston and Weston Farms do not exist for you. You do not contact her in any way. And if I find out you're lying about not threatening her, you won't have to worry about the law coming after you. You'll have to worry about me."

Not waiting to hear Paul's sputtering defense, he stormed out of the office, heading to his car. He felt his phone vibrate in his pocket and pulled it out, surprised to see Colt's name on his screen. Connecting, he barely had a chance to say hello before Colt began speaking.

"Lizzie called in a 9-1-1. Reported there's a man going into her barn with a gasoline can. She said she thought it was Paul Dugan. I've got units heading there now, and Hunter and I are on our way. Where are you?"

Heart pounding, he started his SUV and screeched out of Paul's parking lot. "It can't be Paul. I was just talking to him. Leaving now and heading to Lizzie's. I'm about ten minutes away."

His mind raced as fast as the wheels of his SUV. He had been sure that Paul was the one working with Careena but now was not certain of anything. *Maybe Careena isn't involved.* Whoever was in the barn could have been hired by anyone. *Jesus, they had a gas can.* Glancing at the clock on the dashboard, he hoped Lizzie had not put any of the animals in the barn yet. If someone destroyed her barn, it could be rebuilt. If someone destroyed more of her animals, he was afraid it would destroy her. If someone harmed her...

His tires squealed as he turned a corner too sharply, now just a few minutes away from the farm. *Please, Lizzie, stay in the house with Rufus!*

Not wanting Rufus to dart away, Lizzie snapped the leash to his collar. "Rufus, quiet," she commanded. He stopped barking but quivered as she opened the back door, jumping forward, pulling at the leash.

Hurrying toward the barn, she eschewed the gravel path and stayed on the grass, keeping her footsteps silent. Slipping around to the side, she held onto Rufus' leash as she tiptoed around the front and peeked into the barn. It took a few seconds for her eyes to adjust to the darker interior, but a noise from the back captured her attention.

The man was facing away from her, but she was sure it was Paul. Same build. Same clothes. Same hair color. The gas can was set to the side, and he had a rake in his hand, dragging it through some loose straw, piling it into a small mound.

The two pregnant goats were bleating, and she reacted, no plan in mind other than to halt his progress. Stepping into the doorway, her hands still holding onto Rufus' leash, she shouted, "What the hell are you doing in my barn?"

The man whirled around, and Lizzie stared in wide-eyed, mouth-opened shock. "Dad?"

Robbie Weston's face scrunched into a grimace, a cigarette dangling from his lips as he said, "Shit, Lizzie."

It took a second for his presence to sink in, then she jerked as understanding hit her. "You're the one who's been doing all these things? Oh, my God, you're the one who poisoned my goats? You're trying to destroy my farm?"

He turned to face her fully, and the scent of alcohol drifted toward her. He scrubbed his hand over his face before throwing his arm out to the side. "Yours? This should be mine. All of this. All of this should be mine."

Her gaze jerked around, trying to follow the wild motions of his arms as she tried to follow the path of his words. Understanding slowly dawned on her, filling her with cold reality. "The farm. You thought Papa Beau was going to leave the farm to you?"

"I was next in line. I was his son."

"You didn't even come to his funeral! You haven't been around for years! What on earth made you think he was going to leave it to you?" Her words came out in a rush, her stomach clenching and her heart pounding at the audacity of the man standing in front of her. "You nearly broke his heart. You not only left him, Grandma, and this farm... you walked away from your wife." Slapping her hand against her chest, she added, "You walked away from your daughter! What made you think he was going to leave anything to you?"

He grimaced again, his voice now wheedling. "Oh, hell, Lizzie. You know Dad was a farmer right down to his bones. I never was. I never understood working so hard for so little."

As the reality of the man standing in front of her continued to sink in, it dawned on Lizzie that he was only talking about the farm. He was not denying having abandoned her or her mom. Swallowing past the lump of rejection that once more settled in her throat, her eyes stayed pinned on him. "If you never wanted the farm, then why are you here now? What are you after?"

He startled, his body jerking as though her question shocked him. "Girl, you're sitting on money. Not this damn barn or these fuckin' animals. Hell, not even that house." He waved toward the ground with his forefinger, shouting, "This! This land is worth something. It should have come to me."

"So you could just sell it?" Her rage rose in full force until it crackled in the air all about her.

"Yes, I would've sold it. Finally, I would've had the money that was my birthright all along."

"Jesus, Dad, don't you see? The money is not your birthright. It was the land. If you had appreciated it, worked it, helped Papa Beau, helped Grandma, the land would be yours right now. But only because you understood what it means to have a piece of earth that's been handed down through the years, gifted to you but only to take care of. Not squander it."

Robbie leaned back, his breath leaving in a long, heavy sigh. "My God, you sound just like Dad. So self-righteous. So unable to realize that not everyone wants to kill themselves digging in the dirt."

A tear rolled down Lizzie's cheek and she dashed it away quickly. She started to speak, then cleared her throat and barely whispered, "That's the nicest thing you ever said to me. That I'm just like Papa Beau."

The two of them stood inside the barn built by his grandfather, and a building she knew he had played in as a boy just as she had as a young girl. All the history of their family was spread out all around them, and yet, he was a stranger, not understanding his surroundings.

Rufus nudged her leg and whined, bringing her focus back. Glancing down at the gasoline can setting at her father's feet, she asked, "What now? What are you going to do now, dad?"

His jaw tightened as his lips pursed. "Sign this place over to me, Lizzie. And when I get paid, I'll give you a share."

"Who's your buyer? Paul Dugan? Or is it Luca Giordano? Who's got you doing the dirty work?"

His brows lowered in confusion, and he said, "I don't know anyone named Paul. And Luca may be a big man on the Eastern Shore, but he's like Dad... thinks like him, only bigger. He fuckin' gave up too easy on this place. Now, that daughter of his, she's got a taste for moving up. She wants her place in her own father's kingdom and doesn't mind paying well to get there."

Her breath left her lungs in a rush as she processed his latest claim. "It doesn't matter who's paying you. I'm not signing anything over to you, Dad. You walked away from us. You walked away from Weston Farms. There is not one speck of dirt underneath our feet that belongs to you."

He took a step forward, and Rufus growled, now standing and moving in front of Lizzie.

Sneering, Robbie said, "Just like you to have a three-legged dog for protection." He bent down and snagged the gasoline can from the ground. "Lizzie, you know I don't want to hurt you, but I'm going to do whatever I have to do to make you sign this farm over to me. You don't agree, I'll start with the barn."

She watched in horror as he tilted the can, pouring some of the gasoline onto the straw. "No!" she screamed, dropping Rufus' leash as she dashed forward.

Rufus darted in front of her, his teeth sinking into Robbie's leg. Screaming, Robbie dropped the gasoline can, slinging his arms out to knock the dog away but coming in contact with Lizzie's jaw. Her head snapped back and she crumpled to the ground. The cigarette fell out of his mouth, immediately igniting the gasoline.

Pain exploded throughout her head. Barely able to push herself up, she turned around to see Rufus still battling with her dad as flames began licking through the straw. The bleating of goats hit her ears and she forced her body to her knees, gasping for breath. Coming to a stand, she staggered past the fire toward the gate to let the pregnant goats free.

"No, Lizzie," her dad yelled as he reached to grab her arm, trying to pull her back away from the fire.

The sound of sirens filled the air, and she jerked away from her father's grasp. "We've got to get them out!"

Not knowing if he was working with her or against her, suddenly, her father pushed her to the side and grabbed the gate, jerking it open. Rufus, as though knowing what needed to be done, ran inside the pen and nipped at the goat's heels until they ran past the flaming straw, through the barn to safety.

Head dizzy, she dropped to her knees, unable to stand. Her father cried out her name again as he started to lift her but staggered back as another man forced his way forward through the flames, scooping Lizzie into his arms.

Thick, black smoke billowed all around, but when Lizzie opened her eyes against the pain in her head, Scott's ravaged face was in her sight. Unable to see what else was going on around her, she could hear the shouts of others.

"Did the goats get out? Rufus? The barn—"

"Shhh, babe," he shushed, rushing her out of the barn.

She began to struggle, and he carefully set her down, keeping his arms around her as they turned and watched what was happening. Rufus was right at their feet, leash trailing behind him and his tongue lolling out of his mouth. Head still pounding, she cried, "We've got to make sure the animals are safe."

Grabbing Scott's hand, she staggered toward the two

goats, thankful that they let her grab them by the neck. With Scott's help, they made it to the field where the other goats were, a safe distance from the burning barn. Pushing them through the gate, she turned and looked toward the alpacas, seeing them safely tucked away in their pasture as well.

"The pigs," she shouted over the cacophony.

"Fuck," Scott cursed before rushing toward the back of the barn where the pigs were kept in their pen. She raced after him, grateful to find two of the deputies were ready to assist. It was not easy, but they managed to get the pigs into the same field where the goats were, knowing they would be safe there.

Several more sirens were heard in the distance, and soon fire trucks pulled past her house, straight to the barn. She stood to the side and watched as the fire-fighters managed to keep the fire from spreading but were unable to save the barn.

She stared numbly at the scene playing out before her, feeling Scott's presence at her back as he stood closely, wrapping his arms around her. He pulled her tight, and he shook as she heard him mumble. "Jesus, baby, thank God you're safe."

Reaching up, she grabbed onto his forearms wrapped around her chest, wanting to hang on to his solid strength. "I'm okay, Scott. I'm okay. The animals are okay. We're going to be fine." Rufus barked nearby and she dropped to her knees, hugging him. "Oh, Rufus, you're a hero!"

Scott leaned down, ruffling his dog's fur. "Looks like you're the man of the hour, Rufus."

Colt and Hunter walked by, flanking a man in hand-cuffs. He looked up, his face dejected as he said, "I'm sorry, Lizzie. I didn't mean to hurt you."

Scott's jerked as he growled, "Who the fuck is he?"

Moving slightly so she could turn to look up into his face, she inhaled a shaky gulp of air before blowing it out and said, "That's my father. Robinson Weston."

29

For the next several hours, Scott's phone rang continuously, all of their friends wanting to know how they could help. He appreciated their concern but finally asked Lia to start a phone tree because he wanted to focus on Lizzie.

Scott would not leave Lizzie's side, unnerved by her calm. He wanted her to go to the ER, but Zac had checked her out and other than a bruised, swollen jaw, she insisted she was unharmed. Her focus was on walking around the pastures, assuring that all of her animals were safe, and then peace settled over her, even when she made the announcement about her father.

Shaking his head, he still could not get over the shocking news and wanted to keep a close eye on her, not believing that it did not affect her more than she was letting on.

The firefighters stayed for a while, making sure there were no live embers left to flame again. The back and side wall of the barn closest to the pastures remained standing, but the rest of the structure was destroyed.

Her father had been placed in the back of a Sheriff's vehicle and carted off to the county jail at Easton. Hunter had followed, planning on being a part of the interrogation. Colt escorted Scott and Lizzie into her kitchen, where they found Carrie with a pot of coffee ready for them.

Carrie immediately enveloped Lizzie into a hug, then served everyone coffee in travel mugs. "I know you're going to have to go to the Sheriff's Department to give your statement," Carrie began, "but I've had the coffee at the station, and this will be much better."

Scott smiled his appreciation as Lizzie accepted the preferred mug, offering another heartfelt hug to her friend. Once at the Sheriff's Department, Lizzie asked Colt if Scott could remain with her, and he agreed. The two of them were ushered into a small room reminiscent of so many police stations they had seen on TV shows. Colt explained the procedure and then he allowed his detectives to conduct the interview.

Scott sat quietly by Lizzie's side, holding her hand as she relayed the events of the day carefully, almost unemotionally. She answered each question presented to her, and Scott's anger ratcheted up at the relaying of the events inside the barn. Even when she said that her father tried to pull her out of the burning barn, Scott found no sympathy for the man who should have done everything to protect her to begin with.

After giving her statement and answering all questions,

Hunter and Colt came into the room and sat down. Staring at his friends acting in their official capacity, Scott gave Lizzie's hand a squeeze, wondering what was coming next.

"Your father—"

"Please, call him Robbie or Mr. Weston," Lizzie interrupted. Giving the first flash of emotion she had shown in the last couple of hours, she winced as though in pain, then amended, "Actually, don't call him Mr. Weston. Please, just refer to him as Robbie."

Colt and Hunter's gazes shifted quickly to Scott before moving back to Lizzie, both men nodding.

Hunter began again. "Robbie has confessed to cutting your fence line in hopes that some of your animals would get out. He has also confessed to bringing the azalea plants into your pasture, knowing that it would be poisonous, and cutting the outside pen enclosure, planning that the goats would get to it. And, of course, he has confessed to everything that happened today. His intention was to wreak havoc for you so that you'd be more willing to sell. And he has admitted that he had been working with Careena Giardano in hopes that when you agreed to sell, it would be to Giardano Farms."

Scott kept his gaze on Lizzie, trying to gauge her reaction. She winced again slightly, then shook her head.

"I don't know Careena. I only met Luca Giardano when he came by after Papa Beau's funeral to say that he would be interested in buying my land."

Hunter continued, "Of course, we're still investigating, but according to your... um... Robbie, he never met Luca Giardano."

She sucked in her lips but said nothing, simply nodding her head slightly, her hand still tucked into Scott's.

As they were escorted out of the room, Scott asked, "What happens now, Colt?"

"Hunter will be going with a few deputies to the Giardano Farms to bring in Careena for questioning. Robbie reported that she used phone calls, text messages, and emails as well as a few meetings in person. We're in the process of verifying that, but from what we can tell, she'll have little defense."

The two men looked at Lizzie standing at the end of the hall with Carrie, who had followed them to the station. Colt said, "She's strong, but she's not showing a lot of emotion right now."

Nodding, Scott agreed. "I know, and that's got me worried. You got any advice for victims?"

Pulling a card from his pocket, he handed it over. "Here's the number for Victims Assistance. If she prefers to talk to someone she knows, Zac's wife, Maddie, is a counselor. As for you, stay close. Let her know that you're there when she needs to get it all out. Right now, I'd say she's focused on her animals and the farm. But it'll hit her who was responsible, and when it does... well, just be there." Colt clapped him on the shoulder and said, "Scott, you know what it's like to lose something and yet know you were lucky to be alive. I have a feeling that's what will hit her, too."

Shaking his hand, Scott hurried down the hall,

wrapping his arm around Lizzie while thanking Carrie. As they walked to his vehicle, she was quiet, and he kept glancing to the side, wondering what she was thinking. Afraid to ignore, and yet, afraid to ask, they drove home in mostly silence.

Not waiting on him to assist, she climbed down from the passenger seat and immediately headed toward the back. Her feet stumbled ever-so-slightly as she passed the blackened shell of her former barn, hurrying past until she stopped at the pasture gates, the animals crowding near her.

Coming up behind her, Scott placed his hands on her shoulders and said, "The metal bin that held the feed appears unharmed. Let's get them fed, and they can stay out here tonight."

She nodded, and together they walked back to the scorched area around the bin holding the food. Working side-by-side, they fed all the animals before heading back to the house. Once inside, she moved to the refrigerator and opened the door, staring inside.

Scott watched her stand, motionless, one hand on the open refrigerator door, her gaze blank. Suddenly, she began to shake violently, and he rushed to her, catching her before she fell to the floor. Her mouth was open as tears ran down her face, but no sound came forth until finally a great sob was forced from her lungs.

"M... m... my own fa... father..."

It was an awkward descent to the floor, but he managed to get her into his lap, his arms wrapped around her tightly, feeling her shudder. Rubbing her back, he murmured words of comfort, hating every painful hitch of her breath. Finally, her crying slowed, and she heaved a deep breath.

"Let it out, baby," he encouraged.

It took another moment of silence before she spoke. "He was so full of anger that Papa Beau didn't include him in the will."

It was on the tip of Scott's tongue to interrupt, ranting about the ridiculousness of Robbie's *poor me* attitude, but he clamped his jaw tight, knowing that Lizzie needed to speak freely without interruption.

"Papa Beau would have been so horrified at what Robbie tried to do. When I stared at him out in the barn, it was as though I was talking to a complete stranger. I guess he really was."

"Lizzie, baby, you're right. He was a stranger. In the end, he didn't want you to be physically hurt, but he was so blinded by his own desires. I remember Beau talking about him once with me."

At that, she immediately twisted in his arms, holding his gaze, her face filled with curiosity.

"He told me that the farm had always been in your blood but never in Robbie's. He actually said that Robbie was very lazy, often getting in trouble as a teenager and young man."

Letting out a deep sigh, she admitted, "I heard he and Papa Beau arguing the night he left. To be honest, it was after a fight he had with Mom where he accused her of ignoring his needs to work on the farm or take care of me and she argued back that one of them had to work, which just made him angrier. Then he told Papa Beau that he wanted his share of the land and was told that the farm would not be given to someone who did not care about it. He stormed out that night after packing a bag, and I never saw or heard from him again until today. I don't even know where he's been all these years." Blowing out a breath, she shook her head. "I guess he was just lying in wait for Papa Beau to die."

Scott's arms pulled her tighter as she dragged in another shuddering breath before letting it out slowly. She leaned her weight against him for another moment before shifting to stand. He followed, watching as she snagged a tissue, wiping her face and blowing her nose.

"Honey, Colt gave me the number for Victims Assistance and mentioned that Maddie was a counselor. I want to make sure that you're going to be fine, and I want you to call someone if you need them."

Watching her carefully, he could see thoughts moving behind her eyes, but remained silent to give her a chance to process his request.

After throwing away her tissues, she stepped into his embrace, and they stood in the middle of the kitchen, arms banded around each other with her cheek resting against his chest.

"Right now, I'm not going to waste any more time thinking about what he did to me. But I promise that I'll talk to Maddie if I need to. But, for the immediate future, Scott, I want to focus on the farm. Taking care of the animals, figuring out a way to get the barn rebuilt." She jolted, then quickly added, "Oh, my goodness. I need to call the insurance company."

Pressing her cheek against his chest again, he said, "We'll do that first thing in the morning. They'll send out someone who will look at everything, check the police report, and then they'll have a settlement for you to get someone to rebuild the barn."

"I guess it's a good thing the weather is nice so the animals will be comfortable," she sighed. "I hope it won't take long to get a new barn up."

Thinking about the number of phone calls that had come in that day, Scott did not think it would take long at all but did not want to get her hopes up. Instead, he simply held her close, kissing the top of her head, offering his strength to her.

Lizzie had found sleep easier than she thought she would. The long cry had exhausted her, and Scott fixing comfort breakfast food for dinner had almost made her comatose. But now, in the middle of the night with Scott sleeping with his arm draped across her, she had woken and could not settle her mind.

She had allowed Scott to chat with their friends, not feeling in the mood to rehash the events with everyone. Grateful that she had friends who cared, the ache from her father's actions still penetrated deeply. Mostly, she was glad that Papa Beau had not lived to see how low his son had sunk.

The one person she had talked to was her mom, hating to call her but knowing it was the right thing to do. Jane had been horrified at Robbie's actions, bursting into tears at the thought that Lizzie could have died. She finally convinced her mother to put Richard on the phone where she assured him that she was all right and being taken care of. Accepting their promise that they would be back in the United States by Christmas, she gave them both her love.

Now, the full moon was casting faint light across the bedroom as she carefully slipped from under Scott's arm and slid from the bed. Moving first to the bathroom, she took care of her business before going downstairs, avoiding the few steps that creaked.

Not hungry, she still headed to the kitchen, recognizing that it had always seemed to be the heart of the house. Memories of family meals over the years, her grandmother baking, her mother cooking, and Papa Beau dressed in his overalls, a big smile on his face as he called out his greetings.

As she glanced around the familiar room, she realized she had very few memories of her father... in this room, in this house, or on the farm. While she did remember a few of the arguments, her grandparents and mom had shielded her from most of that.

Turning as she stood at the sink, she glanced at the view through the window, the moonlight casting the farm in a lovely glow. She sighed, knowing that it would be a pain to rebuild the barn but not an impossibility. The animals were safe, and she planned on calling Sam the next day to check on her pregnant goats.

Moving to the kitchen door, she stepped down into the yard, the patio stones cool under her bare feet. As she continued walking, the grass cushioned her footsteps and she stopped halfway through the yard. Turning in a circle, she spread her arms wide, knowing that her family's farm encompassed all the land that she could see.

Her gaze stuttered to a halt when she spied Scott standing just outside the kitchen door, watching her. Taking in all the glorious beauty that was him, she appreciated the wide shoulders, muscular abs, lean hips, long legs. As he stalked toward her, it dawned on her that even with his prosthesis showing underneath his drawstring shorts, she never thought about it. It was part of him. Just one of his legs.

As he approached, it suddenly hit her that he had lost so much and yet accepted all that came, the good and the bad.

So much like Papa Beau.

Stopping directly in front of her, he looked down and cocked his head to the side as he asked, "What are you smiling about?"

"I was thinking how wonderful you are, accepting everything that comes in life, and realizing you are so much like Papa Beau."

Brows raised, he slipped his arms around her and said, "That's the nicest compliment I can think of." They stayed embraced for a moment and then he asked, "What are you doing out here, babe?"

Without hesitation, she replied, "I was just thinking that all of this land, all of this heritage, is mine to pass on to my children."

His arms jerked slightly, and he leaned back to hold her gaze. "If you're thinking about the future of this farm and your children, maybe I shouldn't wait any longer."

"I don't understand. Wait for what?"

"I hadn't planned on this right now, but when I looked out the bedroom window and saw you standing here in the moonlight, I knew I wanted to ask you this question."

Face scrunched, she had no idea what he was talking about until he dropped to one knee and said, "I know I'm not doing this right because I don't have a ring, but I don't want to wait to let you know that I love you and want to spend the rest of my life with you. So, if you're talking about children, I want them to be *our* children. So, Elizabeth Weston, will you consent to be my wife?"

Knees buckling, she dropped to the ground, tears of happiness streaming down her face. "Oh, yes!" she cried as they cupped each other's faces, their lips meeting, sealing their vows.

Later, lying in bed after they made love, she realized he had taken her worst day and turned it into something beautiful.

30

TWO WEEKS LATER

Walking back from feeding the alpacas, she stood at the small field and watched the goat kids frolic. The sun was shining with only a few white clouds dotting the blue sky. She inhaled deeply, pleased to no longer smell charred wood, but instead, the scent of freshly-mown grass mixed with the earthy farm smells met her nose.

Smiling, she turned and walked past the newly graded area where the barn used to stand. Two local farmers, former friends of Papa Beau's, had come by the previous week with their tractors and plows to knock down what was left from the burned barn. After hauling the refuse away, they returned to clear the land, making it smooth and ready for a new barn.

The insurance check had come through much quicker than Lizzie expected. She supposed with the police having the confessed arsonist in custody, the insurance company was able to expedite the claim. She had been pleasantly surprised by the amount, knowing that it would cover the cost of having a new, slightly larger barn built.

She had talked with several construction companies, but unfortunately, none were able to start building right away. She had called a few of her friends, wanting to drive around and take batches of muffins she had made in thanks for all of their concern, but it seemed everyone was busy on this beautiful Saturday morning. She knew there was not an AL ball game since Scott was still inside the house. In fact, now that she thought about it, it was odd that he had not already joined her since he usually helped with the animals.

Heading toward the back door, she was suddenly met with the sounds that she had heard once before, only this time louder. Glancing up the road, she saw a long line of pickup trucks, SUVs, and cars. And at the end of the line was a big rig flatbed truck piled high with lumber. She stood with her mouth hanging open as the huge truck passed by before turning into her lane and she spied the logo for Giardano Farms on the side.

Arms wrapped around her from the back, and she jumped, looking up to see Scott resting his head on her shoulder. Seeing his smile, she said, "I'm almost afraid to ask what's going on!"

"Get ready for an old-fashioned barn raising, sweetheart."

No words met his announcement other than her breath rushing from her lungs. She lost count of the number of vehicles that pulled into the drive, parking in front and to the side of the house. As people began to pile out of their vehicles, they waved toward her and

Scott as several of them helped to direct the big rig driver toward the area where the wood would be delivered.

"And before you ask, Lizzie, all materials have been donated by Luca Giardano. I've talked to Colt, and while at first, Luca denied that his daughter could have been involved in anything so nefarious, when the evidence came forth, she finally confessed. It seems her actions completely gutted her father."

With her hands holding onto his forearms still wrapped around her chest, she said, "Weird, isn't it? It was my father and his daughter that schemed together, leaving the two of us devastated."

"I hadn't thought about it like that, but you're right," Scott agreed. Giving her a squeeze, he added, "Luca has donated all the materials for your new barn. He contacted me, uncertain that contacting you directly would be the right thing to do. He told me that he had considered Beau to be a neighbor and friend and wanted to do anything he could to try to make up for his daughter's actions. I informed him that you were getting an insurance check that would cover everything, but his words were for you to take that money and use it however you wanted. The barn was his gift."

By now, she watched as a line of people walked by, mostly friends and neighbors, although a few she did not know, head to where the barn would be built. To the side was a huge gathering of more friends and some people she recognized from the Auxiliary, already setting up makeshift tables.

"Mitch, Grant, Lance, and Ginny have to take shifts,"

Scott explained, "since Baytown has to have a couple of officers on duty at all times. Same with Colt and Hunter. Carrie's working the breakfast service at The Diner, but she and Jack will be here before lunch. Callan had morning duty with the Marine Police, but he'll be here early afternoon. Pretty much everyone else is here. We recruited a couple of the older members of the American Legion who've built barns before to give us direction. Some of them worked in construction anyway."

She recognized Aiden, Brogan, and Zac as well as Josh and Joseph. Scott pointed out the parents of some of their friends, all joining in the activity.

Katelyn and Jillian came over and asked if they could help with the animals. Jolting into action, Lizzie replied, "Yes! Let's move them to a further pasture so they aren't as upset over the noise." She soon found that she had an entourage of helpers, including some children, all wanting to see the goats, alpacas, and pigs. There was not much she could do for the chickens and hoped they would not be so upset they would stop laying eggs, but if so, she would deal. The barn raising was worth any inconvenience to the animals as long as they remained safe.

Scott headed over to the building site, and Lizzie flitted back and forth between the house and the barn, finding her attention pulled in many directions. At one point during the day, she had a number of helpers in the kitchen making soap and lotion, but she continually looked out of the window over the sink, stunned at how quickly the barn was taking shape. There was no sexism during the work with a number of women hauling wood and hammering.

Soon it was time for lunch, and Lizzie stood to the side watching some of the older Auxiliary women oversee the others hustling to fill the food-laden tables. She tried to count how many people had shown up, but with some coming and going she lost count at forty. The laughter and camaraderie ensued, and suddenly overcome with emotion, she quietly slipped around the side of the house, desperate for a moment of privacy. Swallowing past the lump in her throat, she swiped at the few tears that escaped down her cheeks.

Sucking in a cleansing breath, she let it out slowly, once again dabbing at her eyes to make sure no one could see that she had been crying.

"Ms. Weston?"

Jumping, she whirled around and saw Luca Giardano standing nearby. At first glance, his outward appearance was very much like the first time she had seen him. Silver hair still neatly combed. Khaki pants with a navy shirt, the farm's logo embroidered on the pocket. Stepping closer, she could see that his face appeared to have aged even more than from the years of working in the sun on his farm.

"Mr. Giardano, I understand that the building materials are from you. Thank you—"

He lifted his hand dismissively, shaking his head. "Please, Ms. Weston. No thanks are needed. It was the least I could do under the circumstances, and I wish it could be more. I had suggested to Mr. Redding that I pay to have the barn rebuilt, but he assured me that there were already volunteers ready to perform the task." His gaze shifted from her past the numerous vehicles in her drive to the beehive movements of all the people at work. Looking back at her, he said, "I see he was right. I'm not surprised."

Nodding, she said, "My grandfather had many good friends."

His head tilted, and he smiled ever-so-slightly. "Yes, he did, but so do you. I have no doubt, Ms. Weston, that many of these people are here for you. That says a great deal about who you are as a person. And I'm proud to have you as a neighbor, just as I was your grandfather." His hat was still in his hands, and he took a step back. "Well, I just wanted to ascertain that the materials were delivered—"

"Would you like to stay for lunch? There's plenty of food," she rushed, the invitation surprising her as much as it appeared to surprise Luca.

The lines on his face softened, and he said, "I don't think so, not this time. I'm still coming to terms with what happened. But, if the invitation stands for a later date, I'd love to."

His gaze shot over her shoulder, and she did not have to look to know that Scott was approaching. He came to stand next to her, his arm around her in a show of support, but he remained silent, letting her continue her conversation.

She leaned her weight slightly into Scott before smiling up at Luca. "Mr. Giardano, you're welcome at Weston Farms any time."

With another small smile, Luca inclined his head and walked back to his truck.

Scott's arm about her shoulders squeezed. "Everything okay?"

"Yeah, honey. Everything's okay." With that, she allowed him to guide her back toward the gathering, her smile wide and her heart light as she looked around. She knew if he was looking down at her right now, Papa Beau would be smiling in return.

Two Years Later

Scott left the office, anxious to be home. From the moment he first laid eyes on the large, white farmhouse, he knew it felt like a true home. Now, he could not imagine living anywhere else. Soon, he drove past the Weston Farms sign, turning onto the gravel drive.

For the past two years, the farm was running successfully, both for the alpaca fleece and goats. Lizzie continued making her goat milk products and had even begun breeding goats. She had a yoga instructor that ran two goat yoga classes per week, weather permitting. The farm was also a destination for birthday parties and days where people could come to pet the animals and learn about animal care. Lizzie kept the charges low for those events but still made money due to their popularity.

A number of cars were just pulling past him, leaving the farm. He climbed from his SUV, anxious to see Lizzie, grinning as soon as he spied her standing on the back patio smiling toward the customers leaving goat yoga class. The instructor was saying goodbye to Lizzie, cooing over the bundle in her arms—their one-month-old son, Beau.

The instructor tossed him a wave as she climbed into her car, but Scott's eyes were filled with his wife and son. Bending to take her lips in a kiss, he then placed a sweet kiss on Beau's forehead. "How did it go today?"

"For the first day having the farm open again after having Beau, it went fine. Of course, I didn't have to do anything except just make sure the goat kid pen was ready. The instructor did everything else."

Brow furrowed, he asked, "You didn't overdo it, did you?" He knew Lizzie was more than capable but worried about her trying to do too much. Her mother and stepfather had come for the first week to help out before needing to go back to their home. Scott and Lizzie had hired a part-time farmhand who came early to see the animals in the morning before going to work at Giardano Farms. Then he would stop by to check on the animals in the evening before going home.

Smiling, she lifted a hand and touched his cheek, saying, "Stop worrying, Scott. Beau and I are adjusting just fine."

They turned to walk into the house but stopped as they heard the crunch of gravel indicating an approaching vehicle. As Luca Giardano came into sight, they both smiled and waved. Several months after Careena had been arrested, Luca had approached Scott and Lia to look over the financial records of Giardano Farms. Lia, being a forensic accountant, quickly found that Careena had been stealing from the company, another blow to Luca.

He climbed from his truck and walked toward them, his gaze resting on the bundle in Lizzie's arms. Greeting them with a wide smile, he looked down at a sleeping Beau and whispered, "Congratulations once again. What a beautiful little boy." Lifting his gaze to Lizzie, he reached out and touched her cheek, saying, "Your grandparents would be so proud."

Scott wanted Lizzie off her feet and invited Luca to come inside with them. Over the past two years, Lizzie had opened her heart and her home to Luca. Careena was never mentioned, but Scott knew that she was still in prison, as was Robbie.

They moved to the kitchen door, where she settled into a padded rocking chair that they had placed near the table. Offering a glass of iced tea to Luca, Scott quickly poured one for him, getting water for him and Lizzie.

"I don't want to take too much of your time," Luca began, "but I just had to come by to see your son." He glanced down, his hands shaking slightly. Reaching inside his jacket, he pulled out an envelope and said, "I have a gift for you. It's both in memory of your grandfather and in celebration of the birth of your son."

Scott glanced toward Lizzie but could see from her scrunched expression that she had no idea what Luca was offering. Scott carefully took Beau from her arms, freeing her to reach for the envelope. He watched as she opened it, looking at the contents while showing him as well. It took a moment for his mind to settle on what his eyes were seeing, but as he heard Lizzie gasp, it struck them both.

"I'm giving you back the acres that your grandfather had sold to me. It's a gift, free and clear."

Lizzie's mouth opened and closed several times, no words coming forth. Finally, she managed to sputter, "Luca, I don't understand."

Smiling, Luca replied, "My dear, it's quite simple. I want you, Scott, and your son to have your full heritage of the entire original Weston Farm that's been in your family for generations."

Scott, inhaling the fresh baby scent of his son, loved the idea that he would have his heritage. Hearing a quick intake of breath, he looked over, seeing a single tear slide down Lizzie's cheek. Holding Beau with one arm, he slid his free one around Lizzie, pulling her close.

Looking at Luca, he said, "This is very generous of you."

"No, it's just the right thing to do. Always on a quest for more sent the wrong message to my daughter. This is my way of rectifying that." He stood, and Lizzie immediately jumped up, rushing to him.

Throwing her arms around him, she said, "Thank you. Thank you so much."

Luca kissed her cheek before shaking Scott's hand.

Bending, he kissed Beau's head before turning to leave. "I can see myself out. Take care and I'll see you soon."

Wrapping his arm around Lizzie, he bent to kiss her, her lips warm against his. They had a few more weeks before they could become intimate again, but he did not mind waiting. Just being with her, and now their son, made not only him but his whole world whole again.

Don't miss the next Baytown Boys novel!
Shielding You

Hannah and Dylan have been characters in each Baytown book as the Police Chiefs of the tiny towns of Easton and Seaside.

As one of the few female law enforcers on the Eastern Shore, Hannah Freeman has to be smart, tough, competent, and dedicated.

That's the easy part.

Hiding her feeling for Dylan Hunt, a neighboring Police Chief has been challenging, but she has no time for unrequited love.

When a hostage situation threatens Hannah, Dylan lets his true feelings known, but will it be too late?

Jaxon

Jayden

Asher

Zeke

Cas

Lighthouse Security Investigations

Mace

Rank

Walker

Drew

Blake

Tate

Hope City (romantic suspense series co-developed

with Kris Michaels

Brock book 1

Sean book 2

Carter book 3

Brody book 4

Kyle book 5

Ryker book 6

Rory book 7

Killian book 8

Saints Protection & Investigations

(an elite group, assigned to the cases no one else wants…or
can solve)

Serial Love

Healing Love

Revealing Love

Seeing Love

Honor Love

Sacrifice Love

Protecting Love

Remember Love

Discover Love

Surviving Love

Celebrating Love

Follow the exciting spin-off series:

Alvarez Security (military romantic suspense)

Gabe

Tony

Vinny

Jobe

SEALs

Thin Ice (Sleeper SEAL)

SEAL Together (Silver SEAL)

Letters From Home (military romance)

Class of Love

Freedom of Love

Bond of Love

The Love's Series (detectives)

Love's Taming

Love's Tempting

Love's Trusting

The Fairfield Series (small town detectives)

Emma's Home

Laurie's Time

Carol's Image

Fireworks Over Fairfield

Please take the time to leave a review of this book. Feel free to contact me, especially if you enjoyed my book. I love to hear from readers!

Facebook

Email

Website

ABOUT THE AUTHOR

I am an avid reader of romance novels, often joking that I cut my teeth on the historical romances. I have been reading and reviewing for years. In 2013, I finally gave into the characters in my head, screaming for their story to be told. From these musings, my first novel, Emma's Home, The Fairfield Series was born.

I was a high school counselor having worked in education for thirty years. I live in Virginia, having also lived in four states and two foreign countries. I have been married to a wonderfully patient man for thirty-five years. When writing, my dog or one of my four cats can generally be found in the same room if not on my lap.

Please take the time to leave a review of this book. Feel free to contact me, especially if you enjoyed my book. I love to hear from readers!

Facebook
Email
Website

Made in United States
Troutdale, OR
09/05/2023

12653952R00205